Why Not?

Leanne Treese

Moxie Publishing

To my daughter, Cassidy, whose awesome sense of humor I use as inspiration in my writing.

Leanne Treese/Moxie Publishing LLC

P.O. Box 5323

Clinton, New Jersey. 08809

Publishers Note: This is a work of fiction. Names, characters, places, and incidents are a product of the author's imagination. Locales and public names are sometimes used for atmospheric purposes. Any resemblance to people, living or dead, or to businesses, companies, events, institutions, or locales is completely coincidental.

Cover Design by JRC Designs/ Jena R. Collins

www. jenarcollins.com

Paperback ISBN : 979-8-9926030-8-8

Ebook ISBN: 979-8-9926030-9-5

Chapter 1

Ellie

"Mom?" Caleb swings his hand toward the box of kittens on the reception area floor. "What's this?" A calico one leaps from the towel-lined box, scurries toward Caleb, and bats his shoelace.

I knew I liked that one.

"What's what, dear?" I say, though I know exactly "what's what." I've been working as a receptionist at Caleb's veterinary practice for nearly a year, mainly—okay, entirely—because of "the incident." I haven't been the best about turning away strays.

"The kittens. Don't tell me."

"You're a vet honey. People who want animals are here all the time." I sweep up the calico kitty and kiss the top of its tiny little head. "Who wouldn't want a cutie like this? I'm calling him Rambo." I turn the kitten, look into his eyes, then maneuver him back toward Caleb. "It's a cute name, right? I think it fits."

"Mom." He spits out the word. After, he rakes his hair, thick and dark like his father's. The tone and the gesture are

1

both things Harrison, Caleb's dad and my husband—*ex-husband*— would do. "We talked about this. I can't keep finding homes for these animals."

"But it keeps working out," I insist. And it does. The pit bull mix puppies, the black-and-white bunnies, the overly exuberant Labrador. The chickens I'd found on the side of the road. All abandoned or given up. All with new owners. "Even Peanut has a home."

"*You* adopted Peanut."

"Well, of course I did. Peanut has one eye. And he's old. Who in the world would adopt an old, one-eyed chihuahua?"

"*You* Mom."

"Exactly my point." I set Rambo in the box and pick up the stack of pet insurance claims Caleb keeps on about. Like processing them is my job. Okay, fine. It is my job. And I'll get to it. As soon as these kittens have new owners.

He lets out a long sigh, and I can almost hear him counting to ten in his head. *I* taught him that, way back when he was a skinned-kneed, freckled-faced little cherub of a boy unable to control his temper. You're welcome, Dr. Caleb Moore.

He blows out a breath and leans toward me. "I wanted to talk to you about something while the techs are on lunch."

"Of course, sweetheart."

"It's the cruise."

"Just forty-eight hours before I go *bon voyage* to the Bahamas." I pump my fist in the air. It feels like forever since I've been on a vacation.

Caleb pulls at the lapel of his white medical coat. "I don't think you should go."

I wave a hand in his direction. "What are you going on about? Of course I'm going on the cruise." I spy the pile of untouched claim forms and pick them up. "It's not these, is it?"

"No." He takes the pile of documents from my hands and

sets them on a different part of the semi-circular reception desk. "Of course not."

"Is it Peanut? Do you not want to take care of him while I'm away?"

"No, Mom. Peanut's fine."

"Then why?"

"How do you know it's not—" he stops a long moment— "a scam."

I hold up my hand. "Don't even—" I start. I've had enough lectures about scams to last me the rest of what might be, at seventy-two, a very short rest of my life.

"Mom," he interrupts, "you have to admit it's a little weird how you won this trip out of the blue. What was it on? Some website?"

"Senior Savers," I say, sitting up so my posture is as straight as possible. "The site provides helpful financial advice. I've very much enjoyed the content." Lie. I hate the content. Things like "Make Your Own Laundry Detergent and Save" or "Increase Your Net Worth with Metal Detectors." Ugh. No. Of course, I wouldn't need to be on the site at all if it had not been for—well, the scam.

"But what if it's a—" He stops, knowing, I guess, how I'll react if he says the 's' word a second time. "What if the cruise isn't what you think it is?"

"It's a seven-day cruise to the Bahamas with a few port stops. The concept is straightforward, even for an old lady like me."

One of the kittens leaps out of the box and Caleb picks her up. "But what if the cruise line asks you for money? Or some man does? Or woman, or whatever?"

I close my eyes tight, then open them. My own version of counting to ten. "I'll say no."

"Will you? If it's for an orphan or some person's child who

3

needs medical treatment or help for some animal?" He pushes the kitten in my direction. "Someone who needs to rehome kittens?"

"Well, that's easy." I take the kitten from his outstretched hand. "I hate orphans, sick children, and animals."

"Be serious."

"I am serious."

I know why he's asking these things; I know he has the right to. I've made some mistakes. Doozies. But I need this trip. I'm seventy-two, but I don't feel seventy-two. I don't feel a day over —I don't even know what age. But not seventy-two. And it doesn't help that Harrison, my ex, got remarried eighteen months ago. At seventy-five! To a woman who—get this—is also seventy-five. He could have at least had the decency to marry someone half his age. Then I could mock him. Instead, Lilith is elegant and sophisticated. I'd bet good money that she's never made her own laundry detergent or used metal detectors to increase her net worth.

So, the cruise. I need it. And I'm going. I reach out and touch Caleb's arm. "Look, honey, I appreciate your concern, but I'll be fine. I've learned my lesson."

He rakes his hair again. "Have you?"

"Yes. Of course."

"And you'll be on guard? Suspicious of everyone?" He leans forward. "Especially of anyone asking for money." He pauses. "Or to see your phone. There are lots of scams with phones these days."

"No money, no phones. Got it."

"And people aren't usually nice. I hate to say it, but anyone nice is a red flag."

"I will avoid nice people like the plague." The kitten leaps out of my hands and tumbles back into the box.

"I'm serious, Mom."

"Me too. I have no intention of cavorting with anyone, nice or not. I've packed a bunch of mystery novels. I'm just going to relax."

"Promise?"

The front door swings open and the two techs who work with Caleb step inside.

"I promise."

Chapter 2

Mark

"You got everything, Dad?" Addison asks. We're in the parking lot of the Brooklyn Cruise Terminal. A monstrosity of a ship, the Carpe Diem III, looms in front of us like a floating hotel.

I pull my small suitcase from her car trunk. "Got everything." A wind gust whips from the Hudson River, blowing my gray hair.

She eyes the suitcase. "That's it? For a week?"

"It'll be fine," I say. It might not be. Whatever. This is not a trip I wanted to take. Addison and Sara gave it to me as a retirement gift after I'd been unceremoniously pushed toward retiring from my teaching job by the new school principal. Things had gotten increasingly digital and computerized; I couldn't keep up.

Addison shifts her gaze from my bag to Carpe Diem III. "The ship looks kind of worn down." She scrunches up her nose. "Sorry. It looked better in the pictures."

"It looks fabulous," I lie. "This trip was a wonderful surprise." A second lie. The trip was not a wonderful surprise, and had Addison not been so excited to gift it to me, there's no way I'd be standing here right now. I like order and routine. I have since I took custody of Addison and Sara, my sister's daughters, when they were just six and four. Routine was required as a single caregiver; I got used to it.

"You have all the notes about Sara?" I ask. Sara has cerebral palsy and still lives with me. Her care can be a lot.

"Yes. I know how to take care of my sister, Dad. We're both in our forties. We'll be fine." Wind whips at us and she pulls her coat tighter. "Better than fine. We're totally going to bond, and I'll love having someone else in the house again. It hasn't been that long since Max."

"I know." Addison never married, but she and her long-term boyfriend Max decided to part ways months ago. Though the decision was mutual, she hasn't had an easy time of it.

She pokes her index finger on my chest. "You're going to have an awesome time."

Awesome time. Right. I've got a dozen non-fiction books on my Kindle and my trusty crossword puzzle book. I'll pass the time. Not sure it will be awesome.

"An awesome time, Dad," she repeats. "You deserve it." She looks at her phone. "Come on. You'd better go. I'm sorry I can't stay to see you off."

I give her a peck on the cheek. "No worries. I don't think I'll get lost on my way to the boat."

I start toward the massive and extremely run-down cruise ship. Others are doing the same. Old people, like me, on this "senior cruise" or whatever it is. Part of me thinks Addison booked the trip in the hopes I'd finally find someone. I won't. And I don't plan to even look.

I pass a woman leaning against a railing looking at her phone, a pile of bright purple luggage pieces spread in front of her. She's wearing a puffy purple coat with a matching hat.

I stop. She looks up from her phone, her eyes a color of blue which stand out in the best possible way. Her cheeks are pink, and the bits of hair that peek out from her hat appear to be blond.

I stare for a moment. The woman pushes off the railing and stands tall. "May I help you?" she asks. Her accent is Southern.

I gesture to the bags splayed about her feet. "I was going to ask you the same thing. Are you going on the cruise? Do you need help getting these to the ship?"

She narrows her eyes. "Maybe."

I tilt my head. "Maybe you're going on the cruise, or maybe you need help with your luggage?"

She looks at her fingernails. Long and bright pink.

I push my hand out in her direction. "I'm Mark. Happy to give you a hand if you need it."

She looks at me a long moment before taking my hand and giving it a limp squeeze. "Okay, Mark. I'm Ellie. I could use the help. But this is just a luggage thing."

Just a luggage thing? What did she think this was? I hold up my hands. "Of course."

I pick up most of her luggage. It's heavy, like she's packed everything she owns. Or possibly a bunch of rocks. I carry the luggage, dragging some of it, to the end of the line of people boarding the ship. "So, where are you from?" She's from some-where in the South for sure.

"Not relevant."

Not relevant? Man. And I always thought Southern people were supposed to be friendly. I stand in silence and my mind wanders to Sara. Does Addison know about indoor swimming at the YMCA on Tuesdays? Did I put that on the list? I did, right? I think so. Maybe?

I reach inside my coat pocket. I'll send a quick text about the class. I feel around for my phone. It's not there. I try my other pocket. Nothing. Ridiculously, I pat all over my body, like my phone might possibly be hidden in my stomach or on a limb or something. It's not.

I bend down and unzip my suitcase. I rifle through the contents like a madman. As I'm throwing my boxers on the ground, I visualize it, my phone, in the cup holder of Addison's car. Crap. C-R-A-P! I look at my watch. It's only been twenty minutes. She could get back here in time to give it to me before we take off.

I look up at Ellie, her gaze fixed on the guts of my small suitcase. "Hey. Any chance I could use your phone to call my daughter?"

"My phone?" Her eyes widen.

"Yeah. Sorry. But I left my phone in my daughter's car, and I really need it. My other daughter has cerebral palsy and -"

She jets out a hand and puts it on my arm. For a moment, I think she's about to say yes, of course, please. Things any normal person would say. Instead, she says, "Absolutely not."

Absolutely not? What? "I need to be in touch while I'm away. I really can't be without my phone."

She folds her arms across her chest. "That's not my problem." She wags a finger at me. "And don't think I don't know what this is."

"What what is?" I look at my watch. "Look, it's just one call. I need to reach my daughter before she gets too far away." We move a few steps in line. I pull, carry, and lug her bags along with us.

"No."

"No? Really?" I shake my head. "Okay. Whatever." I step out of line, grab my suitcase, and jog toward a smiling cruise worker. She's holding blue and white pom-poms and is wearing a button that says, "Go Seniors!"

As I approach, she shakes the pom-poms and yells "Yay!"

I'm momentarily frozen by the ludicrousness of the situation, like it's a dream or an out-of-body experience. Or maybe I'm dead and this is my personal version of hell.

"I'm Brandy!" the cruise worker yells in my direction. "Can I help you, handsome cruiser?"

Handsome cruiser? I'm seventy-two with gray hair and brown eyes and my six-foot physique feels like it shrinks on the daily. I'm not handsome. I'm more of a "not that bad" kind of guy.

I don't acknowledge the condescending "handsome cruiser" remark and explain the situation. I make the call with Brandy's phone (adorned with unicorn stickers!), and Addison assures me she'll turn around immediately. I'm standing in the parking lot when she gets there, decision made.

"I can't do this, honey," I say as soon as she gets out of the car.

"Do what?" In a matter of seconds, understanding passes over her features. "The cruise? Dad no."

I put my hands on her shoulders and look into her eyes. "It was a beautiful idea, and I appreciate it, but it's just not for me. I can reimburse you."

She steps away and holds out my phone. "It's not about the money. It's a thank you. For everything. Everything. All these years." She looks to the ship and back at me. "Please. Please go and just have fun."

I take the phone from her extended hand. "I – "

The ship horn blasts.

Addison puts her hands in a prayer position. "Please. Please go, Dad. Please." Her voice is pleading in a way I've rarely heard it. For some reason, my going on this cruise, me having "fun," is extremely important to her, so much so that she's almost in tears. And her feelings on this relatively small matter? Way more important than mine. I can suck it up.

"Okay, sweetheart. I'll go."

The horn blasts again. I give Addison a wave, walk briskly toward the ship, and ascend the ramp. Brandy is among the crew members as I board, all of whom have pom-poms. They make a pom-pom arch, which I have no choice but to walk under.

Good Lord.

I look around the general vicinity. Ellie is nowhere in sight.

At least I've got that.

Chapter 3

Ellie

An hour after sail-away, and after setting my luggage in the "holding area," I stand at the edge of Ballroom A of the Carpe Diem III. The ballroom is large with a circular wooden dance floor in its center; everything else burgundy and gold. *A lot* of burgundy and gold. Walls, chairs, carpets, pillows, paintings, curtains, frames. Kind of like the space was decorated to look regal for the ship's maiden voyage a million years ago and never ever updated.

I'm trying not to hate it.

I mean, I don't hate it.

It's a little old fashioned and kind of old, but of course I don't hate it!

I'm on vacation. On a Caribbean voyage no less. What's there to hate? I glance around the room. Dozens, maybe a hundred people, all seniors, fill the space, along with a fair number of "accessories for the aged" like canes, walkers, and hearing aids. I'm supposed to wear the latter—Caleb got me a pair that I can turn up and down—but I refuse. I mean, no!

Wearing them feels like giving up. Like I may as well wave a flag that says, "I'm super old and I don't care anymore."

I scan the room for Mark the scammer. Handsome guy. Quite built. And he almost had me until that bit about having a disabled daughter. Yeah, right. You have a daughter with cerebral palsy. Sure you do, Mark. Sure you do.

A woman shifts near me, small with a mop of bright white hair. She pulls an index card from her purse with the word dog on it. We'd all received one upon boarding. "What do you make of these?"

"No idea." I shake my head. "I'm as lost as a puppy in a cornfield."

The woman laughs. "I'm Adel."

"Ellie."

"Where are you from?"

"Fairfield, Alabama, born and raised. You?"

"New Jersey. A little town called Clinton."

"Well nice to meet you, Adel from New Jersey." I pull out my index card and hold it next to hers. Mine says sheep.

"I love dogs," Adel says. "Are you really into sheep or something?"

"I love all animals, sheep and dogs included."

Just then, a half dozen crew members walk from the ballroom entrance through the throngs of burgundy and gold items to the edge of the dance floor. All of them have identical circular buttons that say "Go Seniors!" which seems a little condescending. Right? Or no. No. Friendly. The buttons are friendly. Of course they are.

A man with a name badge that says "Dan" steps to a microphone on a makeshift stage. "Hello Seniors!"

There's a smattering of a response.

"Seniors!" Dan implores. "You can do better than that. I said hello!"

"Hello." The second chorus is slightly more enthused.

He cups his hand around his ear. "I can't hear you, Seniors."

There's little response to this third effort. Adel leans in. "Maybe we can't hear him," she jokes and taps on her hearing aids.

Dan finally gives up the bit. "So, Seniors, we're going to go back in time." He holds up his hand and points to his wrist. "Way back. And play icebreaker games like we did as kids."

Groans from most people, but I'm secretly glad. I *love* ice breaker games. I always have.

"Come on," Dan says. "My kindergartner loves this one."

A few passengers head for the exit. A second cruise member, seemingly wanting to save Dan's shtick, yells, "Come on Seniors! Let's have some fun!" She waves her pom-poms enthusiastically.

Dan takes back over. "Okay. We're going to find our cruise groups, people you'll meet up with daily for meals. How do you find them, you ask?" He pauses for effect. "Well, you're going to walk or wheel around the room making the noise associated with the animal on your index card. Like, if your card says cow, you moo. Pig, you oink. Find others making the same noise. They're in your group. Your group looks for more people making the same animal noise until you find them all!"

A man in a wheelchair near the stage boos.

"Was that a moo?" Dan asks.

"A boo," the man clarifies. "Booooo."

It's silent for a long moment and then someone does yell out "moo." Someone else does too, then a third person. Adel barks. Someone meows. And then its mayhem. People moving, scooting, and wheeling along, making animal noises they prob-ably haven't had a reason to make in years. The game is so over-the-top ridiculous, that it's actually fun. Even the man who booed is wheeling around and oinking.

"Baa."

I pass a man barking.

"Baa."

A woman grabs my arm and says "baa." We both laugh. She introduces herself as Trudy and we link hands and baa together until we find a third (Hank) and a fourth (Aspen). We unite with Brandy, our "cruise counselor" who shares that our group has a fifth who didn't show up for the game. My mind flashes to Mark with his lopsided grin and easy voice. And phone scam! Could he be the missing member? No. No way. He's probably not even on the ship.

Brandy shares that we'll eat breakfast with our "friends" at 9:00 a.m. each morning here in Ballroom A at which time she'll run through the day's activities.

I digest this. I wasn't planning to get up at 9:00 a.m. each day, but I would like to get to know these friends. Hank, a self-described day trader, has provided a week's worth of financial tips in the span of ten minutes. And Aspen has twice mentioned that I have a strong aura. I'll have to find out more about that. Trudy is quiet, but nice. Plus, there's missing number five. Maybe a handsome man. Not that I'm looking.

"Okay, friends," Brandy says. "Time to get to our state-rooms. You are all on the same floor. Follow me."

I blow out a breath. Stateroom = bed, which is exactly what I need right now. It's been a long day, and I'm not wearing the most supportive footwear in the world. The idea of snuggling under the covers of my stateroom bed feels like a slice of heaven right now.

Brandy leads us through the interior of the ship and down a narrow hallway, her peppy ponytail swinging as she walks. "This is our wing!" She hands Aspen a key. An actual key, not a keycard. She gives out keys to Trudy and Hank. "Night friends!" She turns to me. "Your room is a little bigger. It's right down here."

Bigger! Yes. Probably because I *won* it. I can't wait to tell Caleb.

She hands me a key and gestures to the door. "Here it is! Sweet dreams."

"Great," I say and push the key into the lock. I step in, turn on the light, and scream.

There's a man in my bed.

Chapter Four

Mark

A scream.

My sleep-scrambled mind centers on the thought that it's Sara. Sara screaming. Shit. Is she all right? I jolt up, open my eyes, and with some relief realize I am on the cruise, not at home. No Sara. Instead, Ellie, aka the obnoxious woman who wouldn't let me use her phone, is standing in the doorframe.

Nightmare. Has to be. I pinch myself just as Ellie points a finger at me. "Him. What is he doing in here? He's a no good-"

"Come on, Mrs. Moore," Brandy interrupts. "You don't mean that."

Mrs. Moore? I scramble up in bed, pulling a sheet over my bare chest. "There is no Mrs. Moore," I say at the same time Ellie says, "This man is not my husband."

"Come on, guys," Brandy says, not seeming to get what I've already pieced together. Ellie Moore. Mark Moore. The crew member who assigned these rooms thought we were a couple.

"This man is a scammer," Ellie tells Brandy. "Tried to scam me when I got on the ship."

I shake my head. "I asked to use your phone. And I carried all your luggage, which hurt my back, by the way. It's why I'm in here lying down instead of out doing whatever." I fling my hand toward the door.

Brandy looks back and forth between us. "Do you guys need a minute? Traveling can be stressful."

"No," Ellie and I say at the same time.

"I'm not a scammer. She's not my wife. And I need to lie down again because of my back."

"Not in my room." Ellie takes two steps across the tiny room and flings open the mirrored closet, something I hadn't done. Purple luggage pieces are inside. "My luggage. My room."

"You're not married," Brandy says, catching up.

"No, we're not married," I say, calmer. "Look. It's no problem. We just need another room. I'm happy to move. Maybe on the other side of the ship." I look pointedly at Ellie.

She crosses her arms across her chest. "Or off of it."

Brandy bites her lip. "Oooh. I don't know. I need to see what rooms we have left that are habitable." She scrunches her face up.

"Habitable?" I question.

"Redone," she corrects, then repeats the word. "Redone." She pulls the unicorn-themed phone from her pocket and punches in a number. There appears to be no answer, and she puts the phone down. "I'll go find someone and see what I can work out. BRB." She waves and hurries down the hall.

I turn to Ellie, the tiny heels of her shoes making indents in the plush green carpet. "Look. I'll get out of here and figure things out with Brandy. You can have the room. I just need a minute."

Ellie eyes her luggage. "Not a chance."

"Oh, for Pete's sake." I throw up my hands. "I'm not going

to take your luggage. Or anything. What would I even–" I start, then stop myself and take a deep breath. "Look, I'm not decent under here. Give me a minute, and I'll get dressed and go."

She crosses her arms. "You got a snowball's chance in Hades of that happening."

Is this woman for real? I stare at her a long moment. "Fine. I'll stay. I need to rest my back anyway." I meet her eyes. "Because of your luggage." I lie back down and pull the covers up to my chin. "Can you get the light?"

"So, you're just going to stay? In my room?"

"Our room, Mrs. Moore. Now can you get the light, please? I'm tired and my back hurts."

"You can't stay here."

I sit up. "Well like I said, I'll go, but I need a minute alone to dress."

"I don't believe you're not decent."

"Suit yourself."

I move to lie back down just as she steps forward and flings the covers from the bed. She jumps back. "You're naked!"

"Well, thank you for noticing. And with such enthusiasm too. Much appreciated."

"Oh my God." She throws the covers on top of me, her face red. "Okay fine! Just get dressed already and get out." She steps out of the room.

I get dressed as fast as I'm able with the back pain, but I'm laughing as I do it. Her face? Priceless. I grab my small suitcase and step out.

"Do you know if there are clean sheets in the room?"

"Not my problem." I shrug and step past her.

"See you never, Mark."

"Never would be too soon," I retort, feeling like a seventy-two-year-old kindergartner.

The door shuts behind me, the sound of a lock right after it.

I amble down the hall. I've never been the best with directions. I have no idea where to find Brandy or even the deck. One hall weaves into the next and the next, all identical corridors, all infuriatingly narrow. By the time I finally reach a deck, my back is killing me.

I lie down in the closest lounge chair. Stupid. I should never have carried Ellie's luggage. I'm not young anymore. But she was pretty—*is* pretty, in spite of the crazy—and she needed help. Instinct took over. Stupid.

I close my eyes and drift off. I sleep restlessly for hours, waking up and falling back asleep in a cycle of poor rest. When it's completely light out, I give up the fight. My back is on fire with pain which would not be the case if I were home, where I wanted to be to begin with. I'd be doing the morning crossword, drinking black coffee out of my bright yellow Steelers mug, and waiting for two pieces of rye toast to pop out of the Black and Decker toaster I've had for years.

I adjust myself on the lounge just as a group of women, half a dozen maybe, walk on to the deck, all wearing matching pink T-shirts with the words "Fit and Feisty" emblazoned across the front.

They collectively halt. "Goodness," one coos, "you look a sight."

"Are you all right?" another asks.

"I'm okay," I say, then in the next breath, admit that I'm not. Pretending I'm young and okay is what got me into this mess to begin with. "I hurt my back."

There's a collective chirp of sympathy and two of the women are immediately dispatched to get ice and coffee. They return not just with ice and coffee, but a heaping plate of eggs and bacon as well. Not the best-looking eggs and bacon, but food, nonetheless. I've forgotten, temporarily, about my morning crossword and rye toast.

The women crowd around on the surrounding lounge chairs. One puts ice behind my back, another asks if I want sugar or cream. A third tells me they are all in a women's group in Ohio, but that the six of them were the only ones in the group well enough to come. "We're the fit and feisty gals," one says, pulling out her shirt.

Despite my back pain, I enjoy this interaction with the women, all of whom seem to be intensely concerned about my back. They're flirting with me, at least that's what it seems. And *that* hasn't happened in forever. I'm enjoying myself for the first time since I boarded and I let go the tiniest bit. I laugh. I flirt for the first time in decades, probably badly, but I do it. And then, because I must have done something truly terrible in a former life, Ellie—the only person on this ginormous cruise ship that I don't want to see right now, or ever—strolls onto the deck. She's with three others, and I think for a moment that she might not spot me. She's engrossed by something the man next to her is saying. Walking, walking, almost past, almost gone. And then Brandy's voice. "There you are, Mark Moore. I've been looking all over for you."

Chapter 5

Ellie

Mark Moore? I stop. The man who'd been in my room?

No.

After I finally got the room to myself last night, I called Caleb to let him know I boarded the ship, was given an extra big room, *and* about Mark Moore the potential scammer who, for some reason, I haven't been able to get out of my head. I mean, I *did* see him naked which is not the most common second meeting in the world. Anyway, Caleb assured me he would "check into his background" so I'd know once and for all who I'm dealing with. Until I heard from Caleb, I'd planned to stay clear of him.

But here he is. Feet away. Surrounded by a gaggle of women in T-shirts that say "Fit and Feisty." They seem overtly thrilled to be in his company. One takes his coffee and mixes cream into it. Mark takes the mug and smiles widely at her, like she'd just given him a lost scroll. Jealousy blips through me; I register the feeling. Jealous? Of other women attending to Mark? No way. I want nothing to do with him, scammer or not.

"Mark!" Brandy waves our group sign, a picture of a sheep on the end of a long stick. "Mark! Over here."

Trudy leans toward me and says, "I can't believe she's waving that sign."

"I can't believe we have a sign."

She juts her chin toward Mark and his harem. "Honestly, what women won't do these days for a man with a full head of hair who doesn't need a walker." She stares a moment. "He is kind of a looker though, right?"

"I hadn't noticed," I lie. I most certainly did.

Brandy waves the sheep sign with more vigor. "Mark. We're doing the morning walk." She swings the sheep sign toward the four of us: me, Hank, Trudy, and Aspen. "Join us."

"Sorry," Mark says. He lifts his head and looks directly at me. "My back hurts from carrying luggage."

I roll my eyes.

"And from sleeping on a lounge chair," he adds.

Brandy looks from Mark to me and back at Mark again. "So you two didn't make up?"

"We're not a couple," we say in unison.

"I thought you were working on a room for me," Mark calls to Brandy.

"Right." Brandy says the word slowly and in a way that makes it obvious she'd forgotten the issue. "Should be today," she adds.

"Great," Mark says. He does not move from the center of the women. Loving the attention. That's the kind of guy he is. One of these poor women is probably his next target.

"Thank goodness for that," I say and fix my eyes on his.

Trudy grips my upper arm. "Wait. You two know each other?"

"Barely. And what I do know is enough."

He shakes his head. "Don't even start."

"Last chance for the walk, Mark!" Brandy calls. "It may help your back."

"It won't help his back," one of the fit and feisty women says. "He should rest." She adjusts his lounge so it's further reclined.

"Fair enough." Brandy sets down the sheep sign and walks briskly around the edge of the deck, arms pumping. Every few steps she says "let's go Seniors" or "you rock" or "move and groove, Sheep." I think she means the phrases to be encouraging. After not all that long because it's not that big a circle, she reaches the point on the deck where we started. I assume we're going to leave this deck and walk around the edge of the cruise ship, a plan I like for two reasons. First, I want to see the cruise ship, and second, I want to get off whatever deck Mark is on. Pronto.

But instead of leaving the deck, Brandy starts to circle it again, Mark and the women in the center. Fine. Maybe it's a warm-up. Surely, Brandy isn't going to spend the entire walk on this one deck.

As we make the small circle, Hank talks about investment strategy. I barely listen, distracted by Mark's presence. When we reach the starting point for the second time, Brandy continues the circle, Hank continues to talk, and my face goes red. It feels like Mark is watching me, which I know he isn't. He's surrounded by women, duh. But still. It's weird. The *one* man I don't want to see on this entire cruise ship, and I'm walking around him like a planet orbiting the sun.

I interrupt Hank's monologue on index stocks. "Are we going to go to any other decks?"

"Mark is on this deck," Brandy says, as if that's explanation enough.

I increase my stride and move next to her. "But it might be nice to see other decks."

"Nah," Brandy says. "Mark's part of the sheep. He wants us here. Right Mark?"

I look toward Mark and see him laughing with one of the women. "He doesn't want us here," I blurt.

Mark turns from the woman, and I can almost see the inner workings of his mind. "Of course I do!" he insists, looking at me. "All of you being here makes me feel part of the group. Please, keep walking around." He circles his index finger around the deck in demonstration.

"See," Brandy says, her voice triumphant.

Ridiculously, we walk around the deck a dozen more times. Aspen stops on a lounge chair, Trudy goes back to her room until breakfast, and Hank keeps talking. I could leave, of course, but it feels like me leaving would give Mark some sense of satisfaction. Like he's under my skin. Which he isn't, of course. Why would he be?

Once the deck walk is over, Brandy checks her watch and announces that it's breakfast time. We all follow her to the maroon and gold ballroom, save Mark. The fit and feisty gals have brought him plates of food almost non-stop. After breakfast, I return to my stateroom. A man is standing in front of it, a towel in his hands.

I walk a few steps closer and see that it's Mark. My face flushes at the sight of him.

I reach the door and pull out my key. "What are you doing here?"

"Hello to you too."

My face flushes *again* at the sound of his voice. Deep and sexy. Ugh.

"Hello. Is there a reason you're standing outside of my stateroom?"

"Our stateroom. And I'd like to take a shower, if you don't mind."

I put my key in the lock, turn it, and push open the door. "You don't have a place to shower?"

He shakes his head. "I don't have a *room*, remember?"

I'm about to open my mouth and tell him to go to the gym or the pool or something then close it. It's not his fault the cruise mixed up our reservation and haven't gotten him a replacement yet. Plus, it was nice of him to give me the room. The least I can do is let him take a single shower. I push open the door. "Fine. One shower."

"Thanks ever so much." Sarcasm edges his tone.

He steps inside.

"Nice morning with your girlfriends?"

"The best. They were quite concerned about my back."

"Good on them," I say. "Wouldn't think a few pieces of luggage would be that much of an issue."

He widens his eyes. "A few pieces of the heaviest luggage imaginable. What did you put in there? Granite?"

"Just the essentials."

"Essentials like that?" He nods toward my book on the nightstand.

"Exactly like that."

He takes a step toward the book and swipes from the surface. "*The Chocolate Mystery Club?* Is this what you're reading?"

"Yes."

"There's a cartoon on the front. Is it for children?"

"No, it's not for children." I lunge forward and grab the book from his hand. "It's a cozy mystery," I say defensively, glad I didn't leave out my copy of *Scones and Drones*, a book about a baker who solves crimes using her personal drone.

"A cozy mystery?" He sounds genuinely perplexed.

"Yes, a cozy mystery."

"Okay." The word comes out like a question.

I stamp my foot. "Why? What do you read?"

"Not that." He shakes his head, steps in the bathroom, and shuts the door. Seconds later, the shower water starts. I place *The Chocolate Mystery Club* on the nightstand. Book three in a ten-part series, thank you very much. Cozy mysteries are very much in vogue. They're all over bookstores. The fact that Mark doesn't know what they are says a lot more about him than it does about me. Right?

I'm still ruminating on his reaction to the book when he steps out of the bathroom, dressed, towel in hand.

"It's a very popular genre," I chirp.

He brushes damp hair away from his face. "What?"

"Cozy mysteries," I say, and realize that, unlike me, Mark hasn't spent the last five minutes obsessing over our conversation.

"Whatever you say, Ellie." He waves his hand in the direction of the book. "Enjoy it, and thanks for the shower." He opens the door and slips outside.

The door closes shut and for some inexplicable reason, I'm disappointed. Ridiculous. It's not like we'd spend more time arguing over whether cozy mysteries are a thing or not (they are). Plus, why wouldn't he leave? This is my room, not his. Plus, he still might be a scammer. I don't know anything yet.

The door shuts. I find my purse and fish around inside it for my phone. I cram tons of stuff into my purse, a trait friends and family make fun of me for endlessly. Until they need something. Then it's all "thanks" and "good thinking." So anyway, it takes me a few moments and a peek inside the bag before I finally grip the phone. I pull it out and text Caleb: *Did you find anything out about Mark Moore?*

I wait for the telltale dots signaling a text back, then check the time. Caleb is probably driving his daughter Chelsea, my only grandchild, to high school on his way to work. Something his wife Marissa can do but doesn't. Lord knows that one can't miss a Pilates class. I wait a few more moments for a response before calling him. I *need* to know what's up with this man.

"Mom? Everything okay?"

He sounds worried. "All fine, sweetheart," I say. "I was just wondering if you found anything out about Mark Moore?"

"Why? Is he bothering you?"

Yes. "No. I was just wondering."

"I googled him. Couldn't find anything." He pauses. His radio, tuned to the sports news channel, blares in the background. "I think it's fine, Mom."

He says the words as if I'm overreacting. *He* was the one who told me to be on high alert.

"I wouldn't worry about it."

"Okay, honey. I won't."

Chapter 6

Mark

I'm on my way to lunch. I still don't have a room. I need to get this worked out. I don't want to sleep on a lounge chair again and I don't want to ask Ellie if I can use her shower a second time. She's a trip, that one. The sink in her room was absurd. I've never seen so many beauty products in one place. And that book. Cozy mystery? What could be cozy about it?

I step into the dining room, and like I'm wearing a homing device, Brandy senses my presence and waves. Big armed waves that can't be ignored. I hadn't planned to sit with the sheep, but I guess I'll have to. I reach the table and the first thing I notice is that Ellie isn't there. Disappointment swirls through me. I may not like Ellie, but she is a character. Dining in her company would likely be entertaining. The second thing I notice is Brandy, who I need to talk to about my room, is now engrossed in a conversation. I'll catch her after lunch.

I sit in an unoccupied chair and grab a roll from a plastic basket in the center. Today's lunch is "Pita Palooza," and pitas with cold cuts and other condiments are lined up on the buffet table. A cruise worker calls the cow table and a group of people, mooing and laughing, move to the buffet. Despite it being only noon, it appears that the cows have had a few.

The man next to me angles his phone in my direction. "Just bought this stock. It's a beauty. Hank, by the way."

"Mark." I look at Hank's phone, his transaction still on the screen. As far as I can tell, he had purchased 150 shares of something with the initials LMP. "Good choice," I say, though I have no idea if it's a good choice or not. What is LMP even?

"Also bought this." He retrieves his phone, punches a few buttons, then flashes the screen in my direction. There's another stock with the initials DBC and a wavy line under it.

"Great."

He taps at the phone with his index finger. "You should consider getting this."

"Okay." I have no intention of doing this, but if I tell him that, I know he'll start a deep dive on the benefits of the stock. Before he can recommend *another* stock, the cruise worker in charge of the buffet calls "sheep." I stand and spot Ellie making her way across the ballroom. She's in a fuchsia sweater and white jeans. She looks pretty, not that I'm noticing. Okay, I am noticing, but I don't care. As much of a character as she is, Ellie has crazy energy. I need to steer clear.

"Hi y'all," she says to the group and slides into line. We all pile food on our plates, except Aspen, who only gets a salad. "Vegan life," she says, holding her plate in the air.

When our group is back at the table, Ellie slides into the seat on the other side of Hank. He's immediately off to the races with his financial monologue. Ellie exclaims "you don't say" or "I'll be" every now and then, but I'd bet good money that she's not paying a lick of attention to anything he's saying. Then again, what do I know? She might be as riveted as she seems. She might *want* to know more about LMP and DBC and whatever else he's got on his phone screen.

I filter out Hank's voice, take a bite of my turkey pita, and look around. The remaining three women at the table are engrossed in their own conversation. Ellie and Hank continue talking. As a matter of habit, I pull out my phone, open my Kindle app, and start to read. It's what I always do when I eat alone.

Hank gets up and heads back to the buffet line. As soon as he leaves, Ellie looks at me over his empty chair.

"You're not reading at the table, are you Mark?" Her Southern drawl is perfect.

I angle my head toward her. "I am, as a matter of fact."

"A cozy mystery?" she asks with a smile.

"Absolutely not."

"What is it then?"

"*Plagues and Medieval Times.*"

She purses her lips and her eyes dance as if I've given her the best possible gift. "You made fun of my book and you're reading *Plagues and Medieval Times*? During lunch, no less."

"What?" I question, though I know what. I'm reading a book about medieval history when I should be socializing with my cruise mates. "I was a social studies teacher," I say, as if this explains things.

"Goodness." Ellie puts an open hand over her heart. She's wearing a wrist full of bangle bracelets. "I hope you didn't have to teach about plagues."

"I didn't. I just like plagues." I could kick myself after I say the words. Who in the heck likes plagues? But before I can explain myself—I don't really like plagues, I just find them interesting—Hank moves back into the seat between us.

"What's this about plagues?" Trudy picks her head up. It's the first time she's addressed me since I sat down.

"It's just a book," I say sheepishly.

Aspen scrunches up her face. "About plagues?"

"Mark likes plagues," Ellie interjects.

"You *like* plagues?" Hank says. "Like the Black Death?"

"I don't like plagues," I insist. "It's just an interesting part of history." No one speaks and I add, "The book also goes into medieval history. Knights and stuff."

"Huh," Trudy says, and I feel as foolish as I can at seventy-two, which frankly is not all that foolish. One great thing that comes with age is that you care less about what people think. Most people anyway. Against all odds, I find myself caring about what Ellie thinks. I don't want her to think I'm the kind of guy who would rather read about medieval history than converse with people.

Ellie holds up a wine glass. "To knights in shining armor," she says and winks.

At least I think she winked. Did she? Did she wink at me? Should I wink back? I shake my head. Man, I am the worst socializer of all time. No wonder Addison insisted that I come on this cruise.

"To knights in shining armor," the group repeats, but I'm so distracted by the possible wink from Ellie that I sit still, my water glass dormant on the table.

"Mark." Aspen wiggles her wine glass.

"Yes," I say, orienting myself to the present. "To knights." I pick up my water glass and clink it with the others.

I don't read my book for the rest of the meal and try to participate in the conversations. But I'm tired and my back hurts and I just want lunch to be over. But when dessert is put out—miniscule scoops of vanilla ice cream in plastic cups—Dan, who I've gathered is the head cruise employee, announces that there's going to be a trivia competition between groups. The cow table goes wild with moos; there's some half-hearted animal noises from other tables. "Come on y'all," Ellie says. She opens her mouth and lets out a "baa." The others join in. I don't. I can't. It's too stupid.

"Mark?" Ellie looks in my direction.

"Sorry." I shrug. "I'd rather read about plagues."

"You're the worst," she says. But the way she says it? It doesn't seem like she thinks I'm the worst.

Despite Ellie's maybe wink and the remark that seemed like flirting (who knows?), I've reached my interaction quota for the day, and I really need my room. I stand and look around for Brandy but don't see her. Crap. I should have cornered her when I had the chance.

Trivia starts and thankfully goes quickly, though the sheep, myself included, are terrible. Our only winning category is Roller Coaster or Horror Movie, the clues being names like Dragon Fire, Cobra, and Fear Flight. A roller coaster buff in her younger days, Aspen got all fifteen right. But as a team we came in second to last, only beating the dogs. The cows won overall, and their excessive celebratory mooing makes me really want to check out of this lunch and lie down.

I get up to look for Brandy and find her standing with a bunch of the other cruise employees. "Any news about the room?"

For a moment she looks *again* like she doesn't know what I'm talking about, then says, "Oh yes. I've got one. Let me get the key."

She leaves the ballroom and returns with a key. I follow her down several corridors, all of which look abandoned. Unlike the other hallways, there are no anchors on the front of each door, no sounds of people in the rooms. It's creepy. Like we're deserted on a run-down cruise ship.

"The *Carpe Diem III* is a little old," Brandy tells me as we walk. "The last owners ripped out a good number of the state-rooms to modernize, but they ran out of money. The new owners have been redoing them, bit by bit, but they didn't get to all of them yet." She reaches an unmarked and unnamed door, puts a key in the lock, and turns. "This one is mostly done." She makes the statement cheerfully—like the adverb "mostly" is not a huge red flag—and pushes open the door.

The room is not "mostly done." It has no carpet and a cot instead of a bed. A bunch of unplugged power tools and a sawhorse sit piled in the corner.

"I'll take it," I say because this room is better than being a nomad for the next six days. I step inside just as a voice sounds behind me.

"No."

Chapter 7

Ellie

"No," I say again. "Absolutely not."

Mark turns and squints in my direction. "Ellie?"

"Yes," I say like my presence is expected, like I didn't just follow him and Brandy down here, staying far enough back that they wouldn't notice. In fairness, I hadn't meant to keep following them. I wanted to apologize to Mark for accusing him of trying to scam me. Caleb didn't find anything definitive, and frankly, he doesn't seem like a con-artist. I think I got that wrong and I needed to set the record straight. So when he and Brandy kept walking, I got curious and followed. And here I am.

"The bathroom is great," Brandy says, not seeming to think it's weird that I'm here or that I'm giving an opinion on Mark's room. She swings the door open to a small bathroom with shining new fixtures. "See? It's new."

I shake my head. "Nice, but no."

"Excuse me?" Mark says. His eyes meet mine.

"You can't sleep on a thin cot with a bad back. And this

floor -" I sweep my hand across the space. "There are pop-up nails everywhere. And power tools in the corner. There's not even a dresser." I fold my arms across my chest and look at Brandy. "This is unacceptable."

The corners of Mark's mouth quirk up slightly.

"The cruise is overbooked," Brandy says. "This room is the best of what's available." She leans forward and whispers, "Most rooms don't even have toilets. Just holes where they'll be someday."

"Imagine living in a world where every stateroom hole has a toilet over it," Mark says, deadpan. He throws his small suitcase on the cot. "I'll take it."

Take it? No. His back will be a mess. I lunge forward, pick up his bag, and drop it at his feet. "No, you won't."

He raises an eyebrow. "Are you suggesting I sleep on the lounge chair again? Because I hate to break it to you, but sleeping on that chair would be worse than this cot."

"I'm not suggesting you sleep on the lounge chair," I spit out. "I'm suggesting you sleep with me."

I play back the statement in my head just as Mark says, "Wow. That's quite the invitation. I accept."

I flail my hands in his direction, heat running from my chest to my face. "I didn't mean it like that." I stop, interrupted by Mark's guffawing laughter. He collapses on to the small cot and wipes at his eyes.

"Are you quite done?" I say, irritated that my grandiose gesture has been derailed.

"Your face—" He points at me through the laughter, unable to finish.

"Should I leave you two alone?" Brandy asks.

It's hard to tell if she's serious or means it as part of the joke, but either way, the remark elicits a second round of roaring laughter from Mark. "Oh my God," he gasps, seemingly trying to catch his breath. "I haven't laughed like this in forever." He clutches his stomach. "My ribs actually hurt."

I stand, red-faced, though it is, I admit, a little funny. A funny story I'll tell *later*.

He finally catches his breath and calms down. "That's a nice gesture, but I couldn't do that to you. I'll be fine here. Believe me, I've stayed in worse."

I shake my head. "My ex-husband had a bad back. You need a good mattress. The bed in my room, our room, is actually two twins. We'll push them apart." I'd come up with this solution on the fly when I saw the cot. But it makes sense. I mean, it's not like we're going to be in the room a ton.

"Aren't you worried I'm going to scam you?" He rolls his eyes.

I hold up both hands, flexed at the wrist like I'm making a double stop gesture. "I was wrong. I'm sorry. And I know carrying my luggage hurt your back. At least let me make sure you have a good mattress to sleep on."

He lies down on the cot. He shifts his body to the left, and then to the right. "This is pretty bare boned as far as cots go." He sits up.

"If we're not compatible, you can always come back to this room," I suggest.

He laughs again, not hysterical like before, but still laughing.

I stamp my foot. "What?"

"Ellie," he starts. It's the first time he's said my name, and I like the way it sounds. "There is absolutely no way we're compatible," he continues, still chuckling, and my recent affinity for how he said my name diminishes. "No way," he says again, like the idea of the two of us getting along in any way, let alone being compatible, is preposterous. "But you're right. Sleeping on a firmer mattress would save my back. And

I'll stay out of your way, completely." He jets out his hand. "Deal?"

I'm put off, a little, by his hysterics at the thought of getting along with me, but I can't exactly rescind the offer without looking like a total jerk. "Deal," I say and shake his hand.

Brandy looks from me to Mark and back again. "I'm so glad the two of you worked things out," she says. "I hate it when couples fight."

Chapter 8

Mark

I follow Ellie to the room. She unlocks it and swings open the door. I step inside and blow out a breath. Oh man.

I hadn't fully taken it in when I came for the shower, or else it's gotten worse, but the room is a mess. Not *a few things out of place* kind of mess. A *this place has been ransacked* kind of mess. Ellie's clothes, shoes, and assorted beauty products are everywhere. Inside the mirrored closet. Laid across the bed. Splayed out on the floor. Strewn across the dresser. Hanging off door frames. Bursting out of drawers.

"Sorry." She slings a pile of dresses from the bed into the closet. "I didn't realize I'd be sharing a room."

I nod. While this situation isn't either of our faults, she could have just let me stay in the awful cot room. She didn't have to offer to let me stay here. "Thank you."

"Sure. I know from Harrison how bad back pain can be. Anyway, put your stuff anywhere. I'm not that neat, if you can't tell."

I nod and set my small suitcase on a patch of unoccupied

rug. I'm fastidiously neat, and the shambled state of the room is giving me hives.

"Listen," she says, holding up her phone. "I just got a text from Trudy. She wants to meet in Ballroom C. A bunch of people are playing giant checkers. A round robin kind of thing. Want to come?"

"No." The word shoots out of my mouth like a reflex. Lunch, the trivia game, it was all enough for me. And I think my back will feel better if I lie down for a bit. "Thanks for asking," I add.

Ellie waves in my direction, a *your loss* kind of gesture. "Okay then." She opens the door, then twists around and looks at me. "You're not going to sit here alone and read about plagues, are you?"

I hold up three fingers in an imitation of the boy scout pledge. "No plague reading. I promise."

She looks like she doesn't believe me.

"I'm just going to lie down a bit for my back."

"Okay. If you get bored, feel free to read *The Chocolate Mystery Club*." She winks and steps out. The door shuts with an affirmative click. I sit on the bed and the feeling that I need to do something lodges in my gut. My mind races with the chores, tasks, and work that have occupied my days and nights for decades. But there's nothing. I don't have to go to work, not just because I'm on vacation, but because of the "maybe you should retire" conversation with the hip, young principal. I'm not at home, so I don't have any odd jobs to keep me busy. And there's nothing I need to do for Sara; Addison has that covered for the week.

My eyes rest on the items strewn across the dresser. Then those on the floor and in the closets and bursting out of drawers.

Not my mess.

Right?

Not my mess.

I lean back and close my eyes, but I can picture the disarray in my mind's eye. For so long I've lived only with Sara, who pretty much has to be super neat because of me. I am unaccustomed to the messes of others. No caps left off toothpaste. No dishes in the sink. No water droplets on the mirror. No stuff *everywhere*.

I sit up. I could just pick up the clothes on the floor. I mean, left as they are, Ellie's things will get wrinkled or dirty. If I hang them up, I'd be doing her a favor. A thank you. Yes.

I push myself off the bed, pick up a blouse, and hang it in the closet. I do the same with a second blouse, then a sweater, then a T-shirt. I continue the effort until all the clothes on the floor are hanging, in size order, in the closet. The space looks better, considerably so. I could do something with her shoes. It would be easier for her to see what pairs she has if I just threw them all in the closet. Or lined them up in a perfect singular row by color. Potayto. Potatho.

I fix the shoes, and on a roll, move to the dresser and the sink, lining up lipstick tubes, organizing hair products, folding towels. I move to open a drawer, then stop. It's likely her undergarments are in one of them and fooling with those is an invasion of privacy.

I lie on the bed again, my back aggravated by the burst of cleaning. But even with the room neat, I can't get settled. I open my Kindle to the plague book, then remember my promise to Ellie and shut it off. I wonder what she's doing. Is giant checkers fun? Is she doing something else now? Should I have gone with her? I shake my head. Stupid. Ellie, blue eyes and bright smile aside, is not my type. I force her from my mind and my thoughts move to Sara and her care. Addison probably has a bunch of questions. I should call. In fact, I might be doing Addison a favor by calling. That way, she doesn't have to call me and admit she doesn't know something.

I swipe my phone from the nightstand and press Addison's contact. After the initial niceties—yes, the cruise is tons of fun (not) and yes, I'm being very social (definitely not)—I dive into a series of reminders about Sara's care. Things that, deep down, I know Addison knows already.

She doesn't respond and regret piles inside me. All this needless call has done is made Addison feel like I don't trust her.

"Sara's fine," she says flatly.

"Okay. Great." I infuse false cheer into my voice.

"Are you even trying to have fun?"

"Yes," I insist. "I actually have a roommate." I dive into the story, leaving out the part about Ellie thinking I was a scammer and me hurting my back, and try to make the situation seem like a hilarious comedy of errors. I describe the state of the room when I got here. "I've made it so neat," I tell her, "it's unrecognizable."

"You didn't."

"Didn't what?"

"Clean up the room."

"I did. It looks so much better."

"That's creepy, Dad. Most women wouldn't want a stranger touching all their things. You need to put everything back."

"Why?" I scan the neatly arranged closet, the row of shoes underneath. "It's so much more orderly now."

"Dad." She says my name like a long exhale. "She won't want to think you rifled through her stuff. Just put it back. Trust me."

We say goodbye, and she makes me promise not to call again. "I promise."

"And have fun," she adds.

"Sure." I click off the call and I stare at the ordered room. Is Addison right? Will Ellie be upset that I put away her things? Maybe. Probably. God. Of course she will. She'd just gotten over the idea of me being a con artist.

I stand up and scatter her make-up across the dresser. I rumple the bed and throw shoes all over the room, careful to be as disorderly as possible, as much as it kills me. I take the tooth-brush out of the holder, uncap the toothpaste, and unfold the towels. I spread her hair supplies across the sink. After, I move to the closet and pull all the clothes I'd painstakingly hung up off their hangers. I ball them up in my arms, ready to throw, when the door clicks and opens behind me. I turn and my eyes meet Ellie's.

Chapter 9

Ellie

"**G**iant checkers was canceled," I say.

Mark turns around, a wad of clothes balled up in his arms. His brown eyes are wide; his mouth agape. The clothes in his arms are mine.

He drops the bundle at his feet. "I just, things were—" he starts. He stutters out a few more words before blurting, "I couldn't stand the mess, okay? I cleaned everything up and then I called my daughter, and she said that me tidying up the room was creepy and that I should put everything back. So I'm doing that."

"Messing up my clothes?"

"Putting them back where they were." He gestures to the floor. "And I realize now that cleaning up your things was over-stepping." He picks up a shirt and flings it across the room. "I'm sorry. My fastidious nature gets the best of me sometimes."

I shut the door, step over my clothes, and sit on the edge of the bed. I should be mad. I barely know this man and he was all in my business so to speak. Still. He sounds genuine. And I *am* an unabashed slob. It used to drive Harrison and Caleb crazy.

"If you want me to go back to that other room, I under-stand." He tosses a pair of pants toward the dresser.

"Nonsense," I say, and in that split second, I decide to trust my gut. Mark and I may not be compatible as he so chivalrously pointed out, but he's not a bad person. He doesn't deserve to have his back hurt all vacation. "My mother was super-neat," I tell him. "It's a sickness."

I make the statement in jest, but I don't mean it that way. Growing up, my mother was obsessed with cleanliness. Our house never looked good enough to have friends over. We couldn't have dogs (too much hair), or cats (scratch marks), or bake (too messy). Our home was perfect, but it felt more like a hotel. "It's why I am the way I am," I add. "I'd rather have fun than be neat."

Mark lobs my favorite pair of pink shorts across the room. "You can do both, you know."

"Have fun and be neat? Pshaw." I nod my head toward him, a shoe in his hand. "Plus, I think you're having fun being messy, Mr. Mark Moore."

"I am not." He chucks my cover-up in the corner. "My soul is dying."

I snort a laugh, push off the bed, and grab the shoe from his hand. "Okay, Mark. I have a deal for you." I throw the shoe and swipe his small suitcase off the floor. "We're going to make a big mess."

His eyes widen.

"And then we're going to leave it and go to the pool."

"Make a mess and leave? Why?"

"Why?" I unzip his small suitcase and dump the contents on the bed. The items land in neat piles rather than in a scatter. "Because I spent my messy, explorative childhood years with a woman who never let loose. It's not too late for you, you know." I pause. I know me projecting my childhood on to Mark is wrong, but there might just be a super-fun guy beneath that cranky, ultra-neat exterior. And I want to find out.

"You can clean everything up when we get back, if it still bothers you," I offer, and pick up a pair of neatly balled socks. "Deal?" I lob the socks into a corner.

"I think this is absurd, but I suppose I owe you." He grabs a perfectly folded shirt from the bed and drops it on the floor. It lands in a perfect square.

I catch his eye and lift my eyebrows. "Seriously?"

"Fine." He picks up the shirt, unfolds it and tries again.

We pick up and scatter more of his things. When I blurted the idea out, I thought the experience would be much more cathartic, even fun, like a septuagenarian pillow fight with clothes. But it's not like that. Mark looks increasingly pained as more and more items pile up. This clearly isn't the way to get to that fun core I know is in there somewhere. Fine. I clap my hands. "Pool time."

Mark looks around the small space. "Is it messy enough?"

He asks the question sincerely, like I have a chaos meter or keep a mess spreadsheet or something. "It looks cluttered enough that you're starting to break out in hives." I nod toward a red welt on his arm. "So, let's have some fun and we'll clean it all up when we get back." I lean forward and give his arm a light slap. "I'll even help you."

"Great," he says with an edge of sarcasm.

"Rude."

We take turns in the bathroom to dress, Mark taking all of one minute to get ready. When he emerges, I wave my phone. "Trudy said in the chat that the sheep are at the Pineapple Pool."

He pulls open the stateroom door. "I need a moment to digest that sentence."

I snort a laugh.

"And you like them? The other sheep?"

"Why not? Everyone has something to offer, right?" I step through the door. "Hank's got his financial shtick. Aspen pretends to be a vegan and all into health, but I think she's not really. And Trudy? Quiet but strong. I'm pretty sure she was a world leader in a past life." I rummage in my bag for my sunglasses and pull them out. "Oh. And Brandy. Not quite sure the elevator is making it all the way to the top there."

"How do you do that?" Mark steps behind me and the door swings closed.

"Do what?"

"Get to know everyone so quickly."

I shrug and poke the elevator button. "I like people. When they talk, I pay attention."

He steps inside the elevator. "Yeah. Okay. That's the difference. I'm not really a people guy."

"Pshaw." I swing my bag over my shoulder as the elevator doors slide shut. "Everyone is a people person."

When we get to the pool area, we find the other sheep sitting at a table by a questionably green pool, a placard that states "NO SWIMMING" sitting on its edge. We pass by a kid, twentyish, in a lifeguard T-shirt with a white bag labeled "pool chemicals" in Sharpie marker. "Don't worry," he says to the smattering of seniors congregated on the pool deck. "I'm going to shock this baby to kingdom come."

I'm contemplating why it is that that statement does not make me feel better, when Mark says "Gavin?"

The kid's face registers surprise, then recognition, then breaks into a broad smile. "Coach Moore. Wow. I didn't expect to see you here." He embraces Mark in an impressive bear hug.

"Great to see you," Mark says with as much enthusiasm as I'd heard from him yet. "Addison booked the cruise for me. Says I needed to have some fun." He rolls his eyes.

"Fun is good," Gavin says jovially.

I'm still at Mark's side and Gavin's gaze shifts to me.

"Ellie," Mark says, "this is Gavin. He was in my US History class and on my soccer team for the high school. And I taught his dad. First class I ever had." He bumps Gavin on the shoulder. "His family lived down the street from me for a time." He pauses. "And Gavin, this is Ellie, my—" he hesitates for the longest time before saying (drumroll)— "acquaintance."

Acquaintance! I know it's an accurate depiction, but the word feels so sterile, like we just met in the elevator a second ago. Acquaintance, my fanny. "We're sharing a room," I blurt and squeeze Mark's arm.

Gavin's eyes get big. "Oh, well. Congratulations." His eyebrows knit together. "Or have fun. I mean—" He points to the circular button every cruise employee must be required to wear. "Go Seniors!"

Mark doesn't respond, his entire face red as a beet. "Thanks," I say breezily, and take Mark by the elbow. I usher him toward the table where the other sheep are sitting.

He turns back toward Gavin. "Catch up later?" he calls.

"Sure thing, Coach Moore."

He swings his head back toward me and whispers, "What was that about?"

"What was what about?" I ask, feigning ignorance.

"You made it seem like we were—" He stops.

"So what? Unless—" Oh. No. No. Noooo. He has a girl-friend or wife. Crap. Why didn't I consider that? Mark's hand-some. Funny. And neat, a trait almost any woman would like. Of course, he has someone at home. I grip his arm. "You have someone at home," I declare. "I'm so sorry."

"No." He shakes his head. "It's nothing like that. There's no one at home."

"Oh." I puff out a breath and release his arm. "Then it shouldn't matter." I slide into a chair.

"Maybe." He sits next to me and studies the space around us. Everything is either shaped like a pineapple or has a pineapple on it. The pool, the chairs, the table, the towels, the bar, the glasses, the umbrellas. Even the bartender is in on it, wearing a hat shaped like a pineapple. "Good Lord," Mark says, "they really overdid it with the pineapple theme."

"Stop being such a grump." I shake my head and look to the group. "Remember Mark? He's the one who likes plagues."

"I don't like plagues," Mark says, but he laughs as the words come out.

"Hey, hey, hey." Brandy sashays toward the table, a bright orange innertube around her waist. "You Sheep ready for some pool games?"

No one answers. Even I don't, and I love games. But in a green pool that needs to be "shocked to kingdom come?" No thanks.

"No swimmers?" Brandy presses.

"Not in that swamp," Trudy says finally.

Brandy shifts her gaze toward the pool. "Oh." She stands still for a moment, then claps her hands together. "No worries, Sheep. We can play a deck game!"

Chapter 10

Mark

A game?
Another one.
No way. I already played trivia and one game a day is more than enough for me.

Brandy grabs Gavin and the two of them have a brief conversation. After, Gavin zig zags the deck and stops at each person or group who made the unfortunate choice to come to the Pineapple Pool this afternoon. A few congregate around the sheep table, waiting, I guess, for the game instructions. Instructions I will not need.

I push off my chair and salute the group. "I'm out of here."

"Well, aren't you just a dog in a manger," Ellie says, her Southern drawl thick.

She throws a bright smile in my direction. I have no idea what a dog in a manger is; it can't be good. But that smile? I almost change my mind, then I remember the lethal combo of games and people, and wave her off. No way.

"But Mark, I have cruiser coupons." Brandy pulls a stack of rectangular papers from her pocket. "For the winner of this game, I'm giving a dinner upgrade. Steak for two." She holds out what appears to be a computer-generated coupon with an image of a steak on it.

Steak. I'd love a steak. The Pita Palooza lunch was not the best and definitely not filling. And tonight, I happen to know, is a glorified potato bar. The Potato Palooza of all things. The cruise menu tried to make the offering sound fun and festive — "Dress Up Your Spud!" — but I know my way around a cheap meal, and this is it. Yeah. Steak trumps potatoes, no contest. I take a step toward Brandy. "I'm listening."

"Okay, here's the deal. We're going to play bumper cars. We played this game at cruise camp, and it was super fun." She does not elaborate on "cruise camp" but does explain the game. Participants are to pretend to drive invisible cars and when she yells "stop," we bump into the person closest to us. She yells a question, and we both answer it. "It's a great way to get to know your fellow cruisers," she concludes.

"I can't move all that well." A thin, white-haired woman in a T-shirt that says "Super G-Mom" gestures to her cane.

"My balance isn't the best," someone else says.

"I don't want to get bumped," a third person admits.

For me, I can't figure out how anyone could possibly win. And I'm not playing if steaks aren't in the mix.

"Okay, Seniors. Okay." Brandy waves her hands like she's trying to corral a bunch of kindergartners. "If you can't move, just stay where you are. And no bumping into people. Just a tap." She lightly taps Gavin in demonstration.

"And how do you win?" I ask.

Brandy contorts her face and it's clear she hadn't thought about that piece, the most essential one as far as I'm concerned. "Gavin and I will choose the most enthusiastic participant," she says finally.

"Forget that." I start toward the elevator.

Ellie materializes by my side and tugs my arm. "If you play, I'll take you if I win. You can even have my steak."

I whirl around, the blue of Ellie's eyes taking me by surprise for what feels like the zillionth time. "Why would you do that? I'm probably the least fun person here."

"Exactly." She smiles. "And I would give up a steak to see you pretending to drive an invisible car. Or talk to people."

"And you'd go to dinner with me?" This, for some reason, feels like an important detail.

"I would." She shrugs. "Why not?"

I can think of a gazillion reasons why not, the main one being that she would have way more fun with almost anyone else. But steak. I could really use a steak about now. I shoot out my hand. "Deal."

She shakes it. "Deal."

"Okay Seniors!" Brandy yells. "Let's start this shindig. Start driving in three, two, one. Go." She pulls her arm down like it's the start flag in a Grand Prix.

Participants move around the pool, their arms in the air like they're holding invisible steering wheels. Most of the effort is lackluster, but Trudy beeps as she moves. "That's the spirit, Trudy!" Brandy calls, and there are a few more beeps after that. But not from me. I try to do it, I swear, but the game is so ludicrous that I just can't. I walk around the outskirts with my hands at my sides. After what's probably thirty-seconds but feels like an hour, Brandy yells "Stop."

Hank crashes into me. I'll note that it's *not* a tap.

"Favorite childhood memory," Brandy calls.

I work to think of any memory, let alone a favorite one, when Hank leans in and says, "I call Ellie."

I whip my head up and look into his eyes. Green, wide, and intense. "What?"

"Ellie. I'm into her. Dibs." He pushes at my shoulder. I feel like I'm in high school. Should I push back? Fight? Over a woman I just met?

Before I do anything, Brandy says "Go," and Hank's off, moving his hands in a driving motion like a tool. Dibs? You can't call dibs on a person. And Hank's not Ellie's type. Or maybe he is. I remind myself that I don't know Ellie all that well.

"Stop." Brandy says.

I'm closest to the woman with the cane wearing the "Super G-Mom" shirt and stop. "Interesting talent," Brandy calls.

"I can yodel," Super-G Mom says. A second later, she opens up her throat and lets one rip.

The whole deck goes silent.

"Wow," I say finally. "That was something."

Conversations resume around us. "How about you?" she asks.

"I can blink really rapidly." I say quickly, remembering my old party trick. I give a few quick blinks to demonstrate. Super G-Mom says nothing, just stares, and I immediately want to amend my answer. Surely, I have more interesting talents than fast blinking. I scan my mind, but I can't think of anything. Fast blinking. My most interesting talent after seventy-two years of life. Nice. Hank appears in my peripheral vision. I wonder what his most interesting trait is. Better than fast blinking, I'm sure.

"Go Seniors," Brandy yells.

The game resumes and Ellie bumps into me which, after the fast-blinking debacle, is not what I need right now.

"Most interesting place you've visited," Brandy yells and Ellie immediately says "Switzerland."

Switzerland. Not only have I never been out of the United States until now, I barely ever left the tri-state area (Pennsylvania, New Jersey, New York). I'll bet Ellie has been to tons of interesting places. And has more interesting traits than fast blinking. God. There's a reason I don't mingle with others.

Ellie nods at me, a prompt.

"Me too," I blurt and immediately regret the lie. Clearly, if she's been to Switzerland, she's going to want details about my non-existent trip there.

As if on cue, her face erupts into a smile and she says, "I can't wait to catch up about that."

"Yeah," I lie. "Me too."

After a few rounds, the game ends. Surprise, surprise. I don't win. Neither does Ellie. Trudy does and she invites Aspen. So, there's that. No chance of steak. Maybe I could pay for an upgrade?

"Pool's clear!" Brandy yells. It is clear, but for the water to go from slimy green to a bright blue in less than an hour makes me wonder what kind of crazy compounds were in Gavin's Sharpie-labeled bag of "pool chemicals." Not any I want to swim in.

I'll just go back to the room. It would be good to rest my back. I move to tell Ellie my plan when Hank jumps in front of me. Literally. Like he's staking his claim. And though I don't really know Ellie, protectiveness surges through me. Or maybe it's machoism. Either way, I make the decision that, as long as Hank's here with Ellie, I'm not leaving the pool deck.

He lays out a pool towel on a lounge chair for Ellie and sets himself up next to her. I put a cruise-owned pineapple-themed towel on the other side. Hank drones on and on about money-related things, mostly centered around everything he owns or has owned or plans to own in the future. It's brutal and begs the question: Why, if you have so much money, are you stuck on this frugal cruise with the rest of us?

"Don't forget sunscreen," Ellie says and pulls a bottle from her bag. She waves it in my direction, but Hank swipes it from her hands. Whatever guy. I don't burn anyway.

Hank continues to drone on about his portfolio. The combination of lack of sleep and his boring monologue converges and practically forces my eyes shut. Like the best-ever sleep story.

When I wake, there's no Ellie. No Hank. No one I recognize, except Gavin. And my skin is hot. I glance down. And red.

"Got a bit of a burn there, Coach Moore," Gavin calls from a chair by the pool.

"Yeah." I sit up and feel my skin. Warm. Damn. I should have used that sunscreen.

I amble over to him, pull up a chair, and sit next to him. There's one woman in the pool, both her arms on its edge.

"So how are things?" I ask him. His dad died of a heart attack when he was a junior in high school. He'd had a terrible time with it, and I'd tried to be there for him. I was his teacher, his neighbor, and I'd known his family for years. Eventually, his family moved. I exchanged Christmas cards with them for a few years, but eventually we lost touch. This is the first I've seen Gavin in at least a decade.

"Doing okay, Coach Moore. Can't beat this for a job, right?" He gestures toward a perfect blue sky.

"That's for sure. And your mom? How's she?"

His face erupts into a smile. "Doing great. Moved to Clarks Summit."

Clarks Summit is an expensive suburb of Scranton. "I'm so glad to hear that," I say, meaning it. Gavin's mother had some health and financial problems after her husband, Gavin's dad, died. If she moved, especially to an area like Clarks Summit, she must be doing better.

Gavin leans in toward me. "Not sure how to tell you this Coach," he whispers, "but Ellie left with that Hank guy."

I wave my hand like Ellie's whereabouts and company are none of my concern—which, of course, they are not. "We're not really together," I say. "There was a room mix-up."

"Oh. Good." Relief crosses over his features. I'm more than a little touched that he still cares this much about me after so many years.

"Well," I say, pushing off the chair with both arms, "I'd better get going."

"See you around, Coach."

I walk back toward the stateroom, my back aggravated by the movement and my psyche bothered by the fact that Ellie and Hank left together. It shouldn't bother me. Ellie's not even my type. Still. The vision of Hank saying dibs, like Ellie's a possession instead of a woman, irritates me. She must know he's a total tool. Right?

After cleaning up my stuff, I return to the room and lie down for a bit. After, I take a scalding hot shower for back pain, order the room (just a bit), and make my way to the Potato Palooza. If I'm honest, I hope I'll see Ellie. Instead, I see Gavin and Brandy together at a table. They wave in unison, and I wonder briefly if they're a couple. Maybe? Each of them could do worse.

I'm piling on way more than my share of bacon bits when I see them, Hank and Ellie, tucked away in a corner with full plates and empty wineglasses. Just when I'm thinking she's probably not enjoying his company — probably hating it, in fact — she throws back her head and laughs like whatever he just said is the funniest thing she's ever heard. After, she sets her hand over his.

Damn.

Chapter 11

Ellie

The stateroom is pitch dark. I shine my light around the room, remnants of the mess I'd insisted we make this afternoon completely erased: clothing hung up neatly, shoes ordered on the closet floor, my lipsticks lined across on the dresser like silver soldiers. The beds are pushed apart, but Mark isn't in either one. I check the time on my phone: 10:47 p.m.

I haven't seen Mark since leaving him asleep on the pool deck. I'd wanted to wake him, but he was sleeping so soundly, I figured he probably needed the sleep and that we'd catch up later. But I didn't see him at the Potato Palooza or at the senior mixer after.

I get ready for bed and snuggle under the covers. I startle at a stray sound in the hall. Mark? I sit up and look at the door, realizing with a start that I'm hoping it will be Mark, hoping he's back. He's grumpy, but he's sweet in a way and I want to get to know him better. I startle at a second noise, then a third. It's never Mark, and eventually I fall asleep.

When I wake, my gaze snaps to Mark's bed. Empty. Crap. I

don't think he'd sleep on the lounge chair again, or on the cot. Both would hurt his back. He could have spent the night somewhere else. With someone else. It's the most likely scenario, but it doesn't seem like Mark from the little I know of him. So, as has been my lifelong habit, my mind immediately flies to way less plausible explanations. He's sick in the infirmary. He's stuck somewhere on the ship. Maybe he's gone overboard.

My heart drops at the thought of that last unlikely happenstance, and I catapult off the bed. It's implausible, but not impossible. Mark *could* be treading water, right now, at this very moment, and I'm the only one who knows it. Someone should be looking into this. There must be a protocol.

I get ready in a hurry, at least for me, and find Brandy at the sheep table in Ballroom A. There's a pancake bar set up with the same sign as last night, but the word Pancake is pasted over the word Potato. Pancake Palooza. I can't even.

I tug on Brandy's arm. "Is there a protocol for men overboard?" I ask, my voice breathless.

Brandy's eyes go wide. "What? Why?"

"Mark's missing."

She leaps from her seat. "Missing? And you think he's gone overboard?"

Heads turn in our direction just as a voice sounds behind us. "Who's gone overboard?"

"Mark," I say twisting around. "Mark Moore." And there he is, standing in front of me, the voice behind the question.

He smirks. "Mark Moore, did you say? Overboard?"

My face reddens, and Brandy shifts to look in our direction. She juts out her hand and squeezes Mark's shoulder. "Mark! You're okay. Thank God."

I don't say anything, unsure if Brandy's mocking me or if she generally believes he went overboard and somehow returned to the ship in time for breakfast.

"I'm a good swimmer," Mark says finally, "but I'm starved."

He steps away from Brandy and takes a place at the end of the pancake line. I stomp after him. "I was worried about you."

"Why?" He grabs a plate.

I open my mouth and shut it. The adrenaline having calmed in my body, I realize that my jump in logic from *Mark didn't come back to the room* to *Mark's probably gone overboard* missed at least a gazillion steps. Damn. I've always panicked like this, seizing upon the most awful scenario I can imagine and getting myself so jacked up that I don't think straight. Harrison's voice sounds in my psyche: "Stop being so irrational, Ellie."

"I'm touched," Mark says with more than a trace of sarcasm. "But I'm all set. I can take care of myself."

"I know, but—" I start, not sure how to finish the sentence. But what? But I was worried about you. But I wanted you to come back to the room. But I might like you. I step back. I'm not saying *any* of those things. I return to the table empty-handed. I feel like I was stung.

Mark returns with a plate piled high with pancakes and an amount of syrup sure to be a precursor to diabetes. I want to tease him about it; I don't feel I can now. He sits in the furthest possible seat from me, and the stung feeling transforms to one of hurt. I'm hurt. After an admittedly dicey start — my fault, I know — I thought we were hitting it off.

Mark avoids me during the meal, or at least that's how it seems. He talks primarily to Gavin, who seems to have joined Team Sheep. Mark's not in the room after breakfast, and I don't see him in line for any of the day's excursions. I guess he's elected not to go.

So what?

He can "take care of himself" as he's already told me.

The rest of the sheep, and Brandy and Gavin, have elected

to go to Cape Canaveral. I stand in line with them, but I don't want to go. Over several tedious days, I'd seen every inch of the place with Harrison and Caleb, both space buffs. At the last moment, I sneak out of the Cape Canaveral line lest Hank see me (ugh) and get into the one for Cocoa Beach. A beach is more my speed.

When I get to the front of the line, a cruise employee holding a clipboard asks my name.

"Ellie Moore, but I'm not on the list. Any chance there's extra room?"

She shakes her head. "None. Sorry. But there's space on the wax museum tour, I'm pretty sure."

A smiling cruise employee with the nametag "Colby" points in the direction of a nearly empty bus. "Yup. Wax museum's open ma'am."

Wax museum? I wrinkle my nose. Yuck. All those lifeless figures. I take a step backward. Would being on a nearly empty cruise ship be *more* creepy than the museum? Maybe. Plus, this is supposed to be a vacation. I should do something.

The wax museum *could* be fun. I mean, what do I know? I've never been to one. It probably will be fun. There are a lot of them for a reason. They're unique. Cool. Timeless.

Yes! I do want to go to the wax museum. In fact, it's exactly what I want to do; I just didn't know it until now. I step into the bus and greet the other five souls who have elected to go on what's sure to be a one-of-a-kind adventure. Better than a beach. I've been to dozens of beaches. And better than Cape Canaveral for sure.

I settle into a seat near the back. Colby, the cruise employee in charge of the trip, steps on and tells us we're waiting on one more guest. I look out the window, and what do you know, there's Mark. So, he's okay. Good for him. He heads toward the van, and I put together the obvious. Mark is the final guest. Oh.

He steps into the vehicle, and I shrink down in my seat, like it's possible he might not see me in my giant hat and bright turquoise shirt. He does, of course. He meets my eyes as soon as I'm in his line of vision and nods. Then, despite the myriads of empty seats all around me, he sits alone in the front.

Okay.

My mind spins as the bus hurtles along. I thought I'd gotten over being irritated after breakfast, but clearly I haven't. I siphon through my Mark-related grievances, all of which have the same core: he's *ignoring* me. Well fine. Maybe I don't want him in the room then. I should just kick him and his whole neat, nice, crabby vibe right out. His bad back — the reason we're sharing a room to begin with — should not be in my sphere of concern.

After a few minutes, Colby holds up an eighties-style boom box and presses play. He claps his hands. "Come on, Seniors. It's a sing-along!" He begins to sing "Sherry" by The Four Seasons, and not well.

"It's too early for this," Mark complains.

Mark's irritated by the sing-along? It's all the encouragement I need. When Colby gets to the chorus, I enthusiastically join in. We finish "Sherry" and then, along with two others, sing "Walk Like a Man."

The sing-along dies out after three songs, and we ride the rest of the way in silence. When the van pulls to a stop in front of the museum, Mark immediately launches out of his seat. He heads to the bus door like he's escaping a fire.

"Hold up there, senior," Colby says. "We'll all go in together. I've got the entry passes and ones to a special event."

Mark opens his mouth, and I half expect him to say, "I can take care of myself," but he doesn't. Instead, he moves back to his seat and waits for every person to pass before getting off. He straggles so far behind the group that it's like he's not with us.

Once we're admitted, a wax museum employee — Tim — ushers us into a room for Colby's "special event," one where we can make wax models of our hands. "Kind of like the hand molds for babies," he tells us, "but for old people! Volunteers?"

I've always been a huge volunteer, and I shoot my hand up. Tim choses me – yay – and walks me through the steps– lotion, lather, bright pink wax (my choice), and cold water. I repeat this sequence, and when I'm finished, Tim pulls the mold off. The result is a bit creepy, like my hand became loose and independently plunged into a bucket of fuchsia paint. But still, it's a keepsake. Of my hand. That's not nothing.

I wash my hands and move to a bench in the back of the room, the mold gripped in both my hands. Mark is the only person on the bench, and as much as I'm sure he doesn't want me sitting next to him, sitting on the opposite end, or not at all, seems rude. *He* might be rude, but I'm not.

"No wax hand?" I say, sitting next to him.

He shakes his head. "I'm not putting my hand in -" He waves to the area where everyone is crowded around, dozens of hands in the same water and wax. "Who knows how many –"

"Shush," I say, because I know how that statement finishes. Who knows how many people have put their hands in that wax and water? It's not something I'd given one iota of consideration to before now. But now that he's brought it up, it's all I can think about. How many people *did* put their hands in there? Dozens? Hundreds? Three? I have no idea.

"It's probably germ infested is all I'm saying."

"I know what you're saying," I quip, and hold the pink hand in his direction. "But it's neat, right? You don't want one?"

"No, I don't think it's neat, and no I don't want one."

"Why not?" I ask, unable to let it go, or acknowledge that the mold is not, in fact, neat. "Where else can you make a wax replica of your own hand?" I wave the pink mold.

"I really don't know or care." He shakes his head. "Where are you even going to put that when you get home?"

"My kitchen," I say quickly, like I'd thought about it. I hadn't. "I have a nice sunny window by my sink."

Mark snorts.

"What?" I set the model next to me on the bench.

"It's wax." He starts to laugh, and not a little titter. A big-bellied guffaw.

I cross my arms across my chest. "Why is that funny?"

"Because it will melt."

Oh. Duh. Of course it will melt! Wax is meant to melt. My cheeks heat up. "Well, I'll put it somewhere else then," I say, like I have dozens of areas in my townhome that just wouldn't be complete without a creepy fuchsia hand model.

"I'm sure you'll get years of enjoyment out of it," he says, the sarcastic edge back in his tone.

Irritation percolates inside me. What is his deal? I've been super nice to him. Okay, apart from accusing him of being a scammer and making him carry all my luggage. But still. I let him use my shower yesterday. And he's staying in the room we'd agreed was mine.

"What's wrong with you?" I blurt. "And where were you last night?" As soon as the questions leave my mouth, I want to stuff them back in. Neither what Mark's problem is nor where he was last night are my concern.

"What?"

"Never mind." I stand. "I have some wax figures to see."

Chapter 12

Mark

Ellie strides toward the door. A moment later, she circles back and swipes the ugly pink mold of her hand off the bench. "Don't want to forget this," she huffs.

"A neat piece of art like that?" I arch an eyebrow. "Definitely not."

She gives me what I imagine is her best attempt at a dirty look, which she'd hate to know, is cute instead. After, she spins on her heel and stomps out. Almost as soon as she's out of sight, I feel bad. If this were a game of "Am I the asshole?," I know the asshole would be me.

Last night, after seeing her holding hands with Hank at the Potato Palooza, I'd run into Gavin. As luck would have it, he was going to spend the night with Brandy, and he offered to let me stay in his room. Not wanting to see when, or if, Ellie got back to our shared room, I'd accepted. Overnight, I'd gotten over my petty jealousy about the possibility of an Ellie-Hank dynamic. Then I saw her at breakfast, and I don't know, I suddenly *did* care. So, I picked this stupid, unpopular museum trip because I was sure she and Hank wouldn't be on it. And yet here she is. Alone.

One by one, my cruise mates complete their "hands" and move into the museum. I pull up the Kindle app on my phone. This is a perfect time to read my book. On plagues. Ellie would ridicule me if she knew. So would Addison. Or almost anyone. I'm on a vacation excursion and I'm sitting alone reading about plagues. I get through a few sentences, then switch off the app. I can't keep reading. It's too pathetic.

I get up and walk into the museum. I've been a jerk to Ellie all morning. I should find her and apologize. I scan a map and contemplate what wax figures I would go see if I were Ellie. A movie star? Music icon? Television celeb? I check Ryan Reynolds and Lady Gaga and am on my way to Ryan Gosling when I spot her reading the placard in front of Abraham Lincoln. "Wouldn't have pegged you for a history buff," I say.

"Wouldn't have pegged you for a jerk," she quips back.

"Touché."

She grips the pink hand model. "I like history. Not necessarily in the form of wax figures, but the stories, you know. Like I told you, I like people."

"Any favorite time period?"

"Stone Age," she says though I'm pretty sure she's kidding.

"Big fan of Fred and Wilma?"

"The biggest."

"Yabba Dabba Doo!" I say in my best Fred Flintstone imitation.

A smile momentarily creeps across her lips. After, she moves toward Steve Jobs, away from me. I'm not sure if it's meant as a "get lost, guy" clue, but I follow her anyway. "Look. I'm sorry. I saw you and Hank at dinner, and afterward Gavin lent me his room. Brandy." I roll my eyes. "Anyway, I didn't want to get in the way if, you know, you and Hank—"

She spins around, her mouth wide open. "Hank?" She slaps my upper arm. "You thought I was going to bring Hank back to the room? Really?"

My face heats. "Maybe?"

"Hank?"

"He told me he liked you. And I saw you holding his hand at dinner."

"That doesn't mean I like him. I'm a very touchy person." She slaps my arm again. "See? Touchy."

"I know, sorry, I know," I say, because now, I do know. I'd been way off. "Friends again?"

She crosses her arms, a sliver of a smile on her lips. "I don't know. Thinking I'd bring Hank to the room, that's pretty offensive, all told."

"Is it?" I shrug. "He's ripe with financial tips. Might have been worth it."

Her face splits into a bigger smile. "It would definitely not have been worth it. And you're going to have to do something to make up for that error in judgment if you want to resume our friendship."

"And that would be" — I ask, liking how this is going, liking the underlying flirtation.

She waves the pink hand replica in my direction. "You've got to make a hand replica as amends."

My gaze drops to the wax hand. "Oh, come on."

"Hank, Mark. You accused me of sleeping with Hank."

"Okay fair." I shake my head. I can just wash my hands afterward. Really well. "I guess it's a just consequence."

We wind through wax replicas of various celebrities en route to the hand model station. When we reach it, I pull out the coupon Colby had given me.

Ellie swipes it from my hand. "Nope. Let's go."

"But –"

"As much as I know you're going to regret not having one later, I'm not going to force you to make a super neat hand model." She pivots toward the exit. "But it means a lot to me that you would."

Though I don't know if she means me to, I follow her. It's bright outside and warm for January. The space in front of the wax museum is peppered with people in varied Orlando-themed gear. "Are you done with wax figures?"

"For the rest of time." She looks around the space. "I'll just find a place to hang here until it's time to go."

"I'll wait with you." I pause, then realize the offer might be pushy. She might want to be alone. "That is, if you want company. Or my company. If you don't, you know, I can just take selfies with some meltable superheroes."

She smiles. "Sounds amazing."

"How much time do we have anyway?" I nod toward her watch, a bejeweled, bangly thing.

"Oh." She holds up her wrist. "This watch doesn't work. I just like how it looks."

I run the phrase through my head, my practical nature fixing on the absurdity of it. "You wear a watch that doesn't work?" I question.

"Yes, because it's pretty. It's never worked. I don't care." She pulls her phone from a large bag with polka dots. "It's almost two hours until the bus leaves. I'd love your company, but are you sure? Could be boring."

I'm certain that spending two hours with Ellie would be anything but boring. Still, we should do something more memorable than just sit and wait. I glance around, the obvious solution clear in front of me.

"Well, we *could* just hang out and do nothing," I say, "or we could go on" — I gesture to the unmissable Orlando Eye, a 400 foot Ferris wheel with enclosed carriages — "that."

Ellie puts a hand over her eyes like a visor and squints at the structure before returning her gaze to me. "Are we allowed? I mean, do we have to tell Colby?"

"Tell Colby? Like get his permission?" I snort. "Absolutely not. He might join us and lead a sing-along." I roll my eyes. Ellie smirks and I tap on her hand model. "Plus, if you wait here in the sun, your hand will melt. The carriages are shady."

"Well, aren't you unexpectedly smooth, Mark Moore."

I nod. "Well, you know what they say. The way to a woman's heart is always through her wax hand replica."

A laugh erupts from her gut. "You win. I'll go."

We stroll toward the massive wheel. A kid on a scooter cuts me off. A woman speaks loudly on her cellphone. A crying toddler throws a tantrum. All three of these things would normally irritate me. A lot, I'm sad to say. But in this moment, they feel insignificant. Just bits of humanity, in all its splendid glory.

Ellie protests, but I buy both tickets. It seems the right thing to do, the chivalrous thing. I was a chivalrous guy once, way back when, and it feels nice to flex that muscle. Feels nice to have someone, even for just two hours, to be chivalrous for.

We stand in line and the sun beats down on my skin, warming it. Muscles I hadn't realized were tight loosen in my shoulders and neck.

"That is one big Ferris wheel," Ellie says, looking up. "I wonder—" she starts, but her statement is interrupted by a chirp from my phone.

"I just need to check and make sure it's not Addison."

I pull the phone from my pocket, sure it isn't her. She said she wouldn't call unless it was an emergency. I glance at the phone; Addison's contact image is on the screen, a FaceTime call. My heart plummets, and I fumble to accept the call.

Addison's face fills the screen. She's smiling.

"What's wrong?" I bark.

The smile vanishes. "What? Nothing. Just wanted to see how you were doing. If you were getting out and about. Hey, is that a Ferris wheel? Where are you right now?"

"Nothing's wrong?" I say, not able to let go of the idea that this call has been made to relate something tragic. "Not with you or Sara?"

"Geez, Dad. No. You just sounded sad when you called the other day. Hey," she says, flipping topics, "did you mess up that woman's stuff like I told you to?"

Ellie moves her head next to mine so she's visible on the screen. "He did."

Addison's face registers surprise on a level I may have never seen. "Oh my God," she says, hand flying over her mouth. "You're there with a woman. Is it a date? Oh my gosh. Wow! A date. I'm sorry to interrupt. Get back to it. Have fun!" She clicks off.

I step forward in line, replaying the last few sentences of Addison's stunned monologue. "Well, that was somewhat humiliating."

"Nah." Ellie waves her hand. "Just because your daughter was astonished that you'd be on a date is no reason to feel humiliated."

"She wasn't *astonished*," I insist, though she clearly was. "And this isn't a date."

She arches a single eyebrow. "She looked and sounded astonished to me. Plus, this *is* a date. It became one as soon as you paid for my ticket."

"It did not. I was just being nice. Friendly."

"Mmm. Well, given that you clearly don't date much—"

"Stop it," I say, half-laughing.

"Anyway," she continues, "you might not know the proto-col, but if one person pays for the other, it's a date." She pulls a ten dollar bill out of her purse and waves it. "Do you want your money back?"

I snort-laugh. "Absolutely not. If this is a date, it's the best one I've had in a while."

"Or only one."

I shake my head. "You are something else."

We reach the front of the line, and the attendant holds open the door to an enclosed cabin. "Lucky you," he says. "You get a whole car."

Ellie slides in and I move in after her, both of us on the side with the best view. The door clangs shut and locks, and after, the wheel slowly climbs upward.

Ellie adjusts herself, her purse, and her pink hand like she's settling in for a while. "Can I ask you something?"

"Is it whether I'm afraid of heights?" I look out the window. "I don't know, but we're going to find out pretty soon."

"No." She taps my leg. "All kidding aside, why does a man like you not date?"

"A man like me?"

She makes a "come on" face before continuing. "Yes, a man like you. You're nice. Tall. Handsome. And you have good mobility. A big plus at our age." She taps on my leg again. "So?"

I want to make light of the question, not answer, not get pulled back to the reality of my dating life or lack thereof. But against all odds, I like Ellie, and I feel like I can trust her. "My daughter Sara has medical needs. It's a big responsibility. All good, but not every woman is up for that, you know, on a permanent basis." When I had dated, every time the subject of Sara came up, the relationship ended soon after. Maybe it was me, but I think it was my caregiver lifestyle. That's how it seemed, anyway.

"I'm sorry."

"Don't be. I love being a dad, and everything that comes

with it. My job provided me with a good living, retirement funds, and some lifelong friends. I like my house, my hobbies, my routine. I'm okay."

"Happy?"

"For the most part," I say, though I'm not sure that's true. I don't get fixated on happiness the way most people seem to.

Ellie shifts her head toward the window, and a serious expression reflects back on the glass. "And the girls' mother?" she asks gently.

I shake my head. "She's not in their life. Drugs. She tried to get clean but never could do it, you know. Ultimately, she thought it would be best if she wasn't in their lives at all."

"Oh," Ellie turns and looks at me. "That's sad."

"Yes," I say. "But we're meant to have fun right now. So how about you? I've got the feeling your dating life is epic."

Chapter 13

Ellie

Epic? Yeah, right. If by epic you mean scammed out of substantial money—the kind that involves an unbearable number of zeros after the one—by Sebastian, my alleged *boyfriend*, then yes, my love life is epic.

"Come on," Mark encourages. "You must have a ton of suitors."

"For me to know." I snap my head toward the window and act as if I'm riveted by the scenery. I do not want to talk to Mark about my love life, especially as it's the opposite of what he clearly thinks it is. "So many lakes," I say lamely.

"I think there's over one hundred in Orlando," Mark adds. "And I didn't mean to pry."

"You didn't. Not more than I did." I lean back in the seat. Mark did share about his relationship; I should let him in a little. "I've struggled a bit since my divorce." I tug on my earring. "Scratch that. I got over the divorce. It's been a long time. I struggled when my husband got remarried. To a woman opposite of me in every way."

"I'm sorry," Mark says.

"Thanks."

"But I feel sorry for your husband."

I tilt my head. Harrison is rich, successful, and remarried to his soulmate. As far as I know, no human has ever felt sorry for him. "Why?"

"Because if his new wife is the opposite of you, she must be incredibly dull."

A smile tugs across my face. "Thank you."

"I mean it."

I internally bask at the unexpected compliment. Of course, Sebastian had been full of flattery, but that had all been fake. The kind of over-the-top fake that anyone, save me, would have seen right through.

Is Mark being fake?

I glance in his direction. He's looking at me with an expression I can best describe as admiration. And one I'd bet my life was genuine.

"What?" Mark asks.

My face goes hot, and I look away. "We should get a good look at this stunner of a view while we're up here. I think I see Disney World."

This prompt, of course, changes the subject. Downtown Orlando is clearly in view as are the one hundred plus lakes. When our rotation comes to an end, we exit the ride. Immediately after, a uniformed employee points a finger at Mark. "Congratulations. You, sir, are today's Lucky Eye Rider." He thrusts a recyclable bag with an image of the wheel on it in Mark's direction. "Enjoy."

"Thanks," Mark says with real enthusiasm and takes the bag. "Ride was tremendous."

"So, what'd you get?" I try to peer in the bag as we walk. I've always loved prizes, raffles, and drawings. I get excited to win almost anything, even stupid things I'd never use, like the coffee mug filled with candy I won at the bank last year. I'd been thrilled at the time; I don't even know where the mug is now. It's something about winning. It makes every object seem more special.

"Well, let's see." Mark stops and sits on a bench. I sit next to him and await the contents of the bag like it's full of jewels.

"We've got an Orlando Eye T-shirt, a bumper sticker, a pen, a stress ball, and oh, look at this." He pulls out a photo of us on the ride in a cardboard frame. "I didn't even know they took that."

"Me either." I take in the photograph. We're both smiling, our heads angled together, a view of greater Orlando in the background. "Good picture," I say, and it is. Even the contrast between my turquoise T-shirt and his black one looks right. Like they belong together.

Mark slips the picture into the bag and hands it to me. "You can have it."

"Really?" I take the bag, thrilled.

"Sure. It's a date, remember?" He gestures toward a nearby ice cream kiosk. "Do we have time for a cone?"

I check my watch. "We do."

The Orlando gear bag tucked inside my polka dot one, I walk alongside Mark toward the ice cream kiosk. It's fun, being here with him. One of the first true vacation experiences I've had since arriving on the ship. "This is so nice," I verbalize just as a panting dog appears on the walkway in front of us. He's small and brown and wearing a collar but no leash. No family either, it seems. Immediately, I bend down and look at his tag. "Willie. Where's your family, Willie?" I look up at Mark. "We need to find his family."

Mark squints at the dog, then looks toward where our bus is parked. "Don't we need to get back soon?"

I stamp a foot. "If your dog was lost, you'd want someone to find you, right?" I scoop Willie into my arms and stand. "Do you have a dog?"

"No. But I had a cat when the girls were younger. Mr. Pickles." He pauses. "The girls named him," he adds.

"And if Mr. Pickles were lost in Orlando?"

"Fine." He pats Willie's head. "Point taken. I guess you have dogs."

"Just one. Peanut. I'd have more if I could." Willie spits up on my shirt. "Poor guy. I think he's dehydrated."

Mark takes a step toward the ice cream kiosk. "I'll get him some water."

We set Willie up with a paper bowl and water in the shade.

"Your shirt?" Mark says, nodding to the new stain.

"It's fine," I say, and it is. I am fussy a lot of the time—okay, most of the time—but never with animals or small children. Spit up, throw up, excrement, it comes with the territory. And it's always worth it.

I sit with Willie while Mark looks around for a place to make an announcement about a lost dog. Willie is friendly and adorable, a cross between a pug and a bulldog, I'd say. I wonder if he'd get along with Peanut? Probably okay. I could take him if he needs a home. If he was abandoned. Or Mark could adopt him. He seems like he could use a dog.

I mentally go through the logistics of sneaking Willie on to the cruise. He'd fit in my bag, and I could hide him in the room. I'd feed him leftovers until I got some dog chow. He's just a little guy. It would be easy.

"Willie!"

I whip my head toward the voice, its owner a small woman barreling toward me, a look of concern on her face. "Willie," she says again. "Willie, where have you been?" She scoops him up and meets my eyes. "Oh my gosh." She kisses his head. "Thank you. Where was he?"

"Just running around. I wasn't going to leave until we found you."

And I most certainly wasn't going to smuggle him out of here in my bag.

Mark reappears and she thanks us again before disappearing into the crowd, Willie in her arms.

"I know we need to get to the bus," I say to Mark. "Let me just use the bathroom." I nod toward a public restroom.

"Sure."

I hurry to the nearest bathroom, take off my stained shirt, and put on the Orlando Eye T-shirt. It's bright yellow with the slogan "High in the Eye" splayed across a decal of the wheel. It's kind of awful but better than smelling like dog vomit. I step out of the bathroom, find Mark, and hold out my arms wide. "What do you think?"

"I think you're pulling that T-shirt off like a queen bee."

I smile. I feel a little like a queen bee in this moment. I might not be sophisticated like Harrison's Lilith, but I'm also not, as Mark pointed out, dull. I stand taller as we head toward the bus.

When we step inside, Colby is already at the wheel. I check my watch. They must have been waiting for us for twenty minutes or more. Colby eyes my t-shirt. "Have a fun ride?"

I don't answer and hop on to the bus, embarrassed I'd made everyone wait. "We saved a dog."

"On the Orlando Eye?" a woman counters.

"After," I insist. I sit and realize how ridiculous the excuse sounds.

Mark sits next to me. He meets my eyes and mouths "Worth it."

The sentiment makes me smile. It was worth it.

Chapter 14

Ellie

O nce we're back on the ship, we immediately go to
our stateroom to get ready for dinner.

"What do you think they'll serve for dinner?" I
call from the bathroom. It's amazing how one afternoon could
so quickly change the dynamics in our relationship. From
barely talking at breakfast to calling out a question from the loo.

"Palooza something," Mark calls back.

"No," I hiss. "They used that already. Three times."

"Just wait."

I open the door a sliver. "You decent?"

"You bet."

I push the door open all the way. "You're in the same
clothes," I blurt without thinking. I know it's pathetic, but I'd
been looking forward to seeing Mark dressed up.

He looks down at his clothes and back up again. "I packed
light. I do have one nice thing, though, if you think I should
change."

I wave my hand, like I'd never, ever considered how he'd
look in nicer clothes. "Of course not. That's silly."

Mark pushes open the door. "Well, let's get to that palooza, then."

"Not a palooza," I say. "Not again."

But it is a palooza. Pizza Palooza. Mark winks at me. "Told ya."

We gather pizza and garden salad, the latter of which is basically shredded iceberg lettuce with carrot slivers.

I follow Mark back to the sheep table. Hank shoots him a look of death and Mark responds with a big smile and says "Dibs." Hank's death look intensifies. I have no idea what *that's* about.

The Cape Canaveral group gives details about their day. Way too many. Like, do I really need to know what each of them had for lunch? During dessert—once again small scoops of vanilla ice cream in plastic cups—Colby takes the stage. "Okay, Seniors. We've got a post-dinner treat in store. The best magician-hypnotist on the high seas today. Give it up for Hubert the Hatifier and his cohort Robby."

Mark leans over. "Oh man, I hate magicians."

I twist around and look at him. "Why?"

"I just do. Always have."

"Well, aren't you a curmudgeon. Who doesn't like magic? Honestly. Plus, Colby just said he's the best on the high seas."

Mark snorts. I move my chair to center my view of the stage.

Hubert and Robby enter the room, the former wearing a cape and a black top hat. He's an older man with shock white hair and ruddy skin. He walks gingerly to the stage. "Hello Seniors!" he says and tips his hat. There's a white rabbit on his head, which he takes down and hands to Robby.

I slap Mark's knee. "See? A rabbit."

"On his head. That's not magic."

Hubert holds up the hat and pulls out a bouquet of flowers. He makes the bunny disappear and reappear.

"See?" I whisper in Mark's ear. "Magic."

Robby hands Hubert a second hat and he makes a show of pouring a container of milk inside and then showing it's gone. He pulls a card and a ball from a third hat, both of which change colors.

I glance at Mark. "It's a hat trick," he says and smirks.

"Stop." I push at his shoulder. "I'm sure he's going to do more than hat stuff."

He doesn't. Hubert is the "Hatifier" for a reason. Every single trick involves a hat, and different hats at that.

"Maybe he's the only magician on the high seas," Mark whispers.

"He's also a hypnotist," I say. "Just wait."

And as if he read my mind, or heard me say it over the thinning crowd, Hubert asks for hypnosis volunteers.

"You should volunteer," I say to Mark.

"Nah. Hypnosis doesn't work on me. *You* should volunteer."

"Me?" I hit my chest with an open palm. As big as I am on volunteering, I wouldn't trust myself under hypnosis. I'd say or do something absurd. I'm sure of it. "No way."

"Hypnosis doesn't work on you?" Hank's voice sounds behind us. "Really?"

Mark meets his gaze. "No. It doesn't."

"Prove it." Hank sets down his glass which somehow seems like a challenge.

"Still looking for volunteers," Hubert says.

"Prove it," Hank repeats. "If it doesn't work on you, what's the difference?"

"Fine." Mark meets his eyes. "I'll do it if you do it."

"You're on."

The two of them volunteer along with two women, and the four participants stand on stage. Hubert takes out the kind of pocket watch I'd always associated with hypnosis, one with a long silver chain and a big silver ball on the end. He swings it back and forth and runs through a progressive muscle relaxation exercise, telling the participants how relaxed they are over and over. It's effective. Even I get sleepy.

After a long moment, Hubert tosses the pocket watch to Robby and turns to the audience.

My eyes rivet to Mark on stage. Despite his insistence that hypnosis doesn't work on him, he looks deeply relaxed. Maybe he's pretending?

Robby produces an iPhone and a moment later "Saturday Night Fever" blares from a portable speaker. "Let's see some John Travolta," Hubert calls and does a few Travolta-like moves. The group, all four, including Mark, start to move and swing their arm diagonally across their bodies, index fingers pointed up.

It's funny. It is. But I can't help wishing Mark had been right. That he couldn't be hypnotized. I don't think he'd like being vulnerable like this.

"Michael Jackson," Hubert says. The music changes to Thriller and participants moonwalk, or try to, across the stage.

"How about the twist?" The song changes and everyone twists.

I try to relax and enjoy the show. It's funny. And I have no idea, really, how Mark would feel about twisting it up on the stage. He might get a kick out of it.

The music stops. "Quick," Hubert says, "you're in a corn maze. Go. Find your way out."

Group members race across the stage, bumping into each other in mass chaos.

Robby produces chairs and Hubert directs the participants

to sit. He then tells them they are glued to their chairs and to try to get out. They do, all of them. Mark tries so hard to free himself from the pretend glue, he looks like he might get hurt.

Hubert runs through a few more ridiculous scenarios. He tells the group they are a rock band, then farm animals, then fish. He stops a woman mid swim. "What's your name?"

"Mary."

"What's your biggest desire?"

"To fly."

"Well fly then Mary."

As Mary flies across the stage, arms flapping, Hubert stops Hank and runs through the same questions. Name: Hank. Biggest desire: money. "Well go count it then, Hank."

Hank goes through a process of counting pretend bills and Hubert stops Mark. "What's your name?"

"Mark C. Moore."

"Okay, Mark C. Moore. What's your biggest desire?"

Mark opens his mouth, and I inhale a breath. I want to know Mark's biggest desire. Of course I do, I'm nosy like that, but I don't want *everyone* to know. And I don't think Mark would either. As he starts to form the first word, I'm hoping he'll say something silly like "chocolate" or "steak" or "winning the lottery." Instead, he says, "A wife and children of my own."

Chapter 15

Mark

Ellie and I lie side by side in the twin beds, streaks of moonlight shining through the slits in the blinds. Something has been off between us since the stupid hypnosis event which, honestly, I can't believe worked on me. I was sure I'd be fine. That I'd just stand there and laugh at the others. But that's not what happened. Apparently. I mooed, swam, and danced on the stage like a moron. Mortifying and probably on film on a bajillion tiny camera phones. Me letting loose like that? It's exactly the type of thing it seems Ellie would love. And yet she's been distant since the show.

"So that was a day, wasn't it?" I say, lamely.

"Sure was."

Her covers rustle and I glance in her direction. A thin beam of moonlight illuminates her form. She's awake. I stare at the ceiling.

"Loved that Orlando Eye," I blather. "Some view, right?"

"Very nice view."

"And your pink hand. Cool."

"It is."

I shut my mouth. If she's angry at me or embarrassed for me or whatever, I wish she'd just say it already. I shift in the bed, away from Ellie, and will myself not to care. I don't care. Or I do, but I shouldn't. I'm just not used to company these days, not used to dealing with the emotions of others. And thank God for that. Lying here wondering what the heck another human being is thinking? It's brutal.

I shut my eyes and breathe deep into my stomach, in and out, in and out, in and out. I feel myself drifting off, everything — Ellie, Hubert, and my ridiculous shenanigans on stage — fading away.

"What did you mean by it?"

I jolt and it takes me a second to piece together that Ellie is speaking. I roll back toward her. "What?"

She sits up. "You said your biggest desire was for a wife and children of your own."

"I said that?" I question, trying and failing to recall.

"Yes. What did you mean by it? I thought you had a wife, or ex-wife, and children of your own."

I'm glad for the darkness, because my eyes widen and I'm sure I look guilty as all get out. Like the scammer she thought I was when we'd met. Of course, I could tell her the truth. That I've never been married, and that Addison and Sara are my nieces, not my daughters. I could tell her my whole sordid past.

I open my mouth to tell Ellie the truth, then shut it. I can't. And I don't want to. I only have a few days with her, and I don't want to mess it up with sordid tales of a past I'm ashamed about.

I sit up and face her. "I guess I'd hoped for a different kind of family life." It's a true enough statement.

Ellie's silent and I grapple again with the idea of telling her the truth. But before I can commit to it, she speaks.

"I get that," she says. "Married life can be hard. And parenting. All of it."

"Yeah," I say, happy the focus is off my statement and on marriage in general. "Did you feel that way? That you wanted your family life to be different?"

"No." She shifts on the bed. "I loved my life as Harrison's wife and Caleb's mom. It was exactly what I always wanted." She pulls the covers up to her chin. "Just not what they wanted."

"That can't be true."

Her eyes stay wide, focused on me. "You're funny, Mark," she says finally. "But I'm a lot. I know that." She grabs a sleeping mask from the nightstand, slips it over her face, and lies down. "We should really get some sleep."

I take the hint and shut my mouth, but Ellie's words crash over me in the silence: I'm a lot. Said like it's a bad thing. I mean, Ellie *is* a lot. But as someone who isn't—someone who, if I were a color, would most definitely be some hue of gray—I like that she's a lot. I like that she has purple luggage, that she wears giant hats, that her watch is bangly and doesn't tell the time. I like that she'd waited to find Willie's owner instead of leaving him there. That she reads those ridiculous books with the cartoons on the cover. That she's willing to try new things. I even like that she jumped to the conclusion that I fell overboard. Not everyone is rational. As I know from being one, rational people are dependable, great in emergencies, and adept problem solvers. But they're not always the people you want to vacation with.

I wake early the next morning, sit up, and peek at Ellie. She's sprawled out on the bed. Her arms are slung wide across it, her mouth agape, a bit of drool at its edge. Her eye mask is askew, and her pink night gown is bunched around her knees. She's not exactly the sleeping beauty of resters. *I* don't care, but

I know *she* will, so I quietly dress and leave the stateroom. I move to the only deck I can find in this labyrinth of a ship, the one I'd slept on the first night, and send her a quick text: *Did not go overboard. See you at breakfast.*

I watch the sunrise in silence and snap a quick photo to show Addison and Sara. And Ellie, I realize. I also want to show the photo to Ellie. A bit after, that same crew from day one, the fit and feisty ladies, power walk on to the deck and stop. They remember my name, ask how my back is, and if I need anything. Just forty-eight hours ago, I'd basked in their attention; I don't care now. I make an excuse to leave.

Surprisingly, breakfast is not another palooza-themed event, but an egg fest with the staff instructed, from what I can tell, to use as many egg puns as possible: have an eggstraordinary day, you look eggscellent this morning, do you want eggstra? It's brutal. Ordinarily I'd shoot straight back to the room, but Ellie is at the sheep table, so I stay and slide into the chair next to her with a plate of eggs. Obviously.

Ellie looks nothing like the drooling mess from earlier. She's wearing the bright blue sweater, one I'm pretty sure I picked up from her floor. Her hair is done, her face made up. She even smells good.

"Morning Mark."

"Morning Ellie." I smile at her, staring way too long before I realize everyone else on Team Sheep is at the table. I've totally ignored them, my smittenness with Ellie more obvious than I want it to be. "And morning to all of you," I say quickly.

During breakfast, Colby, who inexplicably seems to be the lead crew member, takes the stage. "Seniors! Are you eggscited this morning?"

Groans.

"Come on. Are you eggscited?"

More groans. And a few boos.

"Well, you're going to be because we've got an eggstra special activity before we get to our destination tonight."

I lean into Ellie. "How much do you want to bet it's another palooza?" I whisper.

"You're terrible," she says, her tone conveying the opposite.

"It's a scavenger hunt!" Colby pumps his fist in the air. "And we've got an eggstraordinary prize for the winner." He pauses. "A steak and egg dinner for two, free drink vouchers for the evening, and — " he slaps his hands on the podium like a drumroll, "—front row tickets and backstage passes to see Kayko!"

It's silent, except for one person — Ellie. She leaps from her seat, cheering and clapping, like Colby just announced that the prize was a million dollars or a car or something. "I love Kayko!" She continues to clap another few moments before sitting back down, her face flushed.

"Well, you'll want one of these then." Colby waves a stack of papers then sets them on the podium. "It's the official scavenger list. Hunting starts at noon. First person or duo to get photographs of all items on the list wins."

Colby leaves the stage, and I turn to Ellie. "Okay. I have to know. Who is Kayko?"

"He's from American Idol. My favorite." She squeals and grabs my hand. "We *have* to win. You can have my steak. But you need to go with to the concert. Kayko is a real showman."

"Sure," I say, and while I'm not a huge concert fan, Ellie's enthusiasm makes me want to see this guy. "I'll get us a list."

I stand and maneuver through tables and chairs to the winding line behind the stack of scavenger hunt lists. Hank, list in hand, stops in front of me. "I'm going to win and I'm going to ask Ellie."

I digest his words, not sure what he thinks I'm going to do

in response to his statement. Fight him? Protest? Tell Ellie? The whole construct—me and Hank fighting over a woman—is like an absurd, senior-themed, after school special. Even knowing this and knowing that Ellie doesn't like him (her words), Hank's declaration gets my testosterone and competitive juices flowing. And as much as it probably shouldn't, it feels good. Like I'm an extra bit alive.

"Well, I'd better get started then." I swipe the paper from his hand. "Can't have Ellie being subjected to you for a night." I take a step toward the door.

"Hey," he yells, reaching for the paper, "hunting doesn't start until noon."

I continue toward the door. I'm not against cheating to win this thing.

"I'm telling Colby," he yells.

I wave the paper and keep going.

Moments later, Colby's voice sounds from the microphone. "Seems some seniors have gotten an early start on our game. Since you have the lists and to make things fair, we're going to start earlier. Like —now!"

Chapter 16

Ellie

The movement of participants after Colby says "now" is undetectable absent Mark and Hank, both of whom book it to opposite doors of the ballroom. Mark reaches the edge on his side and stops suddenly, like he's just now realized he's forgotten something. Or someone. He circles back to the sheep table. "Come on." He taps his hand in front of my place at the table. "If we're going to win this bad boy, we need to get started."

This kind of situation —one that involves rushing around against a ticking clock — is one I'd normally pass on. I like to take my time with things. Getting ready. Drinking coffee. Eating my breakfast which at this moment, I'm not done with.

"Come on," Mark says urgently. "It's Kayko."

"Fine." I throw my napkin over an uneaten egg. I am the one who wanted to win. And I do love Kayko. "Let's go." I take the list from Mark's hand and scan it as we walk:

1. Bow of the ship
2. Sea-sick patch

3. Towel animal
4. Three items that start with the letter of your last name
5. A painting of the ship
6. Tallest water slide
7. Three cruisers wearing matching T-shirts
8. A pineapple hat
9. A life vest
10. A picture from the highest deck

"Not too bad," I say. Mark speeds up.

"Where are you going?"

"To the Pineapple Pool," he says. "There's that guy up there with a pineapple hat. Right? That happened?"

"Yes, but—" I start.

Mark jogs away from me, looking over his shoulder at me as he does. "I'll grab the shot and circle back."

I cross my arms across my chest. "Okay. But it would be better if you were going the right way."

He instantly stops. "Damn it." He turns around, a sheepish look on his face. "I can never figure my way around this ship."

"I have a weirdly good sense of direction," I tell him, and it's true. It's not a trait that necessarily fits with the scatter-brained rest of me, but I rarely get lost. I always know exactly where I am in relation to everything else. I wave Mark forward. "Come on. This way."

He rushes forward; I grab his shoulder. "No need to rush. Haste makes waste."

"I don't think that fits this context," he says, "but point understood. We'll slow down."

We walk somewhat quickly to the Pineapple Pool, and Mark shoots a picture of the bartender with the pineapple hat.

After, he grabs a stack of towels for pool-goers, slaps them on a table, and starts to fold.

I move next to him. Why is he refolding towels? Aren't we in a rush? I sit in the chair at the table. "So. Whatcha doing?"

"Making a towel animal." He juts his chin toward the list, still in my hand. "What do you want? Elephant or swan?" He shakes his head. "Never mind, swan is faster." His hands move across the towel reams like an artist.

"You make towel animals?"

He answers without looking up, without stopping the flow of the folds. "Long story involving an endless hospital stay, two upset little girls, and a few items in the room."

I nod appreciatively. "Resourceful."

He shrugs. "You do what you have to do, right? My girls still love these. I make them on occasion." He finishes the final fold on a respectable looking towel swan and snaps a shot. "Now what?"

I drop my head to the paper. I'd been so enthralled by the mental image of Mark making towel animals for his daughters in a hospital that I'd forgotten to think about what's next. "Let's do the deck picture. Come on."

A burst of adrenaline shoots through me, and I speedwalk across the deck, Mark on my heels. When we get there, Mark snaps a photo from the highest point, neither of us taking one iota of a moment to enjoy the view. Sacrilege! But it's Kayko. And steak. And, okay, this is fun. We jog to our next target: the biggest slide.

Mark takes a picture, and we move toward the bow of the ship, passing Hank on the way. Hank picks up speed and he and Mark engage in what could best be described as a footrace. I don't know who wins. I get to the bow after them.

"You should get on Team H," Hank says in my direction. "I'm almost done." He waves his phone.

"No way are you almost done," Mark protests.

"You'll see." He dashes off.

Mark shakes his head. "Guy's such a tool. Anyway, we've got to go."

"I need a minute." I plop in a chair. "Let's take a breather and figure out next steps."

Mark opens his mouth, probably to protest, when a voice sounds through the ship's loudspeaker. "Ladies and gentlemen. The fire is out. I repeat, the fire is out."

My eyes go wide. "Fire? Did we know about a fire?"

Mark snorts. "No." He starts to laugh. "We did not."

"What? It's not funny. Someone could have been injured. *We* could have been injured."

"I know, sorry," he says, "but it's so random. Announcing the fire is out? When they never told us there was a fire to begin with."

"The fire is out," the voice on the loudspeaker says again, and Mark loses it. "The fire is out," the voice continues. "For passengers unaware of the fire, it is now out, and you can resume all activities."

Mark doubles over, hands gripped at his sides. He gasps for air in a way that, had I not known he was laughing, I'd have been concerned for his health. "Okay, okay," he says finally, righting himself. "Okay. I'm good. Sorry. That just struck me as really funny." He inhales a deep breath. "Let's get to that ship painting."

"Hopefully, it wasn't damaged in the fire," I say, deadpan.

He snorts and puts a hand on my shoulder. "Stop it, you. And, oh." He reaches into his pocket, pulls out a key, and hands it to me. "Can you get us to this room with your supernatural directional powers?"

I smile and take the key. I like the compliment. Like *being* complimented. Mark's done a good job of that. I study the sticker affixed to the side of the key and figure where the room is based on ours. "Yes. I can get us there."

"Really?"

"Yes, really. Why? Whose room is this?"

"Gavin's. His room has a painting of a ship. I stayed there when — " His voice trails off.

"When you thought I was having a sordid night with Hank." I punch his shoulder. "I still can't believe that. Anyway, do you think Gavin will care if we go into his room?"

"Gavin?" Mark shakes his head. "Nah. He let me sleep there. And he gave me a key. Plus, we'll be in and out. He won't even know."

"Okay then." I lead Mark straight to Room 108.

"You're Batman," Mark says, and I fit the key into the lock.

"Not Batman. I'm more like Wonder Wom—" My voice stops; I freeze.

"What's the matter?" Mark enters the room behind me, his head over mine, both of us staring at the unlikely scene: Gavin and Brandy sitting on the bed surrounded by hundreds of watches.

Chapter 17

Mark

Gavin bolts to his feet. "What are you doing here?"

Brandy rushes to the stateroom door and slams it shut.

"What's all this?" I gesture to the watches.

"Nothing." Gavin grabs a handful of watches and stuffs them into a bag.

"Babe," Brandy says from her post at the door, "there's no point."

I snag a watch from the bed and hold it up to the light. It's an exclusive brand, gold with a black face. Worth a few thousand dollars, at least. I pivot my head toward the bed. There are hundreds of watches. Hundreds of thousands of dollars of merchandise. In Gavin's room? "What's going on?"

Gavin looks to Brandy. "Can we tell them?"

"Do you trust them?"

"Yes," Gavin says without hesitation.

Brandy moves from the door. "They're fakes. We deliver them in exchange for money."

"Wow." Ellie picks up a watch. "These look amazingly real."

"Right?" Brandy's lips split into a smile, and she nods to the watch in Ellie's hand. "I love that one."

"Me too." She sets it carefully on the bed. "It's stunning."

"Do you make these?" I ask. I can't imagine.

Neither of them answer. I get the distinct impression something is wrong and the teacher side of me kicks in. It wasn't that long ago that Gavin was my student, or that I'd seen him riding his tricycle down our street at three years old. A flood of memories of Gavin and his family fills my brain. Trick-or-treating, Gavin always a superhero. Him and his dad playing soccer in their small yard. Neighborhood street parties where his mother always made me an extra dozen empanadas, my favorite. "Are you in trouble?"

"We're not in trouble," Brandy says. "Not yet." She collapses on to the only clear spot on the bed. The watch piles jostle around her.

"Not yet?" Ellie questions.

Brandy inhales a deep breath and explains that her aunt and uncle distribute counterfeit watches all over the world. She tells us that she and Gavin have been doing the Caribbean route for nearly two years.

"What's the Caribbean route?" I ask.

"There are different routes, taking the watches to different buyers. We can pass as cruise employees, so we're on this one."

"For now," Gavin says. "We're about done with this." He looks to Brandy.

"We are," she agrees. "It's nerve-wracking. Always one drop away from getting caught."

I lean against the wall and try to wrap my head around the idea of Gavin and Brandy as criminals. I think I might be less surprised if they pulled out capes and told me they were super-heroes. It just doesn't seem like them.

"I'm using the money we get to help my mom," Gavin blurts. "I bought her a house. I give her money every month." He looks at the floor, then at me. "She needs it, Coach. She really needs it."

Ellie puts a hand on his shoulder. "Bless your heart, sweetheart."

"Thanks Miss Moore." His shoulders relax and he nods his head toward Brandy. "Brandy donates a ton for autism research."

"My sister," Brandy says, by way of explanation.

"We know it's wrong, but we're trying to do good with the money."

"The Robin Hoods of the counterfeit world," Ellie says cheerfully. She picks up another watch and holds it to her wrist.

"You said you weren't in trouble *yet*," I question.

Gavin pulls at his T-shirt. "We're pretty sure the authorities are onto the whole delivery scheme."

"Which is?" Ellie asks, setting the watch back down on its pile.

Brandy adjusts herself on the bed and explains that they take the watches to a drop point on the island and exchange them for a phone with a code that gives them access to the money.

"The set-up is simple, and it's been pretty seamless. But we understand the police on the island are onto it. They're looking for a couple with our description."

"This is our last run," Gavin says. "We just need to unload these—" he gestures to the piles of counterfeits on the bed— "and we're out."

"Out," Brandy affirms.

"Can you just not do this exchange?" I ask. It seems like a logical solution. Plus, something about sending Brandy and Gavin on a criminal mission feels akin to sending puppies to fight a fire.

Brandy shakes her head. "It's already set. My aunt and uncle would be fine with us bailing, obviously, but the other side of this exchange is less amenable. They stand to lose a lot of money if we don't come through."

Ellie picks up another watch. "What about disguises?"

"We wear hats and sunglasses," Gavin offers. "But you can't disguise height or skin color."

"Or the fact that there are two of us," Brandy adds. "They're looking for a couple."

"And if you get caught?" I ask.

Brandy blows out a breath. "Likely prison."

Ellie puts a hand over her heart. "Prison?"

She sounds surprised, but I can imagine counterfeiting at this level is a big deal. Everyone involved in the scheme is capitalizing on the elite branding of legitimate companies. It's wrong. Even if Brandy and Gavin are doing good things with the money they've received.

Silence envelops the room. "Unless -" Brandy starts. She pushes off the bed, moves to the tiny port window, and looks out.

"Unless?" Gavin prompts.

She turns from the window and tips her head toward me and Ellie. "Unless they help us."

My face must register shock because she immediately says, "Just hear me out. The police are looking for a couple. If you walk with us, we'd look like a family. Grandparents and grandkids on a cruise."

"What?" I shoot a look at Ellie. She's staring at the two of them with rapt attention. Like she thinks this is a good idea.

"This whole thing feels like a cozy mystery," she says.

"A cozy mystery? It's a crime."

"Cozy mysteries have crime. And this is one where no one gets hurt." She moves her hand like an underscore. "The Counterfeit Caper."

I open my mouth to say the companies get hurt, but before I get a word out, Brandy continues. "The drop is less than a quarter mile from port. All you need to do is walk with us there and back. You never have to touch the bag, talk to anyone, do anything."

The room falls silent again and I mentally tick off every reason we shouldn't do this. "But it's a crime," I say lamely. It feels like no one else in the room sees it that way.

Gavin shakes his head. "It's not a crime for you Coach. You're just out for a walk."

I look to Ellie, her eyes shining with mischief. She *wants* to do this. "I'm up for a brisk walk," she says breezily, her gaze fixed on mine. "How about you?"

Chapter 18

Ellie

I stand next to Mark, and we look at our reflections in our stateroom mirror. Me in a pink flowery dress; Mark in a navy T-shirt and khaki shorts.

"We look like grandparents, right?"

I grab a tube of lipstick and move away from the mirror. "Are you nervous?" I ask, though I know he is. He'd tossed and turned all night. I know because I was up too, adrenaline rushing through my system in a way it hadn't since Sebastian.

"Aren't you?" he asks, following me to the bedroom.

I drop the lipstick into my bag. "It's just a walk."

"You know this isn't a cozy mystery, right? We know who the bad guys are. Us." He waves his finger between me and himself. "We're the bad guys. There is no mystery."

"Mark." I grab a second tube of lipstick and drop it in my pocket. "Of course, I know this isn't a cozy mystery. It just feels like the kind of setting they have. And Brandy and Gavin would be good characters."

"And it doesn't bother you? The crime part?"

"We're not committing a crime," I insist, though I know we

are—aiding and abetting known criminals. Still, the money Gavin and Brandy get will be used to help real people and causes. I'd watched a true crime documentary about a group like that. They'd called themselves the Hooders, for Robin Hood.

"Do you want me to just do it?" he asks. "A man traveling alone with his grandchildren? That's just as believable as a couple."

"And miss out on the fun?" I lightly push his shoulder.

He angles his gaze to the carpet. "I just don't want you to get in trouble."

"No one is getting in trouble." I'm not sure why I feel so confident about this fact, but I do. The exchange is simple and all we need to do is walk there. Easy peasy. I angle my head toward Mark. He doesn't look convinced. "You'll be helping Gavin and Brandy. Those poor kids just want out of this mess. It's one walk."

He nods, and the expression on his face changes. Like he's convinced. He's not going to do it for the rush; he's going to do it to help his former student and neighbor. That seems like Mark. I link my arm inside his. "Come on, Gramps. Let's go."

We meet Brandy and Gavin in their stateroom to go over the final details. The exchange, as explained, is simple. Gavin and Brandy carry a black backpack with the watches to the drop point. The runner, identified by wearing red and carrying an identical backpack, sits down and says something about the weather. Brandy and Gavin get up, taking the other backpack with them and leaving behind the one with the watches. "Any questions?" Gavin asks.

I shake my head, my body tingling with anticipation. I've read about drops in my books, but I've obviously never seen one.

Mark shifts his weight from one foot to another. "And what are we doing during the drop again?"

"Just walking around, Coach. It's a park."

"Okay." He nods. "Should we talk to each other while we walk? Make it seem more realistic?"

"Sure," Gavin says after a long pause, "that would be good."

After a breakfast where Mark, for the first time on this cruise, eats almost nothing, we exit the ship, descend the ramp, and walk down the dock toward the town. It's a perfect day. The sky is bright blue and the water even bluer. There's a slight breeze and I inhale the smell of the ocean, feel the sun warm my skin. Stores and restaurants in bright pastel colors line the streets and my heart thrums with the anticipation I always get when I see stores. I remind myself that I'm not here to shop, though maybe there'll be time after the drop.

Mark grabs my hand, orienting me back to the present and toward the man now standing in front of our fake family. He's wearing a white short-sleeved shirt and a black hat with a red band around the rim. My heart plummets. The man is a police officer.

"Hey officer," Gavin says smoothly. "How's it going?"

"Fine. And you?"

"A great day in the neighborhood, right?"

"Sure." The officer laughs weakly. "Sorry to ask," he starts, "but there's been some reports of criminal activity involving this cruise line. Out of an abundance of caution and for the protection of the public, would you mind if I checked your backpack?"

Gavin adjusts the backpack on his shoulder but says nothing. Brandy stares at the concrete. And while I know I'm not supposed to talk, I'm just supposed to walk along, I can't help myself.

"Not our bags, I'm afraid," I say in my friendliest, most Southern drawl. "I'm a stickler for privacy. It's a Southern thing. You know the saying — don't show your knickers to strangers." I give him a warm smile. "You understand."

"I—" he starts.

"And it's not like you have a reason to stop us," I add sweetly because I know he doesn't. I haven't read thousands of crime books for nothing. I put my hand on Gavin's back. "Now I've got to get these grands to the beach. Have a blessed day."

We turn away and it's all I can do to walk at a normal speed. I focus on my steps. Step. Step. Step. Step. Step. We're ten paces out, twenty, thirty. Giddy relief floods my body. The further we get, the more it feels like we're going to get away with it. We're really going to get away with it.

"Ma'am," the officer calls.

I stop and puff out a breath. He has no reason to search that bag. I can do this. I plaster a smile on my face and turn around. "Yes, officer?"

"You dropped this."

He holds up a tube of lipstick. The one I'd stuck in the pocket of my sundress for a refresher.

"Thanks, officer," I coo. "I'm not sure what I'd do without my lipstick." We walk toward each other, and I take the tube from his extended hand. I open it and apply some for good measure. "Well don't I feel better already? Thanks, sir." I stuff the tube in my pocket and turn around.

"And ma'am," he says again, and my heart nearly stops.

"Yes, officer?"

"Have a blessed day."

My face breaks into a smile. "You too" — I squint at his name tag — "Officer Kelly."

I turn and we walk for what feels like forever but is actually twenty minutes. We stop and sit on the beach underneath a swath of palm trees, the backpack centered between us like a baby. "We need to stay here a bit in case anyone is watching," Brandy whispers.

"Sure." Time at the beach for any reason is good for me, and this beach especially. The water is crystal clear, the sand white, the sky bright blue. I remove my shoes and wiggle my toes. I pull a bottle from my bag and hold it up. "Sunscreen anyone?"

Gavin takes it. "Thanks."

I peek inside my bag again. "I also have a towel, extra sunglasses, and some water." I pull out a sleeve of crackers and hold them up. "Oh, and these too."

"Thanks girl," Brandy says. "But we're good." She and Gavin move with the backpack baby into the direct sunlight.

Mark leans in and puts his mouth by my ear. "You're amazing," he whispers.

I hold up the sleeve. "They're just crackers."

"No." He smiles and shakes his head. "Not the crackers. Back there. You really saved the day."

"Oh." I flush at the compliment. "I'm sure you'd have done just fine without me."

He shakes his head. "I know I wouldn't have. I totally froze. I couldn't think of a single reason he shouldn't look in our bag." He puts a hand over mine. "Thank you."

I like the feeling of his warm hand on mine. Very much so. Too much so. I remove it and wave in my signature "pshaw" motion. "It's all good," I say, like I'm accustomed to lying to the police in high stakes situations. I think about how I handled myself and sit up taller. Me, Ellie Moore, the woman who panics at everything, whose imagination is on consistent high alert, stayed calm in a crisis.

I lay out the towel from my bag and tap on it. "Come on, sit. I know having sand all over your shorts is driving you crazy."

He stands, shakes the sand off his shorts, and sits next to me on the towel. "How do you know me so well already?"

I shrug. "It's a gift."

"It really is, you know. You're good with people, Ellie."

My first instinct is to push off the compliment. Deny it or denigrate it somehow. But it's true. I am good with people. And it is a gift. "Thank you."

We both lie back on the oversized towel, and a companionable silence settles between us. I'm lulled into relaxation by the sound of the waves, and the warm dappled sunlight shining through the palm tree branches. I shut my eyes, content to be at the beach, to be near a man who said I was amazing, and that I had a gift. I doze off and wake to a hand gently jostling my shoulder. For a split second, I think it's all a dream. I'm not on a beach, not here with Mark because Mark, in my actual life as a divorcée with a fake online boyfriend, doesn't exist. But then I hear his voice. "Come on, Ellie. Time to go."

My eyes fly open, and he's there, smiling. "Ready for part two?"

"As ever."

He stands and holds out his hands. I take them, my skin tingling again at his touch. He pulls me to my feet, and we stand for a moment, his face angled toward mine so we're nearly eye-to-eye. I flush; Gavin's words interrupt the moment.

"We're going to take a bus to the park. It'll lessen the chance of getting stopped."

Mark and I follow them to the bus stop. I see a man and startle. He looks like Caleb. Same hair. Same eyes. I look again. It isn't him. Thank goodness. I can't imagine what he'd say if he knew I was on my way to a criminal drop point. With a man I like, no less. The one he told me to steer clear of.

We take a bus to the park and Brandy points out the drop-off bench. It sits at the edge of a small playground ringed with a chain-link fence. A few kids climb the ladder for a tube slide; others run around in what looks like a game of tag. Brandy and Gavin sit on the bench, the backpack on the ground between them. Mark and I stand together at the side of the park. I stare idly at the kids, random thoughts running through my mind. Things like: This park could really use some safer equipment. Where is that child's mother? Did Mark ever put on sunscreen?

I push the random questions from my mind and scan the surrounding area for a person wearing red and carrying a black backpack. Five minutes pass, then ten, then fifteen. How precise is this meeting time? How long do they typically wait? I tap my fingers on the fence post, impatience flooding my system. This is taking forever. I feel like a kid in line for a ride at an amusement park, like I'll never arrive at the front. Then a youngish woman wearing red shorts and carrying a black back-pack walks straight for the bench.

Mark grabs my upper arm and squeezes it.

The woman slides on to the bench next to Gavin and sets the backpack down. She ties her shoe and says something. Gavin responds, grabs her backpack, and he and Brandy stride away. And that's it. Mark releases my arm. After all I'd built it up in my mind, the real thing feels anti-climactic.

Mark lets out a breath. "Should we catch a bus back to the ship?"

Since all Brandy and Gavin have in the new backpack is a phone, the grandparent ruse is no longer needed. There's no reason we can't and shouldn't go back to the ship. Except I'm not ready yet. I like being here with Mark. And I like being part of this operation, underwhelming as it may have been. "Let's catch up with them and make sure everything's okay," I suggest.

I take a step in the direction they went after the drop. "This way."

Mark waits a moment, then shrugs, and a *what the heck expression* crosses his features. "Sure thing, Ellie Moore. Why not?"

Chapter 19

Mark

I don't really want to meet up with Brandy and Gavin. I've been a step away from all out panic since we saw the watches yesterday and I'm ready to close this short chapter. But I like Ellie. I want to spend more time with her, even if it means checking in on Gavin and Brandy. Or trying to. We may not find them.

As luck would have it (not), we run into them a block away. They're standing in front of a restaurant with an expansive green and white canopy. Large circular tables sit underneath, the entire space adorned with giant ferns. Brandy waves in our direction. "Hey guys." She jerks her thumb toward the restaurant. "Want to get lunch?"

Ellie says yes before I can say no and within minutes we're sitting at a table for four.

"Easy, right?" Gavin picks up a glass of ice water.

"Sure seems it." I hate to admit it, but I'm waiting for the other shoe to drop. "And we just go back to the ship?" I confirm. "There's nothing else?"

"Nothing else." Brandy checks her phone. "But we've got a few hours. Let's enjoy."

We order food and after we exhaust the recap of the day's events, Ellie puts her hand over mine. "Tell me," Ellie says in Gavin's direction, "what was Mr. Mark Moore like as a teacher?"

Gavin waits a long moment before answering. "Tough but fair. I mean, no one really likes history—" he pauses — "no offense, Coach."

I shake my head. "None taken."

Gavin looks again to Ellie. "But everyone loved him, you know. From the worst students to the best ones, he had a way of making you feel like you mattered. And that you could do anything you set your mind to. Even if it was a mind-numbing history assignment." He rolls his eyes.

I laugh but a lump forms in my throat at the same time. I'd always wanted my students to feel like I saw them, that I believed in their ability to be the best versions of themselves. But I never really knew if I succeeded. And after being unceremoniously ushered toward retirement by the district, I figured I hadn't.

"I could see that." Ellie squeezes my hand. "You making your students feel important."

"Thanks," I manage, but I'm unaccustomed to attention and I no longer want to be the center of it. "Enough about me."

The server returns with our food order and Ellie removes her hand from mine. It still feels warm from her touch.

"You heard about me," I say. "Tell us about you."

It's quiet and after along moment, Ellie puts her hand over her heart. "Me?"

Brandy laughs. "Yes, you. The rockstar who singlehandedly got us out of the search this morning. Did you work in criminal enforcement or something?"

She shakes her head. "Nope. Just read lots of crime and mystery books." She says the words in jest, but they feel like a put down.

"Come on, Ellie," I say, lifting my glass. "A woman like you? There's more to you than that."

She stabs a piece of romaine with a fork. "I didn't go to college or anything."

"Girl," Brandy says, holding up her glass. "Neither did I, and look at me now."

"Fine." Ellie clinks her glass to Brandy's. "Before I got married and had Caleb, I worked at Zoo Atlanta."

Gavin slaps his hand on the table. "No shit. Like a keeper?"

"Nah." She waves her hand. "I worked in the gift shop, but I got to know everyone, so I got to see lots of things behind the scenes."

"Like?" Brandy prompts.

Ellie tells us about watching a tiger give birth, feeding a sick meerkat with a bottle, and observing an operation on a zebra. She and some co-workers often stayed after hours and drank, and they always snuck into the zoo galas. "I met Harrison at one. And that was that. We got married and moved to New York for his job."

She says it like her life before Harrison didn't matter. "Did you miss it?"

"Of course. But I got pregnant right away and had Caleb. If there's anything I love as much as animals, it's babies."

I slot in these little snippets of Ellie with the information about her that I already know. I visualize her at the zoo gift shop, feeding a meerkat with a bottle, and sneaking into a zoo gala after hours, hair and make-up done up to the nines. I picture her as a mom and a wife and wonder what in the heck was wrong with Harrison Moore that he'd let a woman like Ellie go.

Brandy's phone chimes with a text notification. She swipes it from the table, and her eyes rapidly scan the text. "Check the bag!" she yells without context. "Check the bag."

Gavin grabs the backpack, unzips it, and pulls out a pile of crumpled workout clothes.

Brandy grabs the bag. "Is there a phone?" She turns the pack over and shakes it. Nothing. In a frenzy, she unzips every pocket, feeling the inside of each with her hand. "There has to be a phone."

Gavin bends his neck, shoulders caving forward. "Oh my God. Oh my God." He repeats the phrase on a loop a few times before lifting his head. "She talked about the weather. It's the same backpack." He smacks his hand on the table.

Ellie's eyes go wide, both of us seeming to piece together what's happened at the same time. The woman whose back-pack they took —the one who now has the bag with the coun-terfeits — is not the runner.

"She'll definitely go to the police," Brandy says. "What else would she do with a bag full of watches?"

My eyes drop to the bag on the floor. "There's a tag," I say, picking it up. "With an address. Sandra Rolle. 14 Rosewood Lane."

Gavin scans the tag. "Worth a chance." He punches what I presume to be Sandra's address into his phone. "It's a twenty-minute walk."

Brandy waves her phone. "What do I tell my aunt? She's asking where we are. The runner's at the bench."

"Tell her to reschedule," Gavin says. "Say we're delayed." He stands and throws a bunch of bills on the table. "We've got to go."

Ellie and I stand. Her eyes meet mine, the question in them clear: Do we continue this escapade or cut out and go back to the ship? Had I been given this scenario pre-cruise, the answer would have been easy: one hundred percent ship. And had I been given this scenario even a few hours ago, the answer would still have been ship. But now I don't know. Every minute I spend with Ellie, every piece of information that fills in the puzzle that's her, makes me more intrigued. Is the wise decision to go back to the ship? Absolutely. But I'm also seventy-two years old and feeling more alive now than I have in decades. And I don't want to give that up. "I'm game," I whisper. "You?"

Ellie shrugs. "Why not? We're in it this far."

Brandy and Gavin hit the pavement and start running.

I nod toward their retreating forms. "I can't keep up with them, but we can follow. 14 Rosewood Lane." I punch the address into my own phone. "Let's go."

Chapter 20

Ellie

Mark and I walk on the edge of a paved street in the direction prompted by his phone. Pastel-colored houses line both sides, the sky a bright blue. I glance at him. He looks more relaxed now than he did earlier, even though the stakes have most definitely been raised. "You good with this?" I check.

"Strangely, yes. I just have a gut feeling everything is going to be all right."

We turn the corner at a turquoise house with a fountain in front. "Me too," I say, though I'm not sure if I mean I'm okay with the counterfeit exchange or with Mark in general. With Sebastian, there was always a feeling in the back of my mind that maybe something was up. A nagging. An instinct. Whatever you want to call it. I don't feel that way now. Whatever is happening with Mark feels like it's right. "I just hope this Sandra woman hasn't opened that bag."

"I can't imagine she hasn't. It had to be heavy, right?"

"Maybe she'll believe a story?"

We walk in companionable silence, and I pivot my head

from one side of the street to the other. "I know it's not the time for this, but I really love the houses here. They're all so unique. And I love the pastels."

"If you were a house, I think you'd be one of these." Mark points to a pink one with a trellis in front. "Maybe that one." He points to a second home, mint green with big porch.

"I'm not sure I like being compared to a house," I joke. "But they're pretty ones." I inspect the homes as we pass. "How about you? What kind of house would you be?"

"Definitely a castle."

"Really?" I bump his shoulder. "Somebody thinks a lot of himself."

"I didn't mean it like that. It's just that sometimes I can be hard to get to know. Hard to break. Like a castle."

"I don't think you're as hard a nut to crack as you think," I say. "I think I know you pretty well."

"Yeah?"

"Yes. A kind guy, bit of a neat freak, with a penchant for steak."

"Not sure about the kind part."

"Not every dad makes towel animals for bored daughters in the hospital." I nod toward a street. "There's Rosewood."

We turn the corner and approach house number 14. Gavin and Brandy are standing in a bush near the front door, their faces angled at a window. I tiptoe over. "For heaven's sake," I whisper, "just knock on the door already and ask for the bag."

"She's probably opened it by now," Gavin says. "How do we know she hasn't called the police?"

"We don't even know if she's here." Mark's tone is no-nonsense. He sounds, I imagine, like he did as a teacher. But he's right. We can't stand, the four of us, in the bushes in front of this woman's house indefinitely. Honestly.

"I'll knock," I volunteer.

As soon as I say the words, the angry face of an older woman appears in the window. Her fist is raised, her mouth spewing out what I can only guess are curse words. She disappears a moment, then reappears at the front door. She's tiny and wearing what can best be described as a housecoat. The stream of angry words are foreign.

I take a careful step toward her. I speak slowly, but given that she's speaking a different language, I'm fairly certain she can't understand me.

Gavin strides toward her holding up the bag. "Bag? Sandra Rolle?"

A voice questions from the street. "Who are you?"

We collectively turn. A woman—*the* woman, the one from the park—turns on to the walk leading to the front door. Her face is flushed, and she has the bag with the watches clutched across her chest with both arms. She says something to the woman at the door, and the torrent of words stop.

"We accidentally switched bags," Gavin says, "back at the park."

Brandy steps forward. "Your address is on this tag." She gestures toward the dangling laminated square with Sandra's address. "That's how we found you."

"We just want to switch back the bags." Gavin moves toward her, bag in hand.

Sandra grips the bag tighter across her chest. "What are you doing with a bag full of watches?" She pauses. "Nice watches. I can't imagine what these are worth."

Gavin grips the tag. "But this is your bag. Your name is on it."

Sandra shakes her head. "There's something weird going on. Please leave." She takes several steps toward the front stoop.

"The watches aren't real," I say. "They're props. A treasure hunt for the cruise."

"And you're going to cost us a nice steak dinner if we can't get them back," Mark adds.

I put my hand on his shoulder. "And believe me, there's nothing this man here likes more than a steak dinner." I pat a flat hand across his stomach. "Like a pig in mud."

Sandra doesn't respond, and she doesn't release her two-armed grip on the bag. Instead, she says something in what I now assume is Creole to the old woman. The old woman speaks rapidly back, hands flying, then disappears inside. Sandra stands on the grass, her legs and feet in an athletic stance. "If they're just props," she says, "then you won't mind if I keep the bag."

I shake my head. "But darling, if you keep the bag, we don't get the dinner. And we really need that steak dinner. Bless those cruise chefs, I'm sure they're trying their best, but the food... well, it's bad enough to knock a dog off a gut wagon. Trust me on this." I take Sandra's black bag from Gavin and hold it up. "Let's switch the bags back and we'll be on our way."

Sandra shakes her head. "I'm happy with this one."

It's silent and still. A standoff. Brandy moves first, swooping down and grabbing a discarded tennis ball from the ground. She throws it in the air and catches it. Then again. And again. Given the situation, the action is odd.

"We'll have to call the police then, I guess," Gavin says. A big bluff. No way do we want the police involved.

Sandra smiles revealing a gap between her front two teeth. "My grandmother has already called them. They should be here any minute."

My heart speeds up and for the first time since I agreed to be a part of this endeavor, I feel the beginnings of panic. I strain my ear for sirens. Brandy is throwing and catching the ball. Honestly! Of all things to do at a time like this.

"Knock it off, Brandy, will you?" Mark says.

As soon as the words leave his mouth, Brandy hurls the ball toward a tree behind Sandra. The ball heads straight for a volleyball-sized beehive, the trajectory perfect. It hits the hive smack in center, and bees swarm the area in a cloud of buzzing. Sandra waves at the flying insects with her hands, the backpack dropping to the ground. Gavin grabs it and runs toward the road, Brandy behind him. Mark and I amble along as fast as we can after them.

"That was crazy," Mark whispers, his face flushed.

"Do you think she really called the police?" I'd be easy to spot in my bright pink sundress.

"I don't hear anything. Maybe she was bluffing. It's not like the watches were hers."

I listen for the sirens another block, then let it go in a way that I typically wouldn't have. Brandy and Gavin are not in sight.

Mark takes a few paces. "What do you think we should do now? Go back to the cruise ship?"

"That makes sense." I say the words, and while I believe them, there's something about the past few hours that I don't want to release. The adrenaline, the attraction, the excitement. All of it has made me feel more alive than I have in years. If I had to fathom a guess, I'd bet Mark is feeling the same way. "I know what you're thinking, Mr. Stone Fortress."

"Yeah?" He stops, shifts his body, and looks at me with a sly smile. "Try me."

"That you kind of want this experience to be over, but not really."

His smile widens. "How did you know that?"

"Because I feel the same way."

We walk toward the main road and talk about the past few hours: the craziness with the police stop, the mixed-up bags, finding Sandra, and Brandy and her perfect shot at the beehive.

It's like reliving the whole thing, but better because we know it ends up okay.

A taxi comes into view. "Where do you think Gavin and Brandy are?" I ask.

Mark raises his hand to flag the taxi. "Heading back to the ship, maybe. Or setting up the real drop."

The real drop. Right. It hadn't occurred to me that the job wasn't done until just now. "They'll miss the cruise."

Mark shrugs. "Not really a loss for them, is it?"

"No," I admit.

"No more Paloozas. No more green pools. No more forced games."

I stamp my foot. "I like the games."

His lips curl into another smile. "Fine then. No more Hank."

"That's a good one," I jest.

The taxi pulls to the curb and for a second I feel like saying what I think Mark wants to: "Let's blow off the cruise and stay here instead."

But my belongings are on the ship and it's not exactly like I'm swimming in funds for hotels or food or anything else. The rational thing to do is get inside the taxi, go back to the ship, and finish out the next few days on the cruise.

The driver's side window of the taxi slides down.

I do have some savings I can use.

"Where to?"

I'm sure I can get my things from the cruise line later.

"Cruise port," Mark says.

He puts his hand on the door handle. I cover it with mine. "Do you want to blow off the cruise?" I whisper.

Mark meets my eyes. He takes his hand off the door handle. "Of course. Do you?"

I shrug. "We're having fun. And who knows when we'll be

in the Bahamas again?" After I say the words, I recognize that I'm using we and not I. But it's true. I'm not just having fun. I'm having fun with Mark.

"Let's do it." Mark tells the driver, and the cab disappears down the road.

With the cab gone, the decision made, my heart dips in my chest. What am I doing? Purposely missing the boarding time of the cruise ship, agreeing to spend time on an island with a man I barely know? I am having fun, but I thought I was having fun with Sebastian too. I stare at the road, doubting myself.

Mark gently touches my elbow. "We can still catch the cruise if you've changed your mind. It's not a problem. I'll just call another taxi."

His tone is gentle and kind and when another taxi comes into view, he raises his hand. I pull it down. I may not have known Mark Moore all that long, but I can trust him. Right? Or no? I thought I could trust Sebastian and look how that turned out. I take a step away from Mark, hating that the old Ellie, the one who wouldn't have questioned herself, who would have dived right in and said why the heck not, is gone.

He guides me toward a bench shaded by a large oak tree and we both sit. "What is it, Ellie?"

I fiddle with my watch, not sure how to answer or if I even want to. What is it? *I like you. I want to stay here. I want to get to know you better. And I miss the version of me that would do all those things without a hitch.*

"You don't need to tell me. Just let me know what you want to do. We have plenty of time."

His voice is tender and understanding and the bubble of doubt in my chest pops. "I just don't know what to think," I say quietly.

He leans his head toward mine. "Think about what?"

I hesitate, then blurt out the words. "About you," I say finally.

"About me?" He shifts back on the bench. "I'm not all that complicated. Retired history teacher. Two daughters. Small town." He pauses. "I've got that weird fixation on plagues though."

I laugh.

"I did lie to you about something though."

My body goes rigid. I knew it. *Knew* it. I knew Mark was too good to be true. "What?" I brace myself for the answer.

"I've never been to Switzerland."

I tilt my head. Switzerland? What does Switzerland have to do with anything?

"During that game the other day," he continues, "I told you my favorite place I'd traveled to was Switzerland. I was just trying to sound exotic. I haven't been there. I haven't even been outside the States until now."

I digest the information, this baby of an untruth. "And that's the lie? That you've never been to Switzerland?"

"Yeah. That's the lie."

A laugh bursts from my gut.

A smile inches across Mark's face. "Why? What did you think it was?"

"That you're a con artist and everything you've told me is false."

He looks up. "What is it with you and con artists, Ellie?"

Chapter 21

Mark

I mean the question as a joke, but Ellie squeezes her eyes shut. Her shoulders slump.

Crap. I internally kick myself. I've always been bad with women, bad at interpersonal communications in general. "I'm so sorry." I put my hand on her leg, then immediately remove it. That's probably not the right thing to do either. "I didn't mean to—" I start.

Ellie opens her eyes and shakes her head. "It's fine. I'll tell you."

"You don't have to tell me anything," I insist. The last thing I want to do is make Ellie feel like she needs to share things she'd rather keep to herself.

She takes my hand. "I want to."

She says nothing for a few moments then spills out the whole story. How, a month after her ex-husband's wedding, she created a profile on a dating site for seniors. How Sebastian, a French businessman, connected with her on day one. He'd been widowed, or that was the story, with a daughter who got married and immigrated to the US. It was his dream to move to the

States and find his daughter. He told Ellie he loved her and that he wanted to move to the US to be with her, even if he never found his daughter. After a few months, he said that he was moving his company to New York so they could be together.

"He texted me seven, eight times a day, sometimes more. He called me his *belle femme*." She pauses. "'Beautiful woman' in French." She rubs at her eyes.

"At first, the monetary amounts he asked for were small. Little bits needed quickly because his own money was tied up in company assets."

I inhale, knowing where this story is going, but not wanting it to get there.

"Then he needed money to find his daughter. And money for office rent. And money to travel here." She shakes her head. "I finally started to feel like it was strange, all these payment requests and when I told him, he totally understood. He sent me a cashier's check from his newly formed American account in the full amount I'd given him, and then some." She angles her head and looks at me, the expression on her face so pained, it hurts me to see it. "I thought it was security. Proof he loved me," she says.

She fills in the rest of the story. She sent Sebastian, or whoever it was, money until she started to run out. When she told him she couldn't send any more, communication stopped. The cashier's check ended up being a fake.

"Ellie, I'm so sorry." I envelop her in a hug without thinking and we stay like that for a long moment.

"Thank you."

"You reported it, right? They're trying to get this guy?"

She nods. "There's an investigation, but cyber scammers rarely get caught. It's been almost a year. I'm pretty sure that money is gone."

God. My feelings vacillate between sadness for Ellie and anger at the perpetrator. "Is there anything I can do?"

"No. But I can tell you're not judging me. I appreciate that." She looks down. "Not everyone has been that way."

"Well, it's not like it was your fault."

She smiles softly. "It kind of was, Mark."

"No," I insist. "He, Sebastian or whoever it was, took advantage of your kindness, of your generosity."

"Of my stupidity."

I grab her hand and gently stretch out her fingers. "You're not stupid. You were blindsided. You'd never conceive of hurting someone. Of course you believed him. It would be against your nature not to."

Her shoulders unfurl the tiniest bit. "Thank you for saying that."

"I mean it." I squeeze her hand. "Now we have a decision to make. Cruise or island?" I shift on the bench. "I'm okay, either way. And if you want me to stay here while you go on the cruise or vice versa, we can do that too. You're in the driver's seat, Ellie."

She keeps her gaze on me a long moment. "Where have you been all my life, Mark Moore?" She says it in jest, but part of me thinks she might mean it. I sit up taller.

"Let's stay," she says finally. "We can get some cheap rooms and eat and dress on a shoestring. Unfortunately, I've become good at that." She smiles.

"I'm game," I say, and I am. Ellie's vulnerability slid into my heart in a way I wouldn't have expected. I already liked her, but it was a surface level like, I realize. I liked her funny Southern sayings, her outgoing personality, her penchant for stray animals. But the Ellie who fell in love with a scammer is more real than the other one, and I feel privileged that she let me see that side of her. It makes me want to protect her, make sure she's cared for like she deserves.

"Where shall we go then?" she asks.

Before I can answer, my phone pings with a text message.

I pull it out and read a text from Gavin. "They made the drop," I tell Ellie, and she squeals. "They want to meet us for dinner."

"Sure," she says.

I smile. It's nice to be making dinner plans, nice to have a woman I care about.

We end up meeting Gavin and Brandy at an oceanside restaurant, part of a bigger, luxury resort. We sit at a round table on a covered, open-air terrace overlooking turquoise blue ocean water and white-sand beaches. Wicker fans spin lazily overhead and the scent of cuisine from surrounding tables infuses the air. The sun, full and orange, dips toward the ocean water. It's like paradise and I wonder why, in my seventy-two years, I didn't travel more. Addison could have watched Sara, or I could have figured out a way for us all to go.

The server stops by with our drinks, and I stop the self-critique. I made the choices I made. No use wishing I'd made different ones.

The server sets down a piña colada with a pineapple garnish and a little pink umbrella in front of Ellie and I internally smile. The drink is very on brand.

"Will you get in trouble for missing the cruise?" she asks.

Brandy swirls her wine. "We'll be fired, but it's fine. We're done with that. Done with this." She shakes her wrist, adorned by an exquisite watch.

"Do we need to contact anyone from the cruise line?" I ask. "Tell them we're not returning?"

Brandy waves her hand dismissively. "On most cruise ships, there's a key system that keeps track of the passengers, but your cruise doesn't have one. On the Senior Savers Cruise Line, the key system is me." She puts a flat palm across her chest. "I'm the one supposed to be keeping track of my sheep. I'm supposed to report it if you don't come back."

"And you won't be there," I supply.

"Exactly. They'll realize, but not until tomorrow. I'll call in then. Tell them you're here and we all missed the cruise and that you'll pick up your stuff and yada yada." She shrugs. "It's not like they're going to turn the ship around and come back."

I take a sip of water. "Any recommendations about where to stay in the meantime?"

"Speaking of that." Gavin reaches in his pocket and slides what looks like a room key across the table. "Stay here for the week." He gestures toward the stunning hotel behind us. "It's all paid for."

Chapter 22

Ellie

I could pinch myself. A room at this gorgeous hotel for a week! I feel like I chose the right door on my favorite old game show *Let's Make a Deal*. The one with the car or the international trip instead of the worthless zonk prize. "A room here for a week must have cost a fortune."

"It's the least we can do," Brandy says. "You really saved us."

Mark swipes the key from the table and looks to Gavin. "You're sure?"

He slaps him on the shoulder. "One hundred percent, Coach."

Mark meets my eyes and mouths, "One room okay?" It might seem like a ridiculous question, given that we've shared a room the past few days, but I appreciate his checking. Our rooming together on the cruise had been borne of necessity to save his back, whereas this, agreeing to share a room on purpose, has a different feel. At least to me it does.

"Good with me," I mouth, and he slides the key into his wallet.

Our server presents us with exquisitely plated cuisine, and the four of us enjoy vibrant discussions as we dine. It's the type of conversation that buttresses a day full of adventure and contrasts immensely with the laundry list of to-dos Caleb typically throws at me at the day's end. Did I remember to send in the insurance claims? Did I pick up my prescriptions? Did I follow up with Officer Stillmore about the Sebastian investigation? He means well, I know, but these types of questions on the daily make me feel like I'm a chore instead of a person. Here, in this moment, I'm not the dizzy mother who must be constantly monitored. I feel valued instead.

The four of us share all four desserts on the menu —chocolate layer cake, raspberry sorbet, carrot cake, and cannoli. When the bill comes, Gavin pays it. "Another thanks," he says. "We couldn't have done it without you."

I should feel strange, even guilty, about his statement, given that he's talking about a criminal enterprise. But I don't. I feel weirdly proud of my role, proud that I assisted in turning a botched exchange into a success. Like a heroine in my own cozy mystery.

"Thanks." I push up from the table and look to Brandy. "We'll see you tomorrow?"

"Sure. Breakfast?"

We set a time to meet, and after Mark and I find our hotel room. He pushes the door open and holds it for me. "After you."

"Thank you." I step inside an insanely beautiful room. I've stayed in a lot of stunning places with Harrison over the years, but nothing like this. It's a corner room with floor-to-ceiling windows. The white caps of the ocean waves are visible in the dark. A king-sized bed with crisp white sheets and a menagerie of fluffy pillows centers the room. A fully stocked bar sits in the corner, a comfy couch and a circular glass table next to it. The bathroom, all white tile, features a soaking tub, double vanities, and a shower bigger than the entire bath in our stateroom.

"Wow." Mark takes a step back. "I've never been in such a grand room."

"Me either." I set my bag down.

We take turns showering and freshening up using the complimentary supplies in the bathroom. Afterwards, we lie side-by-side on the cushy king-sized bed in matching robes with the hotel insignia on the pocket, both of us smelling like soap. If I were younger or not plum exhausted or sure about how Mark felt, I might have tried to start something. But I don't. I'm happy just lying here. I feel safe and cared for in a way I haven't in a long time.

"Tell me something about you," I say. I'm lying on my back, my eyes on the ceiling and its intricate pattern of silver triangles.

"I'd rather talk about you."

I turn to my side and face him. "No changing the subject. I told you about my worst thing. Tell me yours."

"My worst thing? Besides helping commit a crime today?"

I laugh. "That is pretty bad."

"Do I have to give a worst thing? I already feel a little out of my league with you."

"Pshaw."

"I shoplifted once."

I raise an eyebrow. "What did you take?"

"Bottled water. They were under my cart. I forgot to pay for them."

I put my hand under my head and partially sit up. "That's it?" I grab a throw pillow and swat him with it. "You're the worst at this. What's your best thing then?"

"My best thing is the girls," he says. "Watching them grow, being part of their lives."

I nod. "That's mine too, with Caleb. Biggest regret?"

"Not traveling more. I taught European history for decades, but I've never seen Europe. And I've never been to a place like this." He shrugs. "It always seemed like a big hassle to plan, and I didn't want to go alone."

I adjust the lapel on his robe. I don't like the thought of him traveling alone either. I open my mouth to volunteer to go with him, to see the world in our seventies, then shut it. I might want to do that, but I don't know how he'd feel about traveling with me.

"How about you?" he asks. "What's your biggest regret?"

I roll back to my back and look at the ceiling. "Besides Sebastian, I regret letting Harrison call all the shots during our marriage. I wanted to get a job doing something with animals, but he said it would mess up our taxes if I earned too much." I wave my hand. "But it wasn't a bad life while it lasted. I just wasn't ready for after, you know. I didn't expect the divorce."

He takes my hand and squeezes it. "That man was an idiot."

I smile at the ceiling.

"What was your family like?" he asks, and I tell him about growing up in Atlanta, about being an only child. He tells me about his mom, a nurse, and his dad, an appliance repairman. He has a sister. They lost touch. We talk about our kids. What they were like growing up, what they do now. We laugh about our first jobs. We share our favorite movies and books. He laughs at the cozy mystery titles like *Thread on Arrival* and I tease him about his non-fiction reads. We both make a case for being the better cook, but after I explain the intricacies of making Southern grits from scratch, Mark concedes the issue.

"This has been nice," he says, "talking to you like this."

"It has." It's true. The whole scenario — lying in robes and just talking after a long day — it seems intimate without us being intimate and I feel inordinately closer to him than I did just a few hours ago. This man. He's exactly what I've been looking for.

"Thank you, Ellie," he says.

"For what?"

"For shining your light in my direction and letting me bask in the rays."

Chapter 23

Mark

I wake up early, light streaming through the slits in the window blinds. Ellie is asleep on the bed in the hotel robe, covers haphazard, her hair splayed wildly across the pillow. She's snoring, mouth wide open, arms flung out to the sides. Ugly in a way that's endearing. You know you have feelings for someone when unattractive sleep habits become charming.

Despite being happy —is that even the word? No. Too plain. Despite being ecstatic, jubilant, and delighted to be here with Ellie, my mind keeps looping back to our conversation last night. She'd asked me my worst thing and I'd said shoplifting.

A bold-faced lie.

I mean, I did shoplift a case of water, but it wasn't the worst thing I'd ever done. Not by a long shot. I'd used drugs and alcohol to mask my social discomfort in high school and became an addict. I introduced drugs to my sister. And while I turned things around after arrest number five—use of a fraudulent prescription and mandatory jail time—she never got clean. In and out of rehab, each fall after the rebound worse than the last, until she disappeared altogether. She hasn't contacted me or the girls in years. So, yeah, shoplifting a case of water is not my worst thing. Ruining my sister's life is.

I know I should have told Ellie given how important honesty is to her. But I didn't want her to think I'm still that person. I'm not. We only have one glorious week together. If it ends up being more, if our relationship extends beyond the Bahamas, I'll tell her then. But right now, I'm going to soak up every minute.

The *omission* about my past is fine. Right? It was a long time ago. Decades. And I *can* tell her. Just later.

I tiptoe into the bathroom, take a shower, and dress in the same clothes I'd had on yesterday. I check the time on my phone, then FaceTime Addison.

"We're fine, Dad," she says in lieu of hello.

"Well hello to you too."

She pulls the phone farther away from her face. "You sound cheerful."

"I am. I've been comped a week at a hotel in the Bahamas."

Her face lights up. "Really?"

"Yup. Is it okay to stay a bit longer? Maybe a week."

She nods before I even finish the words. "Absolutely." She pauses. "Are you there with anyone?" The question sounds hopeful.

"Ellie is around," I say, purposely vague. "I'm sure I'll run into her."

Addison smiles, the kind where all her teeth show. "Fantastic."

We exchange a few more niceties, and I talk to Sara. She's doing well, happy at Addison's. After the call, I fix myself a cup of coffee from the coffeemaker in the room and sit on the couch near the window. I move one of the vertical blinds and look outside. Ocean waves lap on the white sand, the sun already up in a bright blue sky. Directly below the window is a massive pool, impossibly blue, perfectly ordered lounge chairs and navy umbrellas around it. The restaurant where we'd eaten is to the left, its wicker fans looping lazily over early morning diners.

I glance at Ellie, still asleep. From what it sounds like, she's already traveled the world. Would she want to again? With me? I shake my head. I haven't even kissed the woman for fear she'd tell me to bugger off, and here I am thinking I might just ask her to travel the world. Not yet, but maybe. Things just need to keep going well.

I sip my coffee and watch the ocean waves rise and fall in the distance, white caps on their tips. The repetitious rise and fall of the water mesmerizes me and I lose myself in the present.

Ellie's voice sounds behind me. "Morning."

I turn around. She's sitting up in bed, the hotel robe pulled tight around her.

"Good morning to you. Sleep well?"

"Like a baby." She pushes her hair away from her face. "I didn't snore, did I?"

"No," I lie.

"Okay, good. Harrison used to complain about that."

"Like I said, man's an idiot."

She smiles and a blush creeps up her cheeks.

"Are you still good to meet Gavin and Brandy for breakfast?" I ask.

"Of course. I just need to get ready first."

Ellie moves to the bathroom and emerges in the same dress she'd had on yesterday. "We're going to need to do some shopping."

"I was thinking the same thing. Maybe you could help me pick some things? I'm not the best with clothes."

"Yes, please." She cracks a wide smile. "I've wanted to style you since day one."

I raise my eyebrows. "Really?"

She pushes open the door of our room and we spill out into the hall. "Yes, really. You know you're a handsome man, right?"

My face goes hot. "Says almost no one on earth."

She presses the elevator button, and the silver doors slide open. "Well, I say so," she says, stepping into the car. "You don't doubt me, do you?"

"Absolutely not." I hold up my hands. "Handsome it is."

She laughs and we walk to the restaurant, the weather perfect, our mood light.

"Hi Ellie," the hostess says.

"Hey Annabell. Beautiful morning."

"Sure is."

I follow Ellie and Annabell, once again amazed at Ellie's ease with people. I don't remember meeting Annabell; how did she and Ellie get on a first name basis? I shake my head. That's just how she is. People gravitate toward her.

Annabell seats us at the edge of the terrace. Little yellow birds hop near our table, pecking at crumbs. We order orange juices and coffee and peruse the menu, waiting for Brandy and Gavin. After a few minutes, a man wearing a blazer with the hotel insignia approaches our table. In his hand is a slim gold box. He dips his head. "Mark Moore?"

I nod. "Yes. That's me."

He holds out the box. "A gentleman left this for you at the front desk. He asked that I personally deliver it to you at breakfast this morning."

I set down my coffee and take the box. "Thank you."

He nods his head again, hands behind his back. "Very good sir."

"Looks like a gift." Ellie rubs her hands together.

I shrug. "I guess." I have no idea who the box is from or what it could possibly be. There are exactly four people who know I'm here, and I only told Addison and Sara a few minutes ago.

"Well open it." Ellie shoos her hand in my direction.

"You're one of those people who pulls the wrapping paper off of other people's gifts, aren't you?"

"Yes. So please, take off the lid. The suspense is killing me."

I smile and make a show of slowly removing the lid.

"You're killing me, Mark."

I smile. "Okay fine." I remove the lid all the way and look inside the box. There's a folded piece of paper inside. I motion for Ellie to move closer. She scoots her chair over and I pick up the paper and unfold it. A key falls out. The paper is a letter.

Dear Coach,

Thank you for everything you have done for me over the years and sorry for not saying goodbye in person. By the time you get this letter, Brandy and I will have checked out. By this afternoon, we'll be off the island and on to our next adventure. We're calling it quits like we said. But we wanted to thank you and Ellie properly for yesterday. Enclosed is a key to a safe deposit box located at Mercer Bank on Main Street. If you and Ellie want the contents, take it. If you do not, give the key to Clinton Russell, the bank manager. He'll know how to contact us.

Love, Gavin and Brandy

"Wow," Ellie says in an exhale. "I can't believe they're gone."

"Me either." I reread the letter. "It's very cryptic."

"Another thread of our mystery novel," she says with a smile.

I shake my head. "Only you, Ellie."

The server sets down our breakfasts, just as beautifully plated as the dinners last night. I stab a mango slice.

"What is the most ridiculous thing that could be in the box?" Ellie asks.

I take a sip of orange juice. "Candy?"

"More ridiculous," she prompts.

"Maybe it's a pair of "'Go Seniors!' pins. One for each of us."

"That'd be amazing." She pops a slice of strawberry in her mouth. "Or maybe it's Brandy's sheep sign. The one she carried everywhere."

I slap the table with an open palm. "The sheep sign, yes," I meet her eyes. "I kind of hope that's it."

"Me too. But we'd have to share it."

I shrug. "We could exchange it each month. Meet somewhere in the middle of our houses."

I make the statement in jest — obviously we're not going to exchange a sheep sign every month — but I like the idea of seeing Ellie on a regular basis after the trip, of having a reason to. I push my hand across the table. "Once a month. Deal?"

"Deal," she says and shakes my hand.

We finish our meals and sit at the table after, sipping coffee, watching the little yellow birds peck at our crumbs. "You know we have to go there right now," she says.

"To the bank?"

"Yes, to the bank. I'm dying to see if it's the sheep sign or not. Aren't you?"

"Not really." I shrug like I'm not also curious. "I think we can wait a few hours."

She smirks. "You are lying, Mark Moore."

"Hmmm."

She stands. "Come on. Let's pay this bill."

I pay the bill, and she pulls me through the foyer of the

hotel to the street with the same enthusiasm as a little kid on a mission to get a puppy. We speedwalk to the bank, just a few blocks away. I tell a bank employee I need to get into my safe deposit box, nervous now. What *is* in the box? Do I want to know?

The employee leads us to a back room with floor to ceiling silver boxes. "All yours," she says and exits. I scan the numbers for our box and find it in the third row near the top.

I pull out the key and look at Ellie. "Are we sure we want to open this?"

She widens her eyes. "Yes, we want to open it. I'm about to have a come-apart here, Mark."

I smile, her enthusiasm easing my nerves. I guess that's why they say opposites attract. I need a jolt of enthusiasm now and again. I move a rolling staircase to the space where our box is and step up two stairs. "Okay. Here goes nothing." I put the key in the lock and pull out a slim metal box. I step off the stairs, hold my breath, and look inside.

Chapter 24

Ellie

Mark opens the box, and I peek inside.

Money. The box is full of money.

"Holy cow." I swipe a stack of bills from the box and hold them up to the light. "How much do you think is in here?"

Mark stares at the box. "I have no idea."

I see a paper and pull it from the box. Another note. I hold it out so Mark can read it too.

Mark and Ellie,

Thank you for yesterday. There is ten thousand dollars for each of you in this safe deposit box. It's the amount you can bring into the US without reporting it. It's yours if you want it. If you don't, we understand. Just tell Clinton Russell, the bank manager, to contact us. Have fun.

Gavin and Brandy

Ten thousand dollars. Way better than the sheep sign. Snapshots of what today, what this week, could look like with this kind of money click through my mind. Excursions, expensive dinners, shopping. "Do we want it?" I question. "Why wouldn't we want it?"

Mark sits on a step of the rolling staircase and shakes a stack of bills. "I assume it's from the counterfeits. Taking it would be illegal."

"Would it? We don't know where this money came from."

"It feels wrong." He drops the stack of bills back inside the box and looks at me. "Don't you think?"

"I can't think," I say honestly. "The sight of all this money is skewing my judgment, especially when we're about to go shopping."

He smiles, but it's a weak one. "I think we should put the box back."

I set my bills back in the box and stare at the beautiful pile of green rectangles. Not taking the money is the correct thing to do. I know it is. And despite my actions yesterday, I'm not a criminal. And neither is Mark. Obviously.

He picks up the metal box, climbs the rolling stairs, and fits it back into its place among the safe deposit boxes. He slides it back in but instead of relief, all I can think is: That money is mine. Or it should be mine. I deserve it.

Mark pulls out the key and descends. He puts his hand on the small of my back and ushers me toward the door.

"Wait," I say, turning around. "Hear me out, but I think we should take the money."

He steps back.

"Or at least I want my half," I amend.

Surprise crosses his features. "But"

I hold up a hand. "Look. I was swindled out of way more than ten thousand dollars by an unscrupulous individual who played on my emotions. And no matter what the investigators say, no matter what I try to tell myself, that money is gone. I'll never see it again. This money" - I point to our safe deposit box - "was generated from crime just like money was taken from me by crime, so it seems, to me, like just desserts that I have my share."

Mark looks at the box, and I take a deep breath. "I know ten thousand dollars won't radically change my life, but that money will allow me to have an unforgettable week on this island with a man I've become very fond of." I pause. "And extra money for a rainy day."

Mark averts his eyes from the box. Silence fills the tiny space, my thoughts loud in the quiet. Mark must think I'm awful. I'm not even giving the money to a parent or charity like Gavin and Brandy. I want it to have fun.

"Do you think less of me?" I ask finally.

"No. Of course not." Mark grabs both of my hands in his. "I think you're right. And I think I want my money too."

"Really?" I tip my head. "What changed your mind?"

He smiles. "There's a woman I've grown very fond of too. And I want to have an incredible week with her." He lets go of my hands and puts the key in the safe deposit box. "Come on. Let's go shopping."

We leave the bank, the cash — all twenty thousand of it — in my bag. We go to our hotel room and put most of it in the safe. After, we take a cab to Crystal Court, which as told to me by Google, is *the* upscale area to shop on the island. The space is a mall, half indoors and half out, with gorgeous marble floors and unique store facades, each with a promise of the luxury goods inside. I squeal without meaning to, and Mark laughs.

"So, I take it we'll be here for a while," he says.

"All day," I say, and he groans. "Come on." I pull him toward a men's store. "We've got work to do."

As soon as we get inside, a retail associate greets us at the door. She eyes Mark. "Can I help you?"

"Thank you," I put my hand on Mark's shoulder, "but I've been waiting to style this one for a long time."

She nods appreciatively, her eyes sweeping down his form. "I can see why."

Mark's face goes red. "Here we go."

"Come on." I pull him toward the back of the store. "Let's get you dressed."

Mark sits on a stool while I pull shorts, pants, and shirts from the racks, sizing up Mark as I do it. I pile the items on my arm, one after the other.

He eyes the growing stack. "Do you mean for me to try all those things on?"

"You asked for my help with your wardrobe," I say matter-of-factly. "I'm taking the request seriously."

"So I see," he says as I usher him to a dressing room. He emerges in khaki pants and a light blue button-down shirt. I straighten the shirt and cuff his pant legs, trying to keep my wits about me because, well, ooh la la. A silver fox for sure. And maybe it's because I'm a septuagenarian too, but I like the wrinkles around his eyes, his thick gray hair, the creases near his mouth when he smiles. This is a man who has lived, who has been through heartache, but is here now, looking for a sense of adventure. What's not attractive about that?

He holds his hands out. "Well?"

"You look fabulous. See?" I turn him toward the mirror and go through how all the pieces work together and why, then grab a few for mixing and matching, along with shoes and belts. Mark is a great sport about trying it all on. He models everything, amused, I think, about how excited I am with each look. The only piece of clothing he doesn't show me is the bathing suit I'd selected, telling me I'll "see it on the beach." After we cash out, I release him to the food court and shop for myself. A few hours later, he hails a cab and we stuff ourselves and our things in the back. I squeeze his lower thigh. "Thank you," I mouth. "That was fun."

"For me too," he says. "I can't remember the last time I went shopping."

The cab drops us off at the hotel and we put our new things in the closet and drawers, the room feeling more personalized with actual belongings inside. I sit on the couch by the window and take in the panoramic ocean views. Mark sits beside me. "So, what should we do, Ellie? Sky's the limit."

I grab my phone from the side table and type in things to do in the Bahamas. "Always good to start with a Google search," I say and read down the list. "Flat bottom boat tour, snorkeling, day at the Blue Lagoon Island, pirate museum, swimming with pigs—"

"Wait," Mark interrupts. "Did you just say swimming with pigs?"

I tap on the title in the list and a flurry of images of pigs swimming fill my screen. "Aw. Look how cute they are."

"Not cute." He shakes his head.

"Right." I roll my eyes. "I forgot about your fussy side."

"Pigs wallow in mud."

"Maybe that's why they're swimming. To get clean."

He smirks. "And I suppose that's one of your picks."

"I'm not sure. Though I'd love to see you swim with pigs." I wink. "Especially in that bathing suit I picked out." His face goes pink, and I continue. "You probably want to go to the pirate museum. Aye, matey."

He rolls his eyes. "You would make a terrible pirate."

"Possibly. But am I right? Is that something you would pick?"

"Perhaps."

I slap my hand on his knee. "I have an idea. Why don't we

take turns planning events? We can alternate. Surprise each other."

"I'm game," he says. "Should we be planning things we think the other person would like or things we want to do?"

I shrug. "Doesn't matter. Just cool stuff."

"Just as long as it's not swimming with pigs," he says.

"The pigs are clean, Mark. They're in water. Honestly." I set my phone down. "Anyway, I call that today's shopping counts as an activity planned by me so you, my darling, are up."

He leans back, arms behind his head. "Challenge accepted."

Chapter 25

Mark

"Yes. Mr. Moore." She takes the questionnaire from my extended hand. "I have you and Mrs. Moore down for the couple's evening spa experience at 7:00 p.m." The woman, named Tia, stands. "Let me show you to the dressing space. I assume Mrs. Moore will be joining shortly."

"Yes," I manage. Even though I'd planned this event, and came early to check it was all set, I feel wildly out of place. Everything about this—"The Spa"—including Tia seems peaceful, beautiful, and at ease. The opposite of how I feel. The furnishings in the space are moss green with bamboo accents, all centered around a stone table. In the corner is a stone countertop featuring a tray of cut up vegetables and thick glasses of ice water. Chimes play in the background.

Tia removes a robe and slippers from a closet and hands them to me. Both are warm. I look again at the closet ,which, I guess, is heated. How about that? I let the heated terry cloth warm my skin, so transfixed by the novelty, that I miss Tia's next directive.

"Get changed in here?" I guess and gesture to the huge dressing room she's standing in front of.

"Yes, Mr. Moore. And after, please take a seat. We'll start your experience as soon as Mrs. Moore arrives."

"Sure," I say, not correcting the Mrs. part. Why should I? I like the idea of Tia, or anyone, thinking Ellie is my wife.

I change into the robe, return to the waiting area, and sit. Ellie does not appear and as much as I love the warm robe and even the chimes, I continue to feel out-of-place. I chose the spa because I thought Ellie would like the experience, but now I'm worried it's something she'd rather do on her own. I'm not a spa kind of guy. I've never had a facial or a massage. I don't know what Himalayan salts are. Or a Turkish bath. Is that some kind of hot tub? Or something else? I have no idea.

I stand, decision made. I'll leave. I'll give Tia a note for Ellie and make it seem like the spa day was for her, not us. She'll probably like that better. Relaxing on her own.

I take a step toward my dressing room just as the main door swings open, Ellie and Tia in the frame. "Your wife is here," Tia says gently. I don't correct her. Neither does Ellie.

"Here, Mrs. Moore," Tia hands her slippers and a robe from the closet. "These are for you. You can get changed in any room." She moves her hand across the fleet of doors like a game show host. "I'll give you a few minutes."

Tia exits and I brace myself for the awkwardness of Ellie pretending she's excited about this.

"You dirty dog," she says, and it takes me a second to realize that, in Ellie speak, being a dirty dog is a good thing. "I love spas. A couple's one will be glorious. This" - she waves a slipper and steps into a dressing room - "is going to be hard to top."

She emerges in the hotel robe and slippers. "I can't remember the last time I had a spa day. It feels like a slice of heaven already. Thank you."

"Are you sure it's okay I'm here too?" I ask lamely. "Is it more relaxing to have a spa day on your own? If so, I can—" I point toward the door.

"Don't be ridiculous," she says, picking up a glass of the complimentary water.

I don't know if she means the sentiment or not, but in the next moment Tia reappears and gestures for us to follow her. She brings us to a room for our couples' massage. Two tables draped with brown sheets sit in the center of the space. On each is a plate of folded towels and large flat stones. The room is illuminated by flickering candles and smells like citrus. The sound of ocean waves infuses the area, whether from the actual ocean or a soundtrack, I don't know. Two massage therapists stand in identical white scrubs, a man and a woman. Tia introduces them as Tony and Inga and exits the room. I stare after her, wanting to follow, if I'm honest.

Ellie leans over and whispers, "Don't you dare consider leaving, coward."

I smile, amazed at how well she knows me.

The massages get underway with Tony and Inga directing us to the side-by-side tables and covering our unclothed bodies with heated towels. I turn my head so I can see Ellie. She does the same and we smile at each other. Inga begins kneading my shoulders and, oh, wow, it hurts. I try not to make a face, but man, of all the things I'd expected from a massage, massive pain was not one of them. I check out Ellie's expression to see if she's struggling. Her eyes are closed and she's breathing deeply, completely serene.

Inga presses the ball of her hand into my left shoulder blade. "You are tight," she announces. "Tight, tight, tight." She presses down into my muscles harder and it's everything I can do not to wince. "Such tight muscles," Inga says again. "Why are your muscles so tight?"

Because I just stole twenty thousand dollars.

Because I'm in pain from this massage.

Because I'm lying next to a woman I really like, and I don't want her to think I can't tolerate *a massage*.

"I don't know," I say.

Ellie's eyes fly open. "Are you okay?" she mouths.

"Perfect," I lie.

As the massages continue, I note that Tony is a silent therapist; Inga's the chatty one. Her primary focus is on how tight I am, everywhere apparently, but in between this repeated observation, she asks a plethora of useless questions. Where am I staying? How long have I been here? Where am I from? I hate small talk under the best of circumstances but trying to carry on a conversation while I'm being tortured makes it so much worse. Tortured on two fronts.

"Done," she says finally and slaps the table. I sit up, a towel pooled around my body, relieved. I've worked up a sweat. Ridiculous. Ellie sits up too, but unlike me, she looks peaceful and soothed, like she just had a super-expensive and luxurious spa treatment. At least that's good. If only one of us were to have a nice experience, I'd want it to be her.

Inga waves a finger in Ellie's direction. "This man is tight," she says and points to my shoulders. "Tight, tight, tight."

My face heats; Ellie smirks. "Thank you, Inga," I say dismissively. "I'll work on the tightness."

Tia reappears and announces it's time for our facials, and we follow her out of the room.

"You hated that," Ellie mouths as we walk.

"I did not." I mouth back. The last thing I want is for Ellie to think that I'm not tough enough to endure a *massage*.

Tia stops at a new room and introduces us to a therapist I think of as "Not Inga." Ellie and I lie side by side in our terry robes and Not Inga applies thick mud masks to our faces, then covers our eyes with cucumbers. If it wouldn't seem weird, I'd almost want Not Inga to snap a picture so I could show Addison and Sara. They won't believe it otherwise.

Not Inga scrubs our faces clean and takes us back to the waiting area where we are to meet Tia for our final treatment — hydrotherapy. I look at Ellie. Stripped of make-up, she looks different. Her laugh lines are evident along with crow's feet and the uneven parts of her complexion. An aged face may not fit societal standards of beauty, but it fits mine. Every wrinkle, every imperfection, is proof of life experiences. Beautiful.

Her hands go to her face. "I look awful, I know," she says. "It's always this way after a facial. I'll put my face on when we get back to the hotel."

I take her hands and gently pull them from her face. "You don't have to put any face on. Your face right now is my favorite."

She meets my eyes, her expression vulnerable. "You're lying."

I shake my head. "I'm not."

"Why then?"

"Because it's all you." I stare at her for a long moment, this woman I'm falling for. In more than seven decades of life, I've never felt this way. Never. Then again, I've never met a woman like Ellie Moore.

"What are you thinking?" she asks, her eyes hooded.

"I'm thinking," I pull her toward me, "that I'd really like to kiss you right now."

Chapter 26

Ellie

Mark maintains his gaze and I pull him toward me. Our lips meet in a brief, sweet kiss. He steps back. "I can't tell you how long I've been wanting to do that."

"Me too."

"Yeah?"

"Absolutely." We kiss again, a real one this time. I smile against his lips, and he pulls away.

"What?"

"Nothing," I say. "I'm just happy."

"I'm happy too."

We stand still for a moment, then his arms are around me again.

The door opens and we fly apart. Tia's in the doorway. "Sorry," Mark and I say in unison.

"Used to it." She smiles. "Spa treatments can be aphrodisiacs."

I step away from Mark and adjust my robe. "You don't say."

"You'd be surprised." She shrugs. "Are you ready for the

hydrotherapy session? Inga has stayed on after hours to assist with additional services."

I look to Mark, his eyes wide, and I smile. I knew he didn't like the massage, but he'd never admit it. Men. They're ridiculous. I shift my gaze to Tia. "Is it possible for Mark and me to just sit in the hot tub and relax? We feel we've gotten enough spa treatments for now." I look up at him. "Do you agree?"

His shoulders dip and he smiles. "I couldn't agree more."

We follow Tia to the hydrotherapy room which is, without exaggeration, one of the most stunning and romantic rooms I have ever set foot inside. Wall-to-wall windows feature an unobstructed view of the ocean. Next to the windows is a large in-ground hot tub, bubbling with steam and surrounded by an intricately designed green and blue tile floor. The space is dimly lit by candles on tables and around the pool. Green plants and flowers are all over the space, giving the area a tropical feel. The ceiling, a dome, is adorned with the same tile as the floor. A bottle of champagne on ice sits along with a tray of chocolate-covered strawberries on a nearby table.

"I took the liberty of moving your belongings into these dressing rooms." Tia points to two dressing rooms on the far wall. "The champagne and strawberries are complimentary, and the whirlpool is yours for the next hour. Ring this bell if you need anything." She picks up a small bell next to the strawberry tray, rings it, then sets it back down. "Enjoy." She sweeps out of the room.

"Wow," Mark says as soon as the door shuts. "I have not lived my life the right way if I'm seventy-two and this is my first time in a room like this."

"I think I want to live here." I grab the champagne bottle from the ice bucket. I hold it out to Mark. "Do the honors?"

"With pleasure." He takes the bottle and pops the cork. Champagne springs from the opening in a bubbly explosion.

Mark shakes the excess liquid off his hands, pours us each a glass, and holds his in the air. "To a fabulous evening." He kisses my cheek.

"To our future home," I say, and he laughs. We clink our glasses, sip the champagne, and take strawberries from the tray. I bite into mine. The juiciness of the strawberry and the sweetness of the chocolate collide inside my mouth.

I wipe strawberry juice from my chin with a napkin from the table. "Do you like whirlpools?"

"I would have said no before I saw this one. The main hot tubs I've been exposed to have been at the Y." He looks at the hot tub then back at me. "Not quite the same. You?"

"I love a good whirlpool. Not that you couldn't have guessed that."

"You do give off some serious hot tub vibes."

I pick up another strawberry. "I consider that a compliment. Thank you." I take a bite from the strawberry, then nod toward the tray. "You'd better get in there before I eat them all."

Mark smiles. "Whatever you want, Ellie. I'll do whatever makes you happy."

I stand still, a half-eaten strawberry frozen in my hand. His statement was simple, but the way he said it — that he'd do whatever makes me happy — felt real. Being first in anyone's book has not been something I've felt before. Not with Caleb, but he's my child and that's to be expected. But not with Harrison either. He was always more about himself and his own needs than what made me happy. I was his accessory, until of course I wasn't. I'd thought Sebastian wanted me to be happy but that was obviously wrong. It's amazing that Mark, a man I've met at seventy-two years of age and who I've known less than a week, has made me feel more special than any other man in my life to date.

He gently puts a hand on my elbow. "Are you okay?"

I shake my head. Shake out how Mark just made me feel. We like each other; I'm not blind to that. But the depths that I'm feeling? I'm not sure he's reached that point.

"I'm good," I say and grab a towel. The plushest one on earth, or at least it feels that way.

Mark grabs one after me and makes an audible sigh. "This towel."

"Right? That's why we need to live here."

He puts a hand on my upper arm. "Do we —" He stops and gestures from the dressing room to the whirlpool with his index finger.

I tip my head, not understanding

"I didn't think to pack a bathing suit," he blurts.

I laugh. "Well, you sly dog."

"I wouldn't say sly as much as stupid."

"Well, no worries. There are enough bubbles in there that we can hide ourselves. I'll go *al fresco* if you will."

"You sure?"

"I'm not much to look at these days," I say, "but I'm game."

He touches my face. "You are plenty to look at, Ellie. Probably even more now than when you were younger."

He gives me a tender look. One I want to bottle up and keep with me always.

"So," he continues, "I'm not sure how much of a gentleman I can be once I see you *al fresco*, so how about you go first and get under the bubbles?"

It's my turn to blush and I do. Since the divorce and since Sebastian, all I've felt like is an older woman trying to cling to my youth with make-up and clothes and hair coloring. It never occurred to me that someone would find me attractive *because* of my age. If Mark didn't seem so sincere, I wouldn't believe him, though I'm not sure why. I find his age attractive. Why wouldn't the reverse be true?

"I'll just get, well, you know," I mumble and slip into the small dressing room. I take off my robe and underwear and hang them on a stone hook. I put the towel — still the plushest in the world — around myself and tiptoe out of the dressing area toward the whirlpool. I spy Mark's feet under his dressing room door. I drop the towel and slide naked into the steaming water. It's hot at first, uncomfortably so, but it takes only a few seconds for my body to acclimate. I breathe in the steam and lean back.

"You decent?" Mark calls.

"I'm under the bubbles."

"Coming out." Mark emerges from the dressing room, a towel wrapped around his waist. My gaze drops to his bare shoulders, chest, and torso. His shoulders are wide, and he has biceps like a man who still works out. The hair on his chest is moderate and graying, and his torso has an evident little bulge, both of which honestly make me like him more. Sometimes it's the imperfections that you love about people, not the perfect parts.

Still holding the towel around his waist, he grabs one champagne glass and sets it down by me, then the second. He stands by the side of the tub.

"Should I close my eyes?" I say, almost teasing.

"Whatever you want. It's not like you didn't already see me in my birthday suit."

I squint, thinking, trying to figure out what he's talking about, then my hands fly to my face. Oh God. That first night. When I'd insisted Mark was a scammer and pulled the covers off him. The incident feels like it happened a lifetime ago. "I'm so sorry about that."

"No worries. I've got a scammer aura. I know that."

"You most certainly do not." I tap the water. "Now I'm going to close my eyes, and I'd like you to join me."

I hear the trickle of the water next to me, feel Mark's presence by my side. "All clear," he says, and I open my eyes. He makes a point of stirring up the water in front of him. "Don't want you to take an untoward glance or anything."

I smirk. "I wouldn't dream of it."

"How do you deal with how hot this water is?"

"You'll get used to it."

Both of us lean back and allow the water to swirl around our bodies. Water jets hit my shoulders with just the right amount of pressure, releasing the bits of tension I have left even after the massage. My muscles uncurl and relax. Fatigue overtakes me, the good kind, the kind borne of relaxation.

Mark takes my hand in his and rubs my knuckles with his thumb. I think about the kiss. Or kisses. Maybe the moment was just borne the romantic atmosphere, like Tia said. But, for me at least, there was an emotional component. I'm falling for this guy.

"Ellie," he says, his voice deep and gravelly.

I loll my head to the side. He's done the same and I smile. "Yes?"

He sits up. "I'd really love to kiss you again."

Chapter 27

Mark

"Do you think we were allowed to, you know?" Ellie moves her index finger in a circle. "In the hot tub."

We're in the bed in our hotel room, both of us naked and wrapped around each other. "If by this" — I imitate her finger movement — "you mean sleep together, I'm sure we're not the first."

"Stop it."

"You asked," I say with fake incredulity. She lies against me, her head on my chest, and I move my fingers through her still damp hair.

"I bet you're not tight anymore," she teases.

"Inga would be so proud."

She pushes herself up a little and looks in my eyes. "You didn't like the massage," she says teasingly, "Admit it."

"Fine. I didn't. But Tony wasn't trying to injure you. That Inga had fingers like hammers. I can't believe people pay for those things."

"*You* paid for it."

"Well, I didn't know. Now I do. And never again."

153

She pats my chest. "I'll give you a massage sometime. A gentle one."

"We'll see," I say, though I know if Ellie offered a massage, I'd be all in in two seconds flat. I close my eyes and listen to the sound of the ocean waves. I feel Ellie's heartbeat under my hand. I inhale the scent of her. She smells like the hotel soap but with a special Ellie twist. I love this. I love her.

My eyes fly open at the realization. I'm not just fascinated by Ellie. I don't just think she's a character. And I'm not only enamored by her blue eyes. I am in love with her. I am seventy-two years old and in love. I want to tell her, but if I do and she doesn't feel the same way, it will ruin things.

People, a couple it sounds like, run down the hallway outside our room, laughing and talk-screaming as they go. Their revelry interrupts my musings and reminds me that, notwithstanding how private things seemed earlier in the whirlpool and are now in our snug little room in the corner of the hotel, Ellie and I are not in a solo, forever paradise. This situation is temporary, with just six nights left if you count this one. I can't ruin it by expressing feelings she may not share.

"Have you thought about what we should do tomorrow?" I ask.

"I have," she says and twists her body so that her back is to my chest. She snuggles in and pulls my arm around her so we're spooning. It's uncanny how her body fits right inside my own, like we were made for each other. "I'm going to surprise you."

I kiss her neck. "You're going to make me swim with pigs, aren't you?"

"*Clean* pigs," she says, "and no hints. Now get some rest." She taps my hand.

I hold on to Ellie, feel the gentle rise and fall of her stomach, hear her breathing slow. She's asleep almost immediately, but I stay up as long as I can, leaning into this moment where she's close, memorizing this feeling for a future time, not far from now, when I'll be alone in Scranton and wishing for it back.

Though I stayed up much later than Ellie, I still wake first. I fix myself a cup of coffee, sit on the couch, and look at the ocean through the blinds. Though it's only the second morning, I already like this routine. It's a routine I could get used to, and not because of the view. It's because I'm waiting to spend the day with Ellie.

When she wakes, the only clue she gives me for today's adventure is to bring a bathing suit. "None of that *al fresco* stuff. At least not until later." She winks.

We pack small bags, or rather, I pack a small bag. Ellie shoves a massive number of seemingly unnecessary things (things which will become necessary if I question them, I've learned) into her oversized polka dot bag. We go to the same hotel restaurant overlooking the water where we've eaten all our meals so far, and Ellie greets the staff like long-lost family. I love that about her, the unbridled friendliness I seem to lack. We order our food.

"Any hints now?"

"Nope. We're catching a bus in a half hour," she says, then moves her fingers across her lips like she's locking them. "Other than that, my lips are sealed."

After finishing breakfast, we walk to a small, covered bus stop painted a cheery yellow color. An older couple is there, along with a family of four. It's hot, but not muggy, and the scent of the ocean salt is in the air.

"Where are you going?" A ponytailed little girl, about six and part of the family of four, bounces in front of us.

"Sierra," her mother says, a warning tone.

"It's fine," Ellie answers, then turns to the girl. "It's a surprise."

Sierra's eyes widen. "I love surprises."

"Me too," Ellie tells her then jerks her thumb in my direction. "Him, not so much."

"I like surprises." I don't. I've always hated them, but having a surprise planned by Ellie feels different somehow. Exciting rather than unnerving.

Ellie shakes her head. "He doesn't," she mouths to the little girl.

A colorful bus comes into view and pulls to a stop. It's covered from top to bottom in photographs of swimming pigs. Across the side of the bus, in all capital letters, are the words: Pig Excursions. "Ha," I whisper in Ellie's ear. "I knew it."

She raises an eyebrow. "Do you now?"

The bus takes us to a beach, aptly called "Pig Beach," and I stand, ready to get off and swim with animals who generally live and bathe in mud. I'm not stoked about swimming with them — seems unnatural — but like I said to Ellie last night, I'll do whatever makes her happy.

"Sit back down, you." She pulls on my leg.

"But," I point to the beach and the others descending the stairs of the bus.

"This isn't our stop."

After the "Pig Beach" group disembarks, it's just me and Ellie on the bus. The driver takes us to a marina where we meet a youngish man who introduces himself as Mac. .

Mac leads us to a pristine white boat with a glass bottom, a navy-blue canopy over top. He points out a cooler. "Drinks are in there." He hits a cabinet next to it. "Snacks are in here. Help yourselves."

Ellie and I thank him and grab ice cold waters. We arrange ourselves on a cushy bench overlooking the glass bottom.

"We're snorkeling!" Ellie says the words like she's been holding them back all day. "A private excursion." She leans forward and I smell the coconut of her sunscreen. "Mac told me we might even see a shark."

My eyes widen.

"Nurse sharks," she adds. "Not dangerous at this time of day."

"Wow," I say, not sure how I feel about swimming where the odds of seeing a shark are high. But I don't want to ruin the moment, and if Ellie isn't worried, neither am I. "Great choice," I add. "I've never been snorkeling."

"Not in the tri-state area?" she says with a wink.

"Surprisingly, no."

She leans back against the boat's edge. "I wasn't going to make you swim with the pigs."

"I would have done it if you'd wanted to."

She leans a shoulder into mine. "I know. That's why I wouldn't make you."

Mac starts the boat and maneuvers out of the marina and into the ocean. The boat bounces as it moves and sprays of water dampen our warm skin. I look back at the island. Colorful hotels sit majestically facing the turquoise waters. Palm trees line endless beaches with pristine white sand. Sailboats glide across the surface of the ocean.

Ellie takes my hand, and I sit with her, content. After a short ride, Mac stops the boat in a cove of crystal-clear water surrounded by tall cliffs. "There are some great reefs here," he tells us, throwing down the anchor.

We strip down to our bathing suits. I'm wearing the one she picked, navy blue with tiny sharks on it. She squeals when she sees it. "I knew that would look great on you," she gushes.

"I like yours too," I nod toward her.

She looks down at her body and it feels like she's going to say something disparaging. Some nonsense about how old she looks. I'm ready to dive in, to tell her how incredible she is, inside and out, when she straightens and throws her shoulders back. "Thank you."

She pulls sunscreen from her bag and we both lather up while Mac removes snorkel equipment from a dock box on deck. He goes over the whole snorkeling spiel, reciting it like a rote history lesson. It seems simple enough. Seal your lips around the snorkel and breath in and out. Stay close to each other and the boat. Don't touch anything.

We put on life vests and the snorkel equipment and smile at each other. Ellie hands Mac her phone to take a picture. We move together and I sling my arm around her. I make a note to get a better photo when we're finished snorkeling. When this trip is over, I'm going to need proof that it all happened. Because I'm not going to believe it.

After Mac snaps the picture, Ellie descends the ladder and plunges into the water. "It's warm," she yells. She puts her face in and pulls up immediately. "There are tons of fish down here." She waves a hand. "Come on, Mark."

I jump from the top ladder rung; warm water splashes around me as I break the surface. I move next to Ellie and start to swim, my face in the water. The massive reef is teeming with fish and brightly colored coral that moves with the current. Sunlight streams in from above, illuminating the top level of the ocean water. Ellie points and I follow her gesture with my eyes. Two huge sea turtles swim over the rocky ocean floor, their front flippers propelling them through the water. We swim with them as they pass over a stingray and through a school of stripy fish. We swim a bit then circle back toward the boat. Endless fish of all colors and sizes and patterns dart through coral and swim across the ever-changing oceanic landscape. If I weren't here, experiencing what it looks like under the sea in real time, I wouldn't believe how colorful and vibrant it is. How alive. Pictures don't do it justice.

Ellie breaks the surface, and I follow her lead. We remove our snorkels. "Wow" I say, unable to come up with a better word.

"I know. It's gorgeous."

We spend the next hour gliding through the water together, each of us pointing out finds. Squids, sea urchins, lionfish, clownfish. After a bit, Ellie jabs her finger upward, motioning for me to come to the surface. We both break through the water and remove our snorkels. "I'm pretty sure I saw a nurse shark."

"Really?" Unlike earlier, my worry about the ocean and what might be in it has eased. I *want* to see the shark. "Show it to me."

We put our snorkels back in. I swim a few feet before I see it. A gray behemoth of a shark, ten feet at least, hovering on the bottom, like it's sleeping. I nod at Ellie under water. It feels insane. Less than a week ago, I was in Scranton, moored to my routine. Now I'm swimming directly over a shark with a beautiful woman by my side. I make a mental note to thank Addison for pushing this adventure. It's what I needed.

We finish snorkeling, and not long after seeing the shark, we reboard the boat. We lie on lounge chairs in a sunny part of the deck. The heat from the sun warms my skin and the gentle ocean waves lull my body to sleep. When I wake, the boat is moving, Ellie no longer by my side. I push off the lounge chair and find her standing at the back of the boat, its wake forming symmetrical ripples in the ocean water behind us. I stand next to her. "Hey."

"Hey yourself," she says.

"Good sleep?"

"*Great* sleep. I may have to sleep on a boat from now on."

She smiles and we stand together, the cove behind us getting smaller as the boat moves toward the shoreline. Despite feeling relaxed, melancholy overtakes me. I know we're going back to the Bahamas, back to paradise, but I don't want this experience to end. Or maybe it's not this experience, but this week. I don't want time with Ellie to end and each day, each adventure that passes, is one day closer to saying goodbye. I don't know if she feels the same way. I think she does, maybe, but I need to know for sure. Because if the answer is no, I'll have to get a hold of my feelings somehow. I'm falling too fast.

"Ellie" — I move my body so that I'm looking at her — "what happens after this?"

"After this?" she asks, startling. "I don't have anything else planned but I figured we could get some dinner later. Maybe walk on the beach."

"Yes, to both of those things," I say and take her hands in mine. "But I didn't mean after snorkeling. I meant after this week. Do you see anything between us that lasts longer than five days?"

Chapter 28

Ellie

"I—" I start, then hesitate. It's not that I don't want there to be an "after this." I very much do. It's just hard to trust my feelings. This is exactly how I felt with Sebastian right before things went wrong.

Mark shakes his head. "I don't mean to put pressure on you. I just—" He closes and opens his eyes. "I just haven't felt this way about anyone in a long time." Maybe ever.

I squeeze his hands. Mark isn't Sebastian. And unlike Sebastian, who found every excuse under the sun never to have a video chat, I can see Mark. I see the sincerity in his eyes. I hear it in his tone. This isn't the same. I need to dive in. I need to learn to trust myself again. "You're not putting pressure on me. And I don't want things to be over after this trip."

He lets go of my hands and exhales, so loudly that it makes me smile. And I think my gut is right this time. "How far do you think it is between Rye and Scranton?"

"Two hours and sixteen minutes without traffic." He throws me a sheepish look. "Not that I checked."

I smile.

"I can't move from Scranton," he says. "Not with Sara and her doctors and all." He waves his hands and speeds up his speech. "Not that we were thinking of living together, I just, you know, for the future, wanted you to know that." He shakes his head. "I feel like I'm blowing this. I'm sorry." He puffs out a breath and steps back. "Ellie," he says, enunciating the word, "I would very much like to keep seeing you after this trip. I am happy to drive to Rye or meet you anywhere else you'd like to go. Is that something you'd be interested in?"

"Yes," I say immediately. "I would love that." I step toward him. "And if it comes to it, I don't have any real ties to Rye."

"But Caleb?" he says, and I love that he thought first of my son.

"Caleb's a grown man, married, with a driver's license. He can come and see me."

"And your friends?"

"They can come too," I say. But I know they won't. My friends in Rye are sparse and not the type to travel unless it's on a plane. And frankly, since the Harrison break up, I haven't felt as much a part of the group, like my inclusion was borne of my marriage and without the latter, the former disappears. "Not that I'm rushing things," I add. "I just want you to know."

"That's good," Mark says. "That's good to know."

We reach the shore, and Mac maneuvers the boat into the boat-slip and ties it up. He drives us back to the bus stop and the whole time Mark and I gush about the fabulous time we had. At the bus stop, we give Mac a massive tip, one of the fun things about having a ton of discretionary money. We start back to the hotel, the same path we'd walked this morning. I'd felt great then, but I feel even lighter now that I know Mark feels the same way I do. These next few days are not the end of our time together, but just the beginning.

Mark grabs my hand and squeezes it. "Since we're in our suits already, want to take a dip in the pool?" he asks.

The Ellie of a few days ago would have been worried that I looked awful, which I'm sure I do. My hair is a salty mess, my face stripped of make-up, and this bathing suit shows parts of my aging body I'd typically keep hidden. But the truth is, I would like to go for a dip in the pool more than fix myself up, and Mark clearly likes me just as I am. Not on constant alert about how I look? It's freeing in a way I wouldn't have expected. "I'd love to go for a dip in the pool."

We put our bags down on lounge chairs near the pool, slide into the warm water, and swim up to the bar. We have a drink each — wine for me and soda for Mark. After, we float on pool noodles and talk about our respective hometowns. Mark tells me about Scranton's St. Patrick's Day parade, the largest in the nation, and I tell him about the Rye Bread and Music Festival. He tells me his favorite restaurant is Ale Mary's, but he thinks Casa Belle would be more my speed. I share that I would take him to The Blind Rhino or Henry's, both sports bars. I warn him it's a Giants town, not a Steelers one. We share how each of us would spend a rainy day — shopping for me; reading for Mark. We agree to spend our first rainy day together shopping in a bookstore. With each conversation, with each snippet of new information, more of Mark slides into view. I see myself in his life. Eating at Ale Mary's. Walking through Nay Aug Park. Drinking coffee on his back deck.

After the pool, we return to the hotel room and rinse all the salt and sunscreen from our skin. We sit in our complimentary hotel robes, fresh and clean, the sound of the ocean lulling in the background.

"Come on," I say and pat the bed. "I'll give you a massage."

He lifts an eyebrow.

"A gentle one," I clarify. "Nothing like Inga. No hammers on these fingers." I hold my hands up and wiggle my fingers.

He smiles and lets his robe drop to the floor. "Okay, but only because I trust you." He slides onto the bed.

Still in my robe, I grab lotion from the bathroom, return to the bed, lather his back in gentle circles. After, I lightly press on the muscles in his neck with my fingers, gently kneading. "That's good, Ellie."

"See." I dip down and kiss his back. "I told you."

I work my way from his neck to his shoulders, taking my time, working longer at the tighter spots. From his shoulders, I move to his upper back. When I reach his lower back, he turns over, pulls me toward him, and kisses my neck. I kiss him back and we make love again, my body meshing with his. After, I lay with my head on his chest, and he twirls a lock of my hair around his finger. "You are the real deal, Ellie," he whispers. "I'm so lucky to have met you."

A lump forms in my throat. I feel so cherished by this man, so worthy of love, that I might cry for the intensity of my feelings. "I'm lucky too," I say softly. I fall asleep with my head on his chest, his arm slung around me, and when I wake, it's dark. I'm still lying with my head on Mark; I lift my head to look at him.

"You're up," he says, like it's the best thing ever, me being awake.

"Were you up the whole time?" I shift off of his body. "I'm sorry if you felt like you couldn't move."

"I dozed off a bit," he says. "And I didn't feel like I couldn't move. I didn't want to move." He caresses my cheek.

"Are you hungry?" I ask. We haven't eaten since the boat.

"Starved."

We dress, get a light dinner, then go to the beach. We take our shoes off and walk along the shoreline, water lapping onto the sand and over our feet. Mark takes my hand, and we walk a few blocks before my phone pings. I pull it out of my bag. It's Caleb.

Caleb doesn't have medical concerns like Mark's Sara, but I don't think he'd call me out of the blue while I'm traveling. I need to take it.

"Caleb," I say to Mark, and being a family man and a good dad it's the only explanation he needs. I accept the call and put the phone to my ear. "Caleb, honey. All good?"

"Where are you? Are you all right?"

His tone is two parts worried, and one part exasperated, and I know immediately what this is about. I'd planned to call him about my extended stay, but I hadn't yet. The cruise line must have called him.

"I'm fine. I'm in the Bahamas." I move a few steps from Mark. "Some girlfriends I met on the cruise and we extended our stay. It's absolutely stunning here. Just the bluest waters on earth."

"I've been to the Bahamas, Mom. You have too." The worry in his voice is gone. Now that he knows I'm okay, that there's no emergency, only frustration is left.

"I don't believe your story," he continues. "The cruise would know if you extended your stay."

Damn his beautiful, logical brain. "Okay fine. My girl-friends and I missed the boarding time. I didn't want to tell you because you always accuse me of being scatterbrained, but that's the truth." And it is. Just not all of it. "So, I decided to stay a few extra days. I was going to call you." I look to Mark and smile. "I'm actually having the time of my life."

"I'm glad, Mom." He asks for the name of the hotel, and I tell him the Stardust. It's a small one, nearby. One that, unlike the hotel Mark and I are staying in, could pass as a dive should Caleb look it up.

We say our goodbyes and I switch off the phone.

"Girlfriends? The Stardust?" Mark teases.

I blush. "Caleb doesn't trust my judgment since Sebastian. I couldn't possibly tell him I was here with a man. He'd pitch a fit. I'd never hear the end of it."

"Well, I'll have to make a good impression when I meet him, then."

"Yes, please," I say, warmth flooding through me at the reference.

"That must be frustrating though. To be defined by one mistake."

"Yes." I turn my head and look at him. "Thanks for saying that. I love Caleb but his attitude does get to me sometimes. I mean, name one person in their seventies who hasn't made a mistake, even a doozy? You have, right?"

Chapter 29

Mark

She looks at me, expectant. Did I make mistakes? Doozies? It's the perfect time to tell her about my addiction, my sister, jail. I *should* tell her. Obviously.

"I guess he's just being protective," she says.

"Probably," I say, distracted. I'm almost certain Ellie won't hold my past against me, but unlike the Sebastian scenario, I'm the bad actor in my story. And my sister's still suffering for it. Her children are, too, as good of a parent as I've tried to be in her stead.

"So what do you have planned for tomorrow?" she asks.

I could answer this question, this easy question about what I have planned for tomorrow, and tell her about my past later. Because I will tell her. I love this woman, and just as I want to know all of her, I want her to know all of me. Just not yet. Because the day I planned for tomorrow? She's going to love it.

"I have an amazing day planned for you tomorrow. I can't wait."

I sleep like a log, amazed how easy it's been getting used to sleeping next to another person. I like knowing she's there. In the deep night, I forget sometimes and then I open my eyes and see her lying there, like a gift.

We wake, dress, and eat breakfast. After, we catch a cab, and I make Ellie close her eyes as we near our destination. My heart beats wildly as the cab comes to a complete stop. Unless I've gotten Ellie completely wrong, there's no way she's not going to love what I have planned. I pay the driver, usher her out of the cab, and guide her forward a few steps. "Okay. Open."

She opens her eyes and says nothing. I get it. What I've brought her to doesn't look like anything from the outside. Just a plain building on a sand dune near the beach.

"What *is* this place?" she asks finally.

"The Potcake Palace." I throw my arms out like I'm the owner, then explain that it's a dog rescue. Part of the mission is to socialize the dogs —and get them adopted. To help with socialization, people can sign a dog out for the day. I explain this to Ellie as we walk toward the main building.

"We can take a dog out?" she confirms.

"Yup. All morning."

Her face breaks into a smile. "You've outdone yourself, Mark Moore." She kisses my cheek. "I miss my Peanut. I could really use a dog fix."

"Well, you've got it today. We're in."

Muriel, the woman in charge of the rescue, gives us a small tour, and after, she hands me a ten-week-old puppy named Darnell. His tail wags furiously, like I, the man he met just two minutes ago, is the best in the world. Ellie signs the paperwork and Muriel hands her a bag with toys, treats, water, a pop-up bowl, and a blanket. "Have fun," she says with a smile. "Darnell's a real sweetheart."

"Sure is," Ellie says, her eyes on the little dog in my arms.

We walk out of the building, and I dip my head and inhale the scent of puppy. Ellie sees.

"Puppy smell is one of the best scents in the world," she says.

"It is. Who knew?" I hold Darnell toward her, and she takes the wiggly dog in her arms. "See for yourself."

She buries her head in his fur and hugs him to her chest. "Such a sweetie. I've actually never had a puppy of my own."

"No?" Given how passionate she seems about dogs, this surprises me.

"No. I've always been drawn to rescues that are older or sick. The ones I know no one else will take."

"Ahh," I say. "I get why you like me now. I'm like one of your rescues. The kind no one else will take."

She waves her hand in my direction. "Pshaw, Mark Moore. You're a catch and you know it."

I don't know that I'm a catch and I most definitely don't think it, but we're having too good of a time for me to belabor the point. "Thank you," I say simply.

"Such a cutie." She kisses Darnell on the head and gently sets him down. "Ugh. I'd love to have more dogs, but my condo will only let me have one."

"You wouldn't move?" If being surrounded by lots of dogs is what Ellie wants, then that's what I want for her.

"It's not really in the cards right now." She pulls gently on the leash. "But I do get to see lots of dogs at the vet. Plus, I'm spending time with this little guy. Come on, Darnell," she encourages. "Let's go to the beach."

"You're so good at that." It's amazing that she can so easily look at the bright side. She can't move, presumably because of the money she gave Sebastian, but she still sees what's good about her circumstances.

"Good at what?" Darnell starts to walk, his tail gently wagging.

"Good at looking at the bright side." I fall into step with her.

"Better than being stuck under a cloud." Darnell starts to run toward the beach. "Feisty little thing," Ellie says, jogging with him.

"That makes two of you," I tease.

Once we're on the beach near the water, she lets Darnell off his leash. He runs along the shoreline, paws sinking into the sand, tail wagging. Ellie and I take off our shoes and follow behind in our bare feet. Darnell stops to play in the lapping water, running back and forth in rhythm with the waves.

"He's so happy," Ellie gushes.

"He is. I can see what I've been missing all these years not having a dog." I look at Ellie. I've missed a lot of things, truth be told.

"Dogs are so in the moment." She grabs a small ball out of the bag and throws it down the beach. Darnell bounds after it. "Now that I'm older, I'm trying to savor my moments more. Younger me would be ticking off the whole day, even the whole week, in my mind. Always thinking about what's next and not what's now." She pauses. "I'm trying not to do that anymore." She looks to me. "How about you? Do you live in the moment?"

I think a moment. I'm so routine-oriented at home. It's comfortable, but I don't think I really live in each moment. "I don't think I do," I admit.

Ellie picks up the ball and throws it again. "Why do you think that is?"

"I don't know. It wasn't like something specific happened or it was a choice I made or anything. I just got complacent. Like what I was doing was good enough, you know. I didn't even want to go on the cruise."

"Really?"

"Yes. I only went because Addison booked it, and I didn't want to hurt her feelings. I planned to spend the whole trip reading." Saying the words out loud, I can't believe how short-sighted I'd been.

She throws the ball again. "Reading, yes, about plagues. I remember."

I shake my head. "I'll never live that down, will I?"

"Not as long as I'm around you won't."

Darnell tires of chasing the ball and we find a shady spot under some palm trees. I get him treats and water while Ellie lays out the blanket. He walks in a circle a few times before settling in directly in the center of it. Ellie and I sit on either side of him, and it feels like this could be our life. The two of us, sitting on a blanket on a pretty day, our dog sleeping in the space between us.

"What are you thinking?" she asks.

What am I thinking? I'm thinking about you. About us. I'm thanking the stars above that the Senior Savers Cruise Line made a mistake and put us in the same stateroom. These are the things I'm thinking. I don't say any of them. "It's pretty here," I say lamely instead. I look to the beach, the water a turquoise blue, bits of sunlight dappling on its surface. "You?"

"I'm trying to figure out how I could sneak this little guy into my condo without the association finding out."

I look at the sleeping lump between us. "I'll take him," I blurt.

"What? Really?"

"Yeah." I put my hand on Darnell's back, feel the rise and fall of his breath. "Sara would love him. And I have time now, since I'm retired. I've never had a dog." The more I talk, the more excited I get about the idea of adoption. "I mean, why not?"

"I see no reason." Ellie puts her face down by Darnell's ear. "You are one lucky pup," she whispers, then angles her head upward. "You're sure?"

"Absolutely. And this guy —" he ruffles his fur— "is a sure way to get you to visit me."

"Oh, I was visiting you without the dog." She puts her hand over mine. "But Darnell's a nice bonus."

We sit on the blanket, our time vacillating between easy conversation and companionable silence. When Darnell wakes up, we walk him back to the Potcake Palace. Muriel is thrilled I want to adopt him, and I fill out the paperwork. She gives me instructions for bringing him home and I make the arrangements to get him at the end of our week here. I have no regrets. Taking Darnell home with me seems as right as keeping in touch with Ellie.

We rest in the hotel room after our time at the Potcake Palace, and as it's still my day, I've made plans for dinner. We dress in clothes we'd gotten on our spree. Me in chinos and a dark chambray shirt, Ellie in a lavender dress. When we get to the restaurant I chose, the hostess seats us at a small circular table overlooking the ocean, a small dance floor behind us. Live piano and violin music complement the sound of ocean waves crashing on to the beach. A smattering of stars in an inky black sky sparkle and wink, almost like they were placed there just for this occasion.

The server takes our drink order and Ellie looks out at the view. "Beautiful," she says, her face illuminated by a trio of votive candles in the table's center.

"Yes," I say, looking at her. I can't believe how crazy I am about this woman in just one week. When Sara and Addison were in high school, they watched the Bachelor and Bachelorette, those shows where a man or woman dates a bunch of people at once, hoping to find their soul mate. I'd always thought the premise preposterous; the show nothing more than a ratings grab. Falling in love that fast? No way.

Well, ha ha, karma. Well done. I get it now.

Ellie peruses the menu. "There's a steak entrée here." She leans over and points at the entry on my open menu. "I know that's what you're going to get."

I slap the menu shut. "Nope. I always get steak. You pick for me."

"Me?" She puts her hand on her chest. "Why?"

"Because you have a more adventurous palate that I do. And better taste."

When the server drops off our drinks, Ellie orders us both crab cakes and steamed asparagus.

"Nice choice," I say when the server leaves.

"Crab cakes are my favorite. Do you like them?"

"Never had them, but I'm happy to try." I hold up my glass.

She bumps her glass to mine. "Well to your first crab cake then."

"And to a perfect night."

"Cheers to that." We sip our wine and look out at the view. "I can't believe we're here," she says. "Not just at this restaurant, which is incredible by the way, but in the Bahamas. I can't remember the last time I had this much fun."

"Me either. Favorite part so far?" I ask.

She leans back in her chair and puts her hand on her chin. "Today, of course. I mean —" she shrugs — "dogs."

"Of course," I say. "What else?"

"Probably making my pink hand at the wax museum." She smirks.

"That was quite an epic piece of art," I agree.

"Yeah. How about you? What's been your favorite?"

"I think the game of get to know you bumper cars on the ship deck. That was fun."

"Indeed. I also enjoyed the scavenger hunt."

"Which led us to our foray into crime."

"Which we were quite fabulous at. Me especially," she teases.

"You especially," I agree.

We continue on, reliving the memories of the past week. So many things have happened. From me cleaning her mess in the room, to riding the Orlando Eye, to helping Gavin and Brandy with the drop. Shopping, the spa, snorkeling, drinking at the swim up bar. Romantic interludes. It would take a typical relationship months or even years to build up the memories that Ellie and I have made in less than a week.

The server returns with our meals and more drinks.

As soon as the plates are set down, Ellie leans forward. "Take a bite. I can't wait to see what you think."

I edge off a piece of the crab cake with the side of my fork and pop it in my mouth.

"Well?" she says after less than a nano second. I tick this reaction off as another thing I like about Ellie. She's excited about everything.

"Delicious," I say, though truthfully it tastes a bit spicy. Not that it matters. Given how excited Ellie was for me to try the crab cake, I would have acted enthused even if it was the worst thing I'd ever tasted.

"I'm so glad you like it," she gushes.

During our meal, a few couples congregate on the dance floor, swaying back and forth. I've never been a big dancer. Not at proms way back when or at weddings or bars or anywhere. But Ellie's looking at those dancing couples with a kind of longing that makes me think *she* wants to dance. The least I can do is ask her.

I stand up and extend my hand. "Ellie. Would you like to dance?"

Her face breaks into a smile. "I thought you would never ask."

I take her hand and lead her to the floor. On the way, I run through in my head what I know about dancing. Nothing. I know nothing. I don't know if there are certain steps, or a certain way I'm supposed to hold her. I'm about to tell her this, that I don't know what I'm doing, but then we reach the dance floor and it's easy. I just put my arms around her and sway. If it's not the right way to dance, she doesn't say anything. Her head rests on my shoulder, her body pressed against mine. She seems as content as I am. I think I love this. No, I know I do. And I love her.

I'm emboldened by the wine and the atmosphere and by holding her close. But these days we've spent together have been among the most memorable of my life. Even the clothes she picked out for me have given me a boost of confidence. Enough that I lean down, put my mouth to her ear, and say the words. "I love you, Ellie."

Chapter 30

Ellie

I angle my head up at Mark, the words he'd just said reverberating through me: I love you, Ellie.

I love you, Ellie.

I turn the words around, a verbal gift from a man I know I love too.

"I love you too, Mark," I say into his ear. The words—saying them and receiving them—are like a balm to my soul. After my surprise divorce and after Sebastian, I never thought I'd love again. I certainly never thought anyone would feel this way about me.

Mark pulls me tighter. "You make me so happy, Ellie," he whispers. "You're like all the bright colors in my pack of gray."

"Not all gray is bad." I push gray hair from his face. "This is some nice gray here."

He brushes his lips across mine. "Amazing that you can make gray hair seem sexy."

"Because it is." I tip my head up and whisper in his ear. "Lots of men your age don't even *have* hair."

He smiles and we keep dancing a moment before he pulls back and puts his hand on his throat. "Sorry," he says. "Can we sit down a moment?"

"Sure." I follow him to our table. He sits and takes a big gulp of water from his glass. "My throat feels a little strange. Itchy and like I keep needing to swallow." His Adam's apple moves up and down several times before he takes another sip of water.

"Has this ever happened before?"

He shakes his head while drinking then puts his hand over his throat. He sets his glass down. "It's like there's a sticky lump in the back of my throat."

"Are you having trouble breathing?"

"A little," he says, and then probably because I look completely panicked, he adds, "but I can breathe. It just feels a little harder than it should." He stands and waves his hand. "We can keep dancing. I'm sure it will be fine."

I shake my head, the pieces falling together while I work to keep panic at bay. It's possible, likely even, that Mark is having an allergic reaction to the crab. I'd seen anaphylaxis reactions twice. Once from a cub scout in Caleb's troop who'd been allergic to nuts and inexplicably ate five peanut butter cups. The second time was a woman who I was sitting next to at a charity event. For both, anaphylaxis started just like this, with trouble swallowing.

"Have you ever had shellfish?"

"Sure," he says. "I've eaten clams a lot."

I know from a sea creature obsession Caleb had as a boy that clams are mollusks. Crabs, on the other hand, are crustaceans. Mark could be allergic to one and not the other.

His face turns red. He puts his hand on his chest. "I'm sorry Ellie. I'm not sure what's going on."

"Listen to me, Mark." I work to keep my voice level. "I think you are having an anaphylactic reaction to the crab. I'm going to pay the bill and then we need to go to the emergency room."

I stand and he shakes his head. "Ellie, no. I'm fine. I just need to lie down."

I flag our waiter and hand him a stack of bills, way more than the bill could possibly be. "Sir. We need to go immediately. My companion isn't well. Can you get us a cab?"

"Yes, ma'am," he says, stuffing the money into his pocket. "Right away."

Mark stands and sits back down. "Whoa. I'm a little dizzy." He touches his head and stands again. I take his arm and walk him to the entrance of the restaurant. The cab is waiting for us. We slip in the back seat, and I grip Mark's hand in mine.

"Please take us to the nearest emergency room," I say at the same time Mark says the name of our hotel.

"The emergency room," I say with authority. The cab moves and I turn to Mark. "Listen. This may be nothing, and if it is, we can go back to the hotel, and you can have a big fat *I told you so* moment. But if it is an allergic reaction, you don't know if it's going to be mild or serious until it runs its course and I'm not going to take any chances on something happening to you." I sit back in the seat and grab his hand. "No chances," I say again, under my breath, and I realize how much I mean the words. Finding Mark at my age, having the experiences we've had, growing our feelings so fast? The chances of that happening at all are tiny and it sure as heck won't happen again. So, yeah, I'm not taking any chances that this unicorn of a man is going to have a potentially life-threatening anaphylactic event on my watch.

We get to the emergency room and check in. I'm miffed we don't get seen right away—it's an EMERGENCY—but Mark says it's fine. We take our seats in identical side-by-side chairs in the waiting room. I cross my arms and the panic I'd kept at bay starts to resurface. We need to be seen faster than this. I look around the waiting room, assuming without proof that no one in it is as sick or in as much need of care as Mark. Most people are scrolling on their phones. A few are laughing with the people who brought them. One woman is crocheting a blanket. What the heck? These are *not* emergencies.

Mark touches his throat, hives now evident on his neck. "It's probably good we came," he acknowledges. "It's getting worse."

I don't know what he means by worse, but I don't have to. I leap from my seat and march to the receptionist, a young, obviously bored, girl with a name tag that says Tiffany.

"My husband," I say, because it sounds way more powerful than *companion* or *boyfriend*, "is having difficulty breathing. He needs to be seen by a doctor immediately."

Tiffany gives me a look which is the equivalent of an eye roll. "It's crowded tonight, ma'am. The doctors are doing their best to see everyone as quickly as possible."

"I'm not sure you're understanding," I whisper, my tone ferocious despite the low volume. "My husband is a very important man in the United States. If something were to happen to him on your soil, at this hospital, especially after you were made aware of the seriousness of his condition, well," I look down at my fingernails and back up at her— "I wouldn't want to be in your shoes for the fallout."

Her eyes widen. "I didn't realize," she says, standing. "What does your husband do?"

"He's a retired history teacher," I say honestly, but it doesn't matter. The wheels have already been set in motion and Tiffany's not about to question how important a retired history teacher could possibly be.

"I'll see if there's any way to bring him back now."

"Thank you, darling."

Five minutes later, Mark is in a hospital bed with a nurse taking his vitals. She asks him questions and records his answers into a computer.

"Do you think it's anaphylactic shock?" I ask, the panic evident in my voice.

"It might be," she says. "Best to stay calm. Doctor should be in any moment."

Though it's evident that the advice to stay calm is meant for me rather than Mark, I continue anyway. "Okay but—"

Mark reaches over from his bed and grabs my hand. "I'm okay, Ellie. The doctor will be here soon."

"I'll go see if he's available." The nurse leaves the room.

"I'm so sorry about this." Mark shakes his head. "One moment we're dancing under the moonlight, and the next we're here in the hospital."

I shrug. "That's life, right? It's not like either of us knew you were allergic to crab." I put my hand over his. "I'm so sorry about that, by the way. I guess crabs are a one and done."

"It would appear that way. At least the one I had was delicious."

I smile and just then the doctor appears in the room. She shakes Mark's hand, then mine. "I'm Dr. Roberts."

"Nice to meet you, doctor," Mark says.

I nod without saying anything because I know if I say as much as hello, I'll start blabbing about Mark's symptoms and my self-diagnosis of anaphylaxis. I shut my mouth, tight, while Dr. Roberts asks questions and gives Mark a thorough exam. At the end of it, drumroll, I was right. The nurse administers a shot of epinephrine and Mark is moved to a regular floor for a twenty-four-hour observation. It's after midnight by the time he gets there and the nurse on duty tells me, in so many words, to bugger off.

Yeah.

No.

I plop myself into the chair next to Mark. "I'll just settle in here," I say sweetly. "Never hurts to have another set of eyes and ears."

The nurse, William, shakes his head. "Visiting hours ended at eight."

"And we didn't get here until nine," I say, as if that matters, as if visiting hours can be swapped around.

"And you can come back at nine tomorrow morning," William says matter-of-factly. "Mr. Moore needs rest."

"And I'll make sure he gets it. He sleeps better when I'm nearby." I swivel my head toward Mark. "Isn't that right, love?"

"It certainly is," he says, "but as you know, it's of utmost importance to me that you are comfortable. And that chair you're in doesn't look like the best place to sleep."

"I've slept on worse," I say, though I'm sure that's not true. I've always loved comfy cozy beds and bedding. Still, I'd sleep in a chair for Mark, and I *want* to observe him. These nurses have a ton of patients; I'd just have him. It's a win-win. I'm not sure why William can't see that. "I'll be fine."

"Ellie," Mark says, "please get a cab back to the hotel. Get some rest and come back in the morning. I'll be here, ready for the rest of our week together."

I stand and kiss Mark's forehead. "Are you sure?"

"You don't actually have a choice," William interjects.

I turn my head and give him my worst stare before turning back to Mark.

"You heard him," Mark says, smiling. He knows me well enough now to know what I'm thinking. "Get some rest in a real bed and come back tomorrow."

"Fine." I kiss him again and step away from the bed. The moment I leave the hospital will be the first time I've been without Mark's company in days. It's not something I want. Not now. And not when this trip is over.

"And Ellie," he calls.

I turn. "Yes?"

"I love you."

Chapter 31

Mark

"I love you too, Mark," Ellie says and walks out of the room. Her heels click on the floor in the hallway outside, the sound of them fading as she gets further away. I miss her presence by my side; I've gotten used to it. But I'm tired from the day and from the allergy shot and despite missing Ellie, despite being without her for the first time in days, I fall asleep almost immediately.

Nurse William wakes me in the middle of the night. He takes my blood pressure, temperature, and checks my heart rate with a stethoscope.

"How does he look, Bill?" a whispered voice asks.

I twist my head toward the chair beside my bed. It's been shoved aside, a cot in its place. Ellie is lying on the cot, having just asked the question.

"Vitals are good," William, or "Bill" tells her. "All clear to be released tomorrow."

"Fabulous." Ellie pats my hand.

"What are you doing here?" I whisper.

"Making sure you're okay."

William steps forward. "Ellie came back after you fell asleep. She was quite persistent in her request that she be allowed to stay." He fidgets with the monitor attached to the IV. "So, we made an exception to the visiting hour rules." He turns and looks at me. "As long as you're okay with it."

"I'd never object to her being here, but I'd much rather she'd have slept in a comfortable bed." I shift my gaze to Ellie.

She smacks the cot with her hand. "This is the most comfortable cot I've ever slept on. I can't thank Bill enough for setting it up for me. I've been as cozy as a bug in a rug all night."

Bill shakes his head with what seems like disgruntled affection. "Like I said, she was persistent." He steps toward the door and flicks the light. Even with it off, it's dim, not dark. "Get some rest now. Both of you."

"We will, Bill. Thank you kindly."

"You're welcome." Bill slips out the door.

Ellie shifts in her cot, and now that I know she's here, I feel her presence like a warm blanket. And while I would have been okay if she went back to the hotel, I like that she's here. That she stayed.

I lean over the bedrail and peer at her in the dim light. She's wearing scrubs with the hospital logo instead of her dress. Only Ellie. "I'm glad you're here," I say softly and it's then that I notice it. A towel at the end of my bed folded up to look like a turtle. "Did you make that? The turtle?"

She smiles. "I did. I googled it. Thought it would crack you up."

I pick it up and put it on my lap. "It does. Thank you."

"You're welcome." She reaches up and pats on my bed. "But you need to get some rest now. You heard Bill."

I smile and lie back down, the towel turtle by my side. I have no idea how William became Bill or how Ellie convinced him to let her stay overnight, in a cot with pajamas no less, but

I'm not surprised. Ellie has that way about her. People *want* to do things for her. I know I do.

Bill wakes me early in the morning for more vital checks. Ellie, the deep sleeper between the two of us, remains out on the cot.

"Man," Bill says, adjusting the blood pressure cuff around my upper arm, "that woman really loves you." He presses a button and the cuff squeezes around my arm.

My eyes widen. She told me she loved me, but I didn't fully believe her. Why would a woman like her love a man like me? "What makes you say that?" I ask in the most nonchalant tone I can muster.

"Just that persistence. She wouldn't leave the hospital, kept coming back to the floor to see if you were okay. I tried to tell her you were fine, that the epinephrine did its job, but she wouldn't have it. She had to see for herself." He uncuffs the blood pressure monitor. "One-eighteen over seventy-eight. Good."

He grabs a thermometer, and I automatically open my mouth. He slides it under my tongue, and I close my lips around it.

"She told me you were a unicorn."

I laugh and the thermometer comes tumbling out. "Really?"

"Yup. I asked her what she meant, and she said unicorns were a rare breed of man and any person lucky enough to find one had to do everything in their power to ensure his health and happiness." We go through the rote process of the thermometer again. "That's what got me. The unicorn thing."

The thermometer beeps, and he takes it out of my mouth. "Ninety-eight point four. Good."

"Thanks for letting her stay. And for getting her the cot and pajamas."

"No problem." He nods. "Dr. Roberts is making rounds now. I see no reason for her to keep you any longer, but she has the final say."

"Her and Ellie," I tease.

"Yes," Bill gives a laugh. "Her and Ellie."

By the time Dr. Roberts makes it to my room, Ellie is awake, back in her cocktail dress, and sitting in the chair. Dr. Roberts checks the charts, asks me a series of questions, and rechecks my vitals. "Any questions?"

I have none. Ellie has a bunch. Among them: What should I avoid eating? Do I need an EpiPen? Any activity restrictions? Dr. Roberts takes her time and answers all the questions, some of which, I admit, I'm glad that she asked. The doctor discharges me, and pursuant to hospital policy, I'm brought to the hospital lobby in a wheelchair, a cab already waiting when we get there.

When we get back to the hotel, Ellie and I both nap, neither of us having gotten a decent amount of sleep overnight. We lie side by side on the bed, facing each other. I take her hand; she squeezes mine back.

While I'm not glad I had an allergic reaction or that I had to go to the hospital, it was good to see how things might be with Ellie outside of paradise. It's easy to feel love when everything is going well, when we're surrounded by beautiful scenery, and engaged in fabulous activities, but what about when we aren't? There was nothing romantic, beautiful, or fabulous about being in the hospital, but I left feeling closer to Ellie than I did before we got there.

I fall asleep and when I wake, Ellie is already up, showered, and changed. I sit up. "Sorry. I must have really been out."

"No reason to be sorry," she says. "If you were sleeping, you must have needed it. That's what my mother always said anyway."

"Wise woman." I peek out the window. It's bright and sunny, probably early afternoon. "So, what should we do with the rest of today?"

"No plans," she says. "Let's just see where the day takes us."

"I love that idea."

We head outside and meander around the hotel property. We stop by the outdoor aquarium, amazingly on the same property as our hotel. The massive outdoor area features lagoons with dolphins, sharks, sea lions, stingrays, and turtles. We stop at an employee giving a tour and learn that the dolphins swimming behind him were orphaned after Hurricane Katrina and that the eleven-acre lagoon was made specifically to house them. We also learn that we can sign up to swim or kayak with the dolphins.

Ellie slaps my arm. "We have to do that."

"Swim with dolphins? Sure. We probably need to register. Let's find out."

At the registration desk, we learn that the dolphin excursions are booked for the next four days. It's not a big deal but it makes the finality of this trip a reality. What felt like an endless time with unlimited activities a few days ago is down to just a few, and we can't do everything.

"Bummer," Ellie says. "I would have loved to do that."

"We can extend the trip," I say without thinking. "I'll have to check with Addison, but I think she'll be okay to care for Sara a bit longer. You?" As soon as the suggestion comes out of my mouth, I regret it. It reeks of desperation. Of the truth. I'd rather stay here with Ellie than do almost anything else. I'm almost afraid of her answer.

Her mouth splits into a smile. "I'd love to extend the trip. Why not, right?"

Chapter 32

Ellie

Mark grabs my hand, and we walk back to the hotel. We discuss all the things we want to do with the extended time. Swimming with dolphins, a catamaran ride, island tours. We'll need at least another week, if not ten days. Personally, I'd like to stay here forever.

Mark swings my hand as we walk. "What do you think of a casual dinner tonight?"

I bump his shoulder with mine. "No seafood," I tease.

"No seafood. I'm kind of in the mood for a juicy burger and fries."

"Hard to say no to that."

We approach the hotel, my mind on where we're going to eat and all the things we're going to do for the next however many days. Mark leans down and whispers in my ear. "Hey, do you know that man?"

I look up and see a man jogging toward us waving his hands, a small duffel swinging on his back. In a split second, I recognize who it is, and my heart plummets and leaps in the same moment. Caleb.

I drop Mark's hand like it's on fire. "Caleb," I say with false cheer. "What on God's green earth are you doing here?"

He looks from me to Mark and back at me.

"Caleb," Mark says. "Your son?"

"Yes." I wave my hand between Caleb and Mark. "Mark, this is my son Caleb. And Caleb, this is Mark."

"You're Mark," Caleb says. "Mark Moore."

A look of surprise crosses Mark's features. "That's me. Yes."

A million emotions cross Caleb's face all at once, and I know from over forty years of being his mother, what that look means. He's about to explode.

"Mark. Could you give Caleb and me a few minutes?"

He hesitates only a moment before saying, "Sure." He thrusts his hand toward Caleb. "Nice to meet you."

Caleb ignores his outstretched hand, and I want to disappear. Even though he's in his forties, I still feel responsible for his manners. Or lack thereof. I force myself not to admonish him, not to insist that he shake Mark's hand.

After what feels like a year, Mark drops his hand and gestures to the outdoor bar in front of the hotel. "I'll be at the bar if you need me."

"She won't need you," Caleb says.

Mark looks from me to Caleb and back to me. "Is everything all right?" The concern on his face makes my heart break. He cares about me. It's obvious.

"I'm fine."

"You're sure?"

"Yes," I say, willing him to move along because I know my son and he's about to have a hissy fit with a tail on it and Mark acting like my protector is not helping. "It's all good. I'll meet you in the hotel bar."

Mark walks toward the hotel. Once he's far enough away

that I know he can't hear, I spin around and look at my son. "Caleb!" I admonish. "Why are you acting this way?"

"Why am I acting this way? Why am I acting this way?" He paces, his face red.

If he wasn't my kid and clearly angry with me, I'd shake him by the shoulders. Instead, I inhale and in my calmest mom voice say, "Take a deep breath, honey. You're clearly upset."

"I am upset!" he says. "Do you want to know why?"

"Of course I do." I gesture to a bench by a pretty fountain in the center of the hotel grounds. "Let's sit and calm down."

I walk to the bench, Caleb trailing behind me. Dynamics with him as an adult have been increasingly tough as the years have passed, both of us competing to be the adult in the room.

Once we're seated, he takes a few deep breaths. "Sorry for losing my temper back there," he says, calmer."I was hoping my instincts were wrong."

"What instincts?"

"It's probably best if I start at the beginning." He adjusts himself on the bench so he's facing me. "The other day, after we talked, I called the hotel where you said you were booked. I thought I'd leave you and your 'girlfriends' — he makes quotation marks with his fingers —"some money for a nice dinner as a surprise. But I found out the hotel, the one where you're allegedly staying, is closed for repairs."

I shut my eyes, ashamed that I'd lied. The fact that Caleb found out because he was trying to do something nice for me makes it worse.

I open my eyes, and he goes on to tell me that he'd found me at this hotel on our joint location tracking account and figured I'd gotten the names mixed up. But when he looked it up and saw the hotel — five stars and over one thousand dollars a night — he got suspicious that something was up.

"I remember you'd told me about a guy you'd met on day

one, Mark Moore. The one you thought was a con-artist. Given your history with men like this, I was worried that he might be involved. You asked me to do a check on him that first day, but I just did a cursory one. I'm sorry for that."

"Mark's not a scammer," I say, my heart sinking all the same. There's a reason Caleb flew across the ocean, and it's not: Mark's a great guy, Mom. Go for it.

"I had my buddy from school, a police officer, run a real background check. I'm not sure he's who you think he is, Mom."

"He's a retired history teacher from Scranton, and a divorced father of two girls." I say the words with authority, like doing so will ensure the story matches whatever information Caleb has.

"He was a history teacher, and he is from Scranton," he says, and I wait for it, the but that's going to follow. The one that's going to break my heart.

"But he's never been married, doesn't have any children, and has quite a rap sheet." He pulls a paper from his bag and holds it so I can see. It's a list of criminal infractions.

"Most of the criminal activity is from a while ago," Caleb says, but I'm not listening anymore.

How can this be? Mark told me about his wife. I spoke to Addison. I'd seen pictures of her and Sara.

I push at the papers. "That can't be right. You must have the wrong Mark Moore."

Caleb flips to the second page, a picture of Mark —my Mark — smiles back at me. "It's the right guy, Mom. I'm sorry."

I stare vacantly at his photograph, then take the papers and page through them. Everything Caleb just told me is documented. No wife. No kids. Criminal activity ranging from robbery to drug possession to drug dealing. And fraud. The five letters jump out at me like they are in all caps. Fraud. FRAUD. I stare at the word.

"Mom?" Caleb prompts. He swings a hand around and gives me a half hug. "I'm sorry."

"He hasn't asked me for money," I say weakly. "He knows about Sebastian. He knows I don't have anything."

"You don't have anything yet," Caleb says. "There've been some leads on the Sebastian investigation, but that's not the issue. I don't know what Mark's angle is, but pretending to have a wife and daughters is a red flag." He pauses. "You have to agree with that."

"I don't have to agree with anything," I snip, but all the while Caleb's statement rolls around in my head: pretending to have a wife and daughters. It sounds *so* bad. And strange. Why would he do that? And his past criminal activity? Clearly, Mark was more comfortable with crime than he'd let on when Gavin and Brandy approached us with their plan. Maybe he knew about it? I mean, he did already know Gavin. I have no idea what my piece is in whatever game Mark's been playing, but it's clear I don't know him as well as I thought I did.

Or at all.

I stand up, my thoughts still reeling, my heart breaking into little bits inside my chest. "I need a minute. I'm going for a walk on the beach."

Caleb leaps to his feet. "I'll go with you."

I shake my head. "Just give me a few minutes. This, I — this is a lot." I stride toward the beach without waiting for his reply. My heart drops in my chest; tears collect behind my eyes. I think about Mark. How he feels, how he sounds, how he looks at me. I think about the crinkle in his eyes when he smiles, the tiny bald spot on the top of his head, the deep brown of his eyes. He'd told me he loved me. It had felt so real. I'd felt not only loved, but cherished.

I sit at the edge of a lounge chair set out by the hotel and watch the surf. The waves wash in and out. In and out. In and out. All week long, this sound, the ebb and flow of the surf, has been a balm to my senses. But instead of feeling soothed, I'm tied up in a knot, my emotions all over the place. Sad. Furious. Betrayed. Surprised. And angry. At myself. With Sebastian, I could forgive myself for falling in love. I had no warning. I didn't know there were people out there like him, waiting to prey on innocent people through promises of love. But like the saying goes: Fool me once, shame on you. Fool me twice, shame on me. And yes, shame on me for not leaning into my very first and very real instinct that Mark was not as good a guy as he seemed. The signs were there, and I let some sad and desperate need for love and companionship blind me to them. Again. And while I didn't give Mark any money, I did give him a chunk of my soul.

I stand up, the flux of emotions driving toward just one. Anger. At myself. At Mark. Even at Caleb, as misplaced as that might be. I stride back to the bench where I'd left him standing, I don't know how long ago. He's not there. I scan the immediate area. Nope. I walk toward the bar, and that's where I see them. Caleb and Mark. Together.

Chapter 33

Mark

Caleb slaps the paper on the bar. "Explain yourself," he says. I scan down the criminal convictions, down my personal history. The words *unmarried, no children,* leaping off the page. No. God. I pull at my collar. What must Ellie think?

"I can explain."

"Then do it." Caleb crosses his arms across his chest. He's a bit of prick, but he's trying to protect his mother. And for that, he'll get a pass from me.

"What part?" I ask, realizing there's more than one part of that sheet that warrants explanation. It's the wrong thing to say.

"What part?" Caleb asks incredulously. "Whatever part you lied about. And why don't you tell me what you were doing with my mother while you're at it? She's vulnerable, but you probably knew that."

He finishes just as Ellie pushes through the crowd behind him. When I see her face, I know it's bad. Her expression is hard. Even during that first day, when she thought I was a con-artist, she never looked that way — angry and cold.

"I'll take over now, Caleb."

"Mom, no."

"Caleb," she says in the kind of tone only mothers can use, "sit yourself down at the bar and wait for me. I have some private things to say to Mr. Moore."

Caleb raises an eyebrow at me and shakes his head in a kind of *'you're in trouble now'* look. If I didn't desperately care about Ellie and healing this situation, it might seem funny.

Caleb steps aside, and Ellie taps my personal information with a pink fingernail. "Unmarried. No children." She looks up and meets my eyes.

"I've never been married," I admit. "My daughters are my nieces, my sister's kids. She's a drug addict, out of the picture, and I've raised the girls since they were young. They are like daughters to me, and they asked to call me Dad. Their father has never been in their lives."

Empathy sweeps across her features, but only for a moment. "Why didn't you tell me that?"

"You were so fixated on me being a scammer. I didn't want to add any other ammo into the mix." My words come out frustrated. "Sorry," I follow up. "I should have told you."

"You told me you were married. And all these criminal convictions." She runs her finger down the page. "What about these?"

"I led you to believe I had a wife because it was easier than going back and explaining about raising my nieces. I'm not proud of the criminal convictions. I had a drug issue."

"You had a *drug* issue?" Ellie slaps her hand on the table.

"In my late teens and early twenties. I haven't touched the stuff in years."

"This conviction was six years ago." Ellie points to a spot on the page. Drug possession. I'd covered for my sister, one of the few times I'd seen her in recent years. If she'd been convicted, she'd have gone to jail.

"I covered for my sister."

"Your sister who's been out of the picture?" She crosses her arms across her chest. "That's convenient."

Frustration courses through me, edging on anger because the way all of this sounds is so bad. My feelings for Ellie are real. And my background makes sense if I can just state it without feeling like I'm under attack. "Look," I say finally, "had I known a week ago how my feelings for you were going to progress, I would have done things a lot differently. I thought we were just roommates for a few days. I didn't know it was going to be like this." I pause a long moment, then put my hand over hers on the small table. "Regardless of the mistakes I made, my feelings for you are real, Ellie. I swear they are. I meant it when I said I loved you."

She doesn't respond, but she allows my hand to stay on top of hers. I focus on my breathing, every second that passes without her moving away gives me a bit of hope that she can put all this aside.

Finally, she steps back and pulls her hand away. "I don't know what to believe anymore, Mark." The icy look is gone from her eyes. She looks heartbroken instead, and it's almost worse. "I need time to process all of this. Trust isn't easy for me after what happened." She pauses and gives me a look riddled with deep disappointment. "And you knew that."

I nod. Because I did know. I figured we had lots of time to go over our backgrounds. And frankly I was having way too much fun falling in love to go back and revisit a past I'm not proud of.

"I'm not like Sebastian," I say. "I'd never take advantage of you."

"I don't know that."

"Come on, Ellie," I plead.

"Caleb has a return airline ticket for me. I'm going to pack up my things and go with him."

"Ellie," I start.

"I need time, Mark. You owe me that."

I snap my mouth shut. I do owe her time. At the very least. "Okay."

She walks away, toward the hotel. Caleb hurries after her and puts a hand on the small of her back. I collapse on to the bar stool as the first woman I have ever truly loved disappears inside the hotel.

Chapter 34

Ellie

I settle into my airplane seat next to Caleb, securing the seatbelt across my waist as directed by the flight attendant. I blow out a breath.

Caleb leans over. "Are you all right?" He's asked this same question a few times since we left Mark. I'm not all right. I'm humiliated, confused, and heartbroken. But I'm too embarrassed to get into how deeply I'd fallen for Mark with Caleb. How truly in love I'd felt the past few days. Instead, I'm acting as if the whole thing had just been a crazy madcap fling. Like his lying and having a criminal record were no big deal. A big fat hilarious whatever.

"I'm okay," I say and shrug. "It's not like I was going to marry the guy. We were just having a bit of fun."

"Still," Caleb starts.

I put my hand over his, not wanting to hear the sad statement sure to follow the "still":

Still, you must be upset.

Still, it must hurt that you didn't know.

Still, you must feel like a total idiot.

198

Yes, I'm upset. Yes, it hurts that I didn't know. And, YES, I feel like a total idiot. Not that I'll admit to any of these emotions. "Caleb, I'm fine," I puff out, frustration edging my tone. "Let's get some rest."

I close my eyes and pretend to sleep for the three-hour flight back to New York. But I don't sleep. Instead, I think about Mark, my active imagination running wild. He transforms in my mind from the likable history teacher from Scranton with crinkly brown eyes and an easy smile to a lying substance abuser who'd obviously had some connection to Gavin and his undercover counterfeit ring. God knows what his long-term plans for me were. Maybe I was to be a scapegoat for the crimes? Or he planned to blackmail me for my participation. Who knows? I don't, and that's the whole problem. I don't know Mark Moore, not the real one.

It's pitch-black when we touch down. I've lost all track of time. I don't even know what day it is. I mindlessly follow Caleb through the airport and out to his car.

"Do you think Mark will try to contact you?" Caleb asks once we're going and on the highway.

I look out the window at the sparkling New York skyline. "Maybe. I don't know. If he does, I'll cut him off. I have no reason to stay in touch." I wave a hand, wanting to maintain the facade that my relationship with Mark was no big deal. "Like I said, we were just having a bit of fun."

"Do you think you should get tested for STDs?"

"Caleb!"

He looks at me, then back at the nearly empty road. It's after midnight. "I'm just saying, Mom, you don't seem to know much about this guy. Who knows who he's been with? Better safe than sorry, right?"

"I'll think on it," I say noncommittally, panic teeming underneath my words. STDs! Getting an STD from Mark never once crossed my mind. But Caleb is right. I don't know him, not really. He could have slept with hundreds of women before me. Thousands even. I add STD-carrying sexual degenerate to my new vision of Mark.

"I do have some good news," Caleb says.

I brace myself. The last time Caleb used the term "*good news*" he'd presented me with a new billing system for the vet office. He'd made a big deal that it was color-coded and that *I* could choose the colors. Like getting to pick pink to designate outstanding bills would be a huge mood changer. "Yeah?"

"There's been a break in the Sebastian case."

"Oh." Caleb has been way more invested in the case than I have. It's not that I don't want my money back; it's just too painful to think how stupid I'd been. "Good," I add, then trying to sound more excited, repeat the sentiment. "That's good."

"It is good, Mom. If you recover the money, you won't have to work for me anymore. You'd be able to do what you want. Enjoy your retirement."

"That'd be great," I say without meaning it. Having the ability to do what I want would be great if I knew what that was. But I don't. And any thought I had that I'd find a man to spend my golden years with is out the window after the one-two punch of Sebastian and Mark.

"I brought Peanut to your house already."

"Super," I say, my heart lighter with the thought of the little, brown, tail-wagging bundle of love that will be waiting for me. I'm reminded of Darnell and the morning Mark and I spent with him on the beach. Yesterday morning. It seems forever ago. I wonder if Mark was really going to adopt him. Maybe it was another ruse, another way to get me to fall for him. Because what woman doesn't love a man who loves dogs?

"All your kittens but two got adopted," Caleb tells me.

I visualize the mewing bundle in Caleb's office. "Why not the two?"

"They have feline immunodeficiency virus. FIV."

"Is that a serious condition? FIV?"

Caleb shrugs and turns his car into my neighborhood. "Cats with FIV are more susceptible to other viruses, so they must be kept indoors. People generally misunderstand the illness, think it's easier to spread than it is, so FIV-positive kittens don't get adopted." He pulls into my driveway, parks the car, and shuts it off.

"I'll take them."

"Take who?"

"The kittens."

He steps out of the car and moves to the passenger side and opens the door. He peers at me in the passenger seat, his face illuminated by the car's headlights. "Mom, no. You don't have to do that."

"I want to," I say, seizing on the idea. Two cuddly kittens leaping around my house? It's exactly what I need.

"Come on. Do you really want more pets in the house? Think about it."

"Think about what? Cats are the easiest animals on earth to take care of. They need a home. I have a home. It's a win-win."

Caleb sighs and moves to the back of the car. He takes my suitcases out of the trunk and brings them inside. I follow him in, grabbing Peanut and hugging him to my chest.

"I swear, Mom, I think you love that dog more than me."

"Not you, sweetheart. But I love him more than all other men." The sentiment feels true as I say it. I kiss Peanut's head and set him down on the ground.

Caleb contorts his frame down and kisses my cheek. "Glad you're home, Mom."

"Thanks, honey."

He drives off, and I immediately get ready for bed. I fall asleep easily considering all that has happened over the past few hours. I wake up to Peanut pawing at me. I put on a robe, pad into the kitchen, and get him his food. I spy the sunny windowsill. The one where I'd told Mark I would put my fuchsia pink wax hand. He'd laughed so hard about that, wrinkles crinkling around his eyes. That had been the first time I'd seen him laugh, but not the last. The Mark I thought I knew was a fun-loving guy who takes a while to warm up. But, of course, the Mark I thought I knew doesn't exist.

Don't think about him. Don't think about him. Don't think about him. I mentally repeat the mantra, but the experience is like telling yourself not to think about chickens. As soon as the pledge is made, chickens are the only beings on earth worth thinking about.

My phone pings, and I grab it from the countertop. Hopefully, whoever or whatever it is will steer my thoughts away from Mark. That's what I need. Distraction. I pick up the phone and read the message.

Ellie. I've thought of nothing but you since you left. I am so sorry. I know you said you needed time to process, but I want to let you know my feelings for you are real. My past isn't perfect, but I can explain it all. Please give me a chance. I miss you. M.

I read his words again, and then a third time. Tears prick at my eyes and frustration swirls inside my gut. I want so badly to believe him, it's pathetic. But even if I let him in, if I hear his explanations about his past, how will I ever know if what he's telling me is true? I've already proven myself gullible and naïve. I can't let that happen again. I won't let that happen again.

I start to draft a text back, delete it, start again. Type. Read. Delete. Type. Read. Delete. Type. Read. Delete. I go through the trio of actions over and over but nothing I say seems right.

The tone is off. Or the words aren't right. I set my phone down on my thigh.

I don't have to answer. I don't owe Mark an explanation. And I don't need to leave the door open for more communication. I make a split-second decision, delete the message, and block his number right after.

There. It's done. Mark Moore is out of my life.

Chapter 35

Mark

The swish of my text message flying through cyberspace fills the hotel room. I look at the ocean a moment from the little couch in the corner, coffee in hand, none of it the same without Ellie. She'd probably be sleeping if she were still here. We'd have breakfast at what I'd come to think of as our restaurant, the one with the little yellow birds hopping and pecking at crumbs beneath the tables.

I look anxiously at the sent message on my phone, hoping for a reply. Dots appear. My heart rate speeds up. Please, Ellie. Just give me another chance. The dots disappear and my heart plummets. They reappear, disappear, reappear, disappear. The fact that she's taking her time with the response must be good, right? She's trying to think of the exact right thing to say. If she didn't care about me at all, if I was out, she'd just cut me off. The dots appear and disappear again. Then nothing. I watch the text chat. My investment in the appearance of a group of blinking little dots is so strong, it feels like my life, my future, depends on it. Nothing. Five minutes. Seven minutes. Ten minutes. Nothing. Maybe she got called away. Maybe she needs time to think. Maybe she's still here on the island and is going to surprise me. I watch my phone, feeling like if I put the device down, I'll lose the chance for her to respond. Finally, I can't stand it anymore. I type out another text.

Ellie. I'm here if you want to talk. I'd love to hear your voice. Love you and miss you. M.

I send it off, the sound of the swish once again filling the otherwise silent room. I set the phone down on the end table and lean down, elbows on my knees. I gaze at the floor, hoping for the sound of a ping.

"Ping."

My heart lifts at the sound and I immediately right myself and swipe my phone off the table. A response. Finally. Yes.

Not delivered.

I stare at the two words, uncomprehending. Not delivered. Not delivered? But I'd just sent her a text. I grab my phone and type out – *Did you get my last text?*

Ping. *Not delivered.*

Is your phone working?

Ping. *Not delivered.*

I dial her. Maybe I can get through with a call, leave a message if she doesn't want to talk to me. The phone rings once, then a robot voice: "This caller is unavailable." I try again. Same thing.

I stare at my phone; the obvious issue unfurling slowly in my mind. I can't leave a text or get a call through even though I was able to a moment ago. Because Ellie blocked me. Oh. I shut my eyes. She blocked me. Ellie blocked me. She's not here in the Bahamas about to surprise me. She wasn't thinking about what to say. Forgiveness is not on the horizon. Ellie Moore, a woman I'd fallen in love with in one short week, wants nothing to do with me.

Alarm bubbles up inside me. No. This can't be over. My

feelings — her feelings — they were too strong not to overcome something I can easily explain. When I get back to the States, I could drive to Rye. I could write her a letter. I could show up at her son's vet office with a big cheesy bouquet of flowers and beg for her forgiveness. I feel hopeful for a long moment before I settle down and realize that I can't pursue Ellie in that way. She's put a clear definitive boundary between us. If she wants that boundary removed, she'll contact me.

I sit, numb on the couch with my coffee until it turns cold. I finally get up and go to "our" restaurant. Annabell, the hostess Ellie had somehow gotten to know in the short time we'd been here, smiles warmly. "No Mrs. today?"

"No," I manage, "not today."

"I hope to see her later. She's a light, your Mrs."

"Yes." I swallow the lump in my throat. "She is."

I order the same breakfast I've had for the past several days and eat it, sadness falling over me like thick fog. I pay my bill and walk aimlessly toward the beach. I take off my shoes and walk along the edge of the water, where the surf meets the shore, my feet sinking into the sand. Water splashes over them. It's a stunningly beautiful day. I could stay, even if Ellie isn't here. I'd been mentally lamenting about not having ever traveled. Why not enjoy?

I see a dolphin in the surf ahead, not far from shore. I stop. A bunch of them are playing. A crowd gathers and I watch for a moment, wishing Ellie were here. She would love this. I take a picture with my phone to show her, just in case.

Just a week ago, and for nearly my entire adult life, I'd never minded being alone. I had Addison and Sara, always, but in between the time with them, I was fine reading books, watching movies and sports, following my routines. Pre-Ellie Mark would have been okay here alone. Great, even. I'd probably set up on a lounge chair and read a book or sign up for a tour. I'd have no issue eating by myself at restaurants, no problem walking the beach alone. It would all be just fine.

And now it isn't.

I miss her. Her smile. Her laugh. The silly Southern sayings.

I gaze at the ocean another few moments then turn and walk back to the hotel. My body and heart feel heavy and as much as staying here seems the sensical thing to do for a man who's never traveled, I don't want to be here anymore. This place is too mired with Ellie memories.

I go back to the hotel room and call the Potcake Palace. If there's one thing I'm going to do right on this trip, it's adopt that little dog. I take an Uber to the palace and Muriel helps me make the arrangements to bring Darnell home on the plane. Thankfully, she doesn't ask about Ellie.

Darnell and I fly out that evening, and the next day, I decide to surprise Addison and Sara, both with dinner and the dog. Arranging to see my daughters, and getting ready to have Sara come back home, distracts me from thoughts of Ellie. It will all be fine. I just need to get back into my routine.

I pick up a ton of favorites from Ale Mary's, Darnell in tow. I drive to Addison's, happy to have something to do for the night, excited to introduce them to Darnell. I pull to a stop in front of the house. I set Darnell on the ground with his leash, grab the food bags, and head to the front door.

I ring the doorbell. Footsteps pound on the hardwood floor. "Surprise," I start when the door opens, then immediately shut my mouth.

"Mark." Sharon, my sister, says the word, half-surprised and half-confused. "We weren't expecting you."

"Sharon." I hug her tight. "What are you doing here?"

I try to reconcile her presence. Sharon. Here? Why wouldn't the girls tell me this?

Darnell barks. I'd forgotten he was here.

Addison bounds down the stairs. "Uncle Mark," she says instead of Dad. "You're back." She gives me a hug and a kiss. Still, I have the overwhelming feeling that my unexpected presence is not a good surprise. "And you have a dog?"

"Yes," I look down at Darnell, forgetting for the second time in the span of a minute that he's even there. "He's a potcake."

"He's adorable." Addison bends down and pets his head. "And you brought food?"

"Ale Mary's." I hold up the bag but the feeling that I don't belong overwhelms me. "And you're here," I say again to Sharon.

'I'm here." She pushes the door further open. "Come on in."

I step inside the home I helped Addison move into after her divorce, Darnell trailing behind me. I've come to this home at least one day a week since Addison moved in. I love my sister and I'm glad to see her, but it's been years since I've heard from her. The girls, too, I assume. So, her inviting me in like *I'm* the guest? It's off-putting.

I hand the food bag to Addison and pick up Darnell.

"You look snazzy, Uncle Mark," Addison says. I look down at my outfit, jeans and a button-down shirt. Both are among those Ellie picked out for me that first day of shopping. I'd tell Addison about the shopping excursion, but I'm too taken aback by Sharon's presence here. Also, by Addison calling me "Uncle Mark." What is that? Both girls have called me Dad for years.

"Come on, Sara's in the family room," Sharon says, waving her hand forward. "I'll bring out this food on a tray."

"Sure," I say, then add, "good to see you."

"Thank you, Mark," she says somewhat formally. "You too."

She and Addison walk toward the kitchen, their hair the same color, their height within an inch. Even their gait is the same, which obviously makes sense. They *are* mother and daughter.

I find Sara in her wheelchair in front of a Hallmark movie on the television. Nail supplies, polish and emery boards and little vials of liquid, are on the table next to her. She waves at me with pink-nailed fingers. "Dad!" she says. I give her a hug and a kiss, glad that I haven't been demoted to "Uncle Mark" in her eyes. Her eyes shift to Darnell. "And you got a dog."

"I got a dog," I repeat. "Darnell." I hold him toward her and she pets his head.

Addison and Sharon return with plates, drinks, and the Ale Mary food that had, in the past, always been a hit. But nobody seems particularly excited to dive in. Addison finally puts two wings on a plate. Sharon grabs a nacho. Sara wheels over and takes a hamburger slider. At least that's something.

I pile food on my plate and sit on an ottoman across from Addison and Sharon on the couch. Sara wheels back to where she'd been and switches off the television. Without the movie voices in the background, it's unbearably quiet, the sound of chewing amplified by the silence.

"How was the trip?" Addison finally asks.

"Good. Beautiful." I move to get my phone from the pocket to show them pictures then stop myself. The mood in the room is not a *hey, let's see your pictures and hear about your trip* one. There's something I don't know.

"So, Sharon," I say, thinking her unexpected presence may be at the root of the obvious elephant in the room. "You seem to be doing well."

"Very well," she says. "I've been sober and in recovery for some time."

This is news to me.

"I'm so glad. Nearby?"

"In Wilkes-Barre."

I raise an eyebrow. Wilkes-Barre is just twenty minutes from here. "Why didn't you tell me? I would have come to see you."

She gives a weak smile. "I wanted to make sure I was truly recovered and committed to that recovery before letting you know. You of all people have been down the path of failed recoveries with me before."

"Mom's doing great," Addison comments. She puts her hand over Sharon's in what feels like a show of solidarity. For what reason, I don't know. I've always been supportive of Sharon. I raised her daughters, for God's sake.

I push my irritation at the perceived jab, get up, and kiss Sharon on the cheek. "That's wonderful. Recovery isn't easy. I'm so proud of you."

She nods. "Thank you. That means a lot."

"So, what's next then?" I ask, sitting back on the ottoman. No one answers. I look from face to face to face, trying to figure out what's going on. "What's wrong?" I ask finally.

"Uncle Mark," Addison starts. Hearing her call me "Uncle Mark" still stings, but I brush the feeling aside. Whatever it is Addison wants to tell me, it's hard for her.

"We were planning to tell you this," she continues, "but Mom, Sara, and I have actually been in touch for a few months."

"Oh." I'm not upset by this — she is their mother — but I am hurt. I don't understand why I wasn't included in whatever being "in touch" means. "Is there a reason you didn't want me to know?"

Sharon answers. "Like I already said, you've been through the ringer with me. I didn't want to involve you again. Not until I was sure it was going to stick."

So you involved your daughters? I think but don't say.

"Anyway," Addison continues, "Mom's been staying here with Sara and me this week."

"And loving every minute of it," Sharon interjects with a smile.

"It's been working out really well," Addison says and squeezes Sharon's hand. "So, she's going to stay."

I look from Addison to Sharon. They both seem happy, thrilled actually, with the decision. And while I have reservations with Addison opening her doors to Sharon given her track record, she is her mother. Addison's an adult and she's been lonely since her divorce. Sharon moving in may be the best thing for both of them.

"Well, that sounds amazing." I hop up from the ottoman and give them both hugs. The mood in the room shifts a bit. I guess the news that Sharon moving in with Addison is what was wrong.

"Sara and I will be here all the time," I say and reach out to pat her knee. "Right, Sara?"

She doesn't answer and I realize what Addison's next words are before she says them. "Sara is going to live here," Addison says. "With me and Mom."

"No." I shake my head. "I have everything set up for Sara at my place. We've got our routines all set." I tap her knee again. "Right Sar-bear?"

Sara says nothing and in the absence of her affirmation, I know her answer. She wants to live here.

"I am able to handle everything, honey," I say, thinking this decision is less about me than my age.

"I know, Dad," Sara says.

Her quick response makes me feel worse. Sara and Addison aren't worried about me, their feeble old uncle. They prefer to be with Sharon. And while I know their feelings are justified and natural, the reality stings. I'm being replaced. I lost Ellie. Now I'm losing my girls.

"You can come over whenever you want," Addison says.

"And for *Survivor*," Sara adds, homage to our decades-long tradition of watching the show.

"Sure, of course," I say but the words feel hollow.

"Thanks for understanding, Mark," Sharon says. "I know I haven't been around, but I'm loving this chance to make up for lost time."

"Sure. Right," I say, and the brain fog I've had periodically since Caleb showed up in the Bahamas with his big reveal descends over me like a big ugly cloud. I'm talking, I'm here, but I don't feel like I'm here.

"And now you can do things," Addison says. "Travel. Date." She leans forward. "Did anything happen with that Ellie woman? Did you end up asking her to dinner?"

I dial back my memory and remember my last call with Addison, the one where I'd told her I'd be coming back late. Ellie had been in the room; I'd pretended she wasn't there. "Nah," I say, because answering a question about Ellie on top of everything else would kill me. "I never asked her."

"Bummer. She seemed really nice."

"Yeah," I say. "She did."

Chapter 36

Ellie

"Do not pick up the turtle," Caleb says. We're in his yard at the edge of the small pond that abuts his property. His daughter Chelsea, newly fourteen, is with us. It's been a month since Bahama-gate. Right after I'd blocked Mark's number, a part of me regretted it, but a bigger part of me thinks that I may well have avoided inevitable heartache down the road. If his story about his past was as rock-solid as he'd made it sound, he'd have told me earlier. Or he would have tried to reach me some other way. The fact that he didn't even try makes me think he was either full of crap, or he didn't care about me as much as he said he did. Either way, good riddance, right?

That's the rational way to think about it.

But I'm not the most rational person in the world, so I'm struggling. Which is why I'm here at the edge of the pond focusing all my energy on a turtle.

"He's hurt. See?" I bend down and point to a crack on the turtle's shell. "And I can pick him up. He's not a snapper."

"He's a red-eared slider," Caleb tells me. "And a crack on the shell doesn't automatically mean the turtle is hurt."

"And it doesn't mean he isn't." I right myself and look at my son. "Honestly, Caleb, you'd think as a vet you'd be a little more empathetic to the Lord's creatures."

Chelsea points to the crack. "He's hurt, Dad."

"See," I say. "Your girl recognizes an animal in distress."

Caleb puffs out a breath. "Okay, Mom. He might be hurt. He might not be. But if you pick the turtle up, I one hundred percent know what's going to happen. You're going to add him to the menagerie of animals you've taken in since the trip and then ask me to fix his shell."

"Nonsense." I pull out my phone and do a quick google search. "It says right here, I can patch up his shell with duct tape."

"Mom," Caleb says, exasperated. "You cannot patch up a turtle shell with duct tape."

"It says here that I can." I show him the picture, one of a turtle with a thick layer of gray duct tape on its shell. "And duct tape is way better than leaving him here in the elements with a broken shell." I bend down and scoop him up. His tiny legs flail around in the air. "Come on, sweet thing," I coo. "Let's get that shell patched up."

I walk back across the grass, Chelsea next to me, cooing at the turtle. Caleb jogs to catch up. "Okay, Mom. Fine. I'll go with you to the office and fix his shell. But you have to promise that this is it. No more rescues."

"I don't have that many rescues."

"Peanut. The kittens. The baby bunnies. Those two ferrets that family gave you."

"The ferrets aren't rescues. I'm watching them for a neighbor. They wanted to get their son acclimated to the idea of them before taking them back. They apparently freaked him out."

Caleb snorts. "They're not taking those ferrets back."

"They will."

"I doubt it." We reach his car and assemble inside with the turtle. "Doesn't the Homeowner's Association limit how many pets you can have?"

"No," I lie. I'm allowed *two* pets. But that's a completely unreasonable rule. How would the Homeowner's Association possibly know how many pets I have? I'm certainly not going to tell them.

Caleb pulls to a stop at a traffic light.

"Look, I'm just worried about you. You haven't seemed yourself since the trip. Is it the Mark guy? Is he bothering you?"

"No," I say, cringing at the designation "the Mark guy." I haven't heard from him. I barely thought of him. LIE. "I'm fine, honey. Right as rain."

"And have you thought any more about going on a date with Luis, that friend of Monica's mother?"

Monica, Caleb's wife, gushed about how perfect Luis was for me right after I got back from the trip. I can't imagine what kind of man Monica would think was perfect for me. Not that it matters, because I'm done with men. "I already told you to thank Monica for me, but I'm not dating."

"Ever?"

"Yes, probably. I have enough in my life caring for all these rescues."

Caleb pulls the car to a stop in front of the vet office. "I thought you didn't have that many rescues."

"Of course I have a lot of rescues, Caleb. These animals need homes."

He shakes his head, and we get out of the car and enter the office. I hand the turtle to Caleb, and Chelsea and I take places in the waiting room. She shows me pictures of potential Spring Fling dresses while Caleb *glues* the shell together (like glue is so much better than duct tape). The turtle, now named Flash per Chelsea, needs to be kept dry and out of the wild while his shell heals. I volunteer to home him and Caleb grabs supplies for me from the back room.

When we get to my house, Chelsea wants to help settle Flash and see the rest of the rescues. We all pile inside my condo and Caleb sets up a tank for Flash in my already messy living room. I feel judgment ooze out of him as he does it. He's neat like his father, and like Mark, who I am very much *not* thinking about. Not the way he ordered his shirts by color, or lined up his shoes in size order, or carefully folded his socks into perfect squares.

I grab Chelsea's hand. "Come on. I'll show you the latest." I bring her up to the spare bedroom where I'm housing a cat, Lucille, that Caleb doesn't yet know about. I'd gone to get cat food at the pet store, and there she was. Rescued from a sewer with four kittens, poor sweet thing. Already given shots and a clean bill of health. So, I adopted her. I mean, what's one more?

I leave Chelsea with Lucille and return to the kitchen. Caleb is picking up pieces of mail piled on the kitchen counter and dropping them.

"You do open your mail, right?"

"Of course I open my mail. It's mostly ads targeted to seniors." I grab the unopened envelope from Caleb's hand and make a show of opening it. "This is an ad for a senior living community." I take another envelope and tear it open. "This is an ad for senior vitamins. And this—" I pick up a third envelope, slide my finger across the seal, and pull out a letter— "is from the Homeowner's Association." I start to read. Oh. Crap.

Caleb moves behind my shoulder, the letter in his view.

Apparently, someone – multiple people! – have reported that I have more than the allowable two pets living in my "dwelling."

I wave the paper. "Someone told on me. Can you believe that?"

"People like rules, Mom. They get bothered if you don't follow them."

"It's ridiculous. They're my animals in my home. They're not bothering anyone." I drop the letter. "It's just a warning anyway. None of my babies are going anywhere." I scoop up Peanut and cradle him to my chest. "Right, Pea?"

Caleb swipes the letter from where it landed on the floor. "You have sixty days to comply with the two-pet maximum or they are going to take legal action."

My heartbeat speeds up. Legal action? Over a few pets? What is the world coming to? "I can't get rid of any of them. They count on me. Plus, people don't want rescues. You say that all the time."

I must sound as panicked as I feel because Caleb's demeanor changes. "We'll get it sorted out. In the meantime, why don't I take Flash?"

"No," I say with such force it would seem Caleb was trying to take my child rather than a turtle I'd found outside a few hours ago. "You can't take Flash. He needs me."

Caleb sits on the couch. "Are you sure you're okay, Mom?"

"Yes," I insist, but I know how pathetic I must look. Mending my broken heart with a menagerie of rescued animals. But caring for them is the only thing keeping me going right now. They need me. And I need to be needed. "Really, sweetheart, I'm fine."

"And no more rescues?"

"No more rescues."

Chapter 37

Mark

"I'm sorry, Mark," Lee Martin, the young principal I'd worked with before my forced retirement, slides my resume across the table at the coffee shop. "You're a great teacher, but the history department is full."

"It doesn't have to be a history class," I push, hating the fact that I sound desperate. "It could just be an elective."

Trying to fill my empty days with something, I'd created a class that would use iconic world landmarks as touchstones for history. For instance, I would discuss the Eiffel Tower's connection to the French Revolution or Chinese history as it relates to the Great Wall. My premise was that, by pairing historic events to familiar landmarks, it would make them more interesting to learn about.

Lee takes a sip of coffee and sets down his mug. "It's a great idea, Mark. Really. There's just no room in the budget."

I pick a piece of my croissant off, pop it in my mouth, and swallow. "Look, Lee," I start, knowing how pitiful my offer is going to sound before it even comes out of my mouth. "I have everything I need. I'm not looking for extra income. I'm just looking to fill my day with something meaningful." I pick up the folder with my new class idea. "And I think this is it." I pause. "What I'm saying is — I'll teach it for free."

The look of sympathy that passes over Lee's face is so palpable that I wish I could stuff the offer back in. I know it's pathetic. But I don't have Sara's care to structure my days, and things are going so well for Sharon and the girls, that I don't want to get in the way by coming over all the time. This freedom would have been perfect if I had Ellie in my life, but I don't. I've tried to contact her a few times by phone, but I get the same response: *Message failed* or "Caller not available." I'm still blocked.

"That's a generous offer, but it doesn't work that way, you know, with the district."

I wave a hand, like it's no big deal, like this class is not what I'd been pinning my hopes on as a remedy for my spiraling loneliness. "I get it, yeah. Just thought I'd throw it out there. You know, just in case."

"Yeah. If the budget increases, I'll be happy to bring up the idea to the district."

"Thanks," I say, but I know he's just being kind. I'm not even sure, sitting here, that the class is a good idea after all. Are kids nowadays even familiar with these landmarks? I'm a history teacher and I've never seen any of them in person. Only in pictures.

Lee throws a few dollars on the table, stands. "Good to see you. Don't be a stranger now." He shakes my hand.

I pick up my folder of ideas for the class and force a smile. "You either. Thanks for the time."

"And enjoy your retirement," he says, and takes a step toward the door. "Have some fun."

I smile but say nothing. Have fun? Right, Lee, sure. I'll pick a bushel of fun up at the store. Because a man who just offered to teach a class for free surely has lots of opportunities for fun and enjoyment. I shake my head. Idiot.

I walk through the Scranton streets toward my car. I pass a trash receptacle and drop the folder inside. I stare at it a moment, then pull it back out. Chances are, I'll never need this, but I'll keep it. Just in case.

I continue toward my car, parked by the town's University. Every person, it seems, is walking fast toward something or someone, some task or class or activity. This might be an assumption, but it feels real, and right or wrong, it amplifies my loneliness. I hurry to my car, not wanting to be around others, like being alone will somehow be an antidote to the sadness welling up inside me.

I get in my car. I need to shake this off. It's Saturday and still early, so I pick up a dozen donuts, taking care to pick the girls' favorites, and drive to Addison's house as a surprise. I won't stay long, just a quick hi, but long enough to remind me I do have people in my life. I'm not entirely alone.

Once at the house, I get out of the car and stand on the doorstep, a weird déjà vu of last month's scene, when I'd come with dinner from Ale Mary's. I push that memory away and ring the doorbell. No answer. I peer inside the rectangular window on the side of the door. No people. I shift my gaze to the driveway just as the garage door sounds. Addison backs out, Sara and Sharon in the car with her. I walk toward the car, balancing the dozen donuts on my hand.

Addison rolls down the window. "Hey Uncle Mark." Sharon and Sara wave.

"Hey ladies. I thought I'd swing by and drop off these donuts." I hold the donut box up.

Addison's face scrunches up. "Oh. Sorry. We're going to the spa."

The word spa automatically makes me think of Ellie and our time in the Bahamas whirlpool and my heart dips.

"Did you want to come, Dad?" Sara asks.

"No," I say automatically. Being at a spa will only remind me of Ellie. Maybe someday I'll be able to think about her fondly, think about our times together and smile, but that time is not now. "Thanks for asking." I walk toward the car. "At least take the donuts." I hold out the box.

Addison makes a pained face. "We're all on a cleanse, sorry."

"A cleanse?"

"Drinking water and eating only certain foods to get the toxins out of our system," Sharon says.

Addison pushes the box toward me. "Donuts aren't on the list," she jokes.

"Right," I say, stepping back. "Call us later," she says, waves, and backs out. The car disappears around the corner.

I stand alone with the box of donuts, and an overwhelming feeling of sadness rains down on me. I have no purpose. I'm no longer a teacher. No longer a caregiver. And the glimpse of life with Ellie—about how it would feel to share my golden years with someone—was only that. A glimpse. And one that has made me feel a thousand times worse than if I'd never had it at all. Before I didn't know what I was missing.

I drive home by rote and take my folder and the donuts inside. Darnell greets me, the only bright spot in my life right now, but of course even he is mired with memories of my time with Ellie. I wouldn't have him if it weren't for her.

I pet his head, dump the donuts in the bin, and lay the folder on the kitchen table. I page through the pictures of the landmarks I'd chosen. The Eiffel Tower in Paris. The Taj Mahal in India. The Colosseum in Rome. The Great Pyramid of Giza in Egypt. The Statue of Liberty in New York City.

Amazing that in seventy-two years of life, I'd only been to one of these. Good old Lady Liberty.

I shut the folder. The rest of the day looms before me, long and lonely. I open the folder again and line up the landmark pictures across my kitchen table. I look at each one, picturing myself there, seeing it in person and jolt. Could I see them in person? I pull out my computer and start a search.

I could. I still have money from the long-ago counterfeit watch episode, plus my savings, and I'm healthy. Sara doesn't need me. And neither do Addison or Sharon. I'm sure they'd watch Darnell if I went exploring.

A sliver of excitement courses through me, the first I've had since returning from the Bahamas. If nothing else, traveling through Europe, seeing all the sights I've read about for years, would get my mind off Ellie Moore.

Before I can lose my nerve, I log on to the airline site and book my first trip.

Chapter 38

Six months later

Ellie

I sign the last paper and Linda, my realtor, hands me the key. "Congratulations. I know you've been renting, but it's officially yours now."

I clasp my fist around the key, the metal hard and cold against my skin. "Thank you."

"It's a wonderful thing you're doing," she says. "How many animals do you have there again?"

"Twenty right now. But there's always room."

Linda puts my purchase documents in a file and smiles. "Isn't your tagline something like that?"

"Ellie's Animals: There's Always Room at the Inn." I move my hands like I'm underscoring the words.

"Love it," Linda says. We both stand and she gives me a half hug. "Keep in touch."

I take the documents from her hand. "Sure will." I leave the realtors' office. When I get inside my car, I could pinch myself. The past six months have been wild. The FBI caught the ring Sebastian was a part of. The criminal case is still going on, but my lawyer settled the civil one out of court. I received all the money I'd given Sebastian and extra for pain and suffering.

The settlement was enough that I left my job at Caleb's vet practice, something he was way too elated about, and rented an old farmhouse with a barn. I moved in with my menagerie of animals and Ellie's Animals sprung to life. It's a rescue, with the goal of adoption for every animal there. I've become skilled at matching pets and owners. I matched Flash the turtle with a boy desperate for a pet but who had massive allergies. I matched one of the rescue bunnies with a special ed teacher who brings him to her classroom, and a second with a little girl, my neighbor's daughter, smart as a whip and obsessed with bunnies. I love doing it. It's like setting people up on a perfect blind date, one you know won't end up in heartbreak because animals just don't hurt people the way humans do. Love them and they'll love you right back. The owner of the farmhouse, with whom I matched a shaggy stray dog, loved the concept and sold me the property for a song. And now it's mine. MINE.

I pull into the driveway and stare at the home. White, big, in need of a paint job but with good bones. I get out of the car, make way up the brick path, and step on to a rickety but still usable front porch. I stop to pet Lucille, one of the cats, and then open the door. I step through the foyer and into a large, sunny kitchen with a massive island. Maude — one of my room-mates — stands behind it with a knife, ingredients strewn in front of her.

I'd inherited Maude and her grandson back when I'd first rented the farmhouse. They'd been the existing tenants, but had not renewed the lease because they couldn't afford it. Maude was my age but had temporary custody of her fifteen-year-old grandson Sam, bless her heart. Sam had been bullied at his old school and Maude was trying to give him a fresh start in Rye. But after a year, renting was just too expensive to be practical. They planned to move back to the old area.

Yeah.

No.

That wasn't going to happen. Not when I had four whole bedrooms and needed help with the rescue. I'd asked only one question of Maude: Do you mind rooming with a few cats? Maude had smiled broadly. Turned out she loves animals almost as much as I do. Sam, too. He has a way with dogs, especially the tough ones. And he's a whiz with social media; he posts on all our platforms.

I hold the house key over my head. "It's official."

Maude drops her knife, moves around the island, and envelops me in a big hug. She steps back. "Congratulations, Ellie. That is so exciting!"

"It is." I throw my purse on the counter and drop the key in the junk drawer. "Anything new since I left?"

"There's always something new." She pushes back ash-gray hair with long fingers. "You didn't think you'd leave for a few hours without something happening, did you?"

I pick Peanut up off the floor. "I guess not. So, what is it?"

"Follow me."

She gestures toward the living room, and I follow her tall form into the space, Peanut in my arms. There's a cage in the corner. I step toward it and peer inside. Two small, gray animals sleep huddled on a pastel striped blanket.

"Chinchillas," Maude says without me having to ask. "Lenny and Squiggy. Owner couldn't care for them anymore."

I stare at the little sweeties, tiny chests moving up and down with their breaths. Adorable. "Couldn't care for them or didn't want to? Honestly." I shake my head. "Doesn't matter. I've got a perfect owner in mind for these two." I glance at the chinchillas, make a mental note to ask Caleb what they should eat, and sweep back toward the kitchen.

Maude follows me, one of her signature floral kimonos flowing behind like a cape. "Is the potential owner Doug Lambert?" she asks teasingly.

I set Peanut down. "Absolutely not." Doug, a retired banker, has asked me out several times over the past few months. "I'm done with men, remember?"

I'd told Maude, a widow, about Harrison and Sebastian. But not Mark. I tell myself it's because the big reveal—Mark's a liar—happened only six months ago, but deep down, I know it's more than that. My feelings for Mark came on fast, but they were deep, and the way things ended shocked me in a way that the breakups with Harrison and Sebastian didn't. With those two, there had been glimmers of something amiss. Harrison staying at work late a lot; Sebastian increasing his monetary asks. But with Mark, there was none of that. I'd have bet my life on his being a stand-up guy. One night, I pulled up his Facebook page, something I swore I wouldn't do and did anyway. On it there was a new picture, just one, of Mark in front of the Taj Mahal. *In India.* I'd stared at his image a long time before clicking off the page. The answer I needed was clear: Mark was not pining away for me. He'd moved on.

"So, who's the lucky owner of the chinchillas then?" Maude asks, interrupting my thoughts. She returns to her place behind the island, preparing the food for our animals with special diets.

"Sam."

"My Sam?" She puts her hand over her chest.

"Hear me out." I hold up a hand. "I know he's helping take care of all the animals here, but I think it would be good for him to have these little ones just for himself." I pause and try to read Maude's expression. Sam's been doing better since moving here, according to Maude, but he's still a bit of a sad sack a lot of the time. Having pets of his own may move the dial in the right direction. Animals have done that for me more than once. Heck, they're the only things that keep me going most of the time. "It's hard to feel sad when a bunch of animals think you're the greatest thing ever. Of course, if you don't think it's a good idea" I start.

Maude shakes her head. "No. It's a great idea." She balls up the food into individual servings and wraps them in plastic. Milo, a black and white rescue cat, jumps on the counter; Maude picks him up and pets his head. "He'll love them. I'm sure of it."

I am too. I'd thought for a while that Sam would benefit from having his own pet and was waiting for the right ones to come along. I have a few others in mind for the right pets too. Shane, my hairdresser, is just itching for a big dog to hike with, and I'm fairly certain my old neighbor from the townhouse (the one who told the HOA about my excess pets when I lived there) would positively love a cat. But it must be the right cat, snuggly and loving, the kind that would let you pick him or her up like a baby. That personality is rare among strays, but I've got a new one. Ginger Root, an orange tabby with extra toes. She may be the perfect fit.

Out the front window I see the mail truck pull to a stop at the bottom of the drive. I push open the front door and greet Alex, the driver, at the same time he exits. I move to the truck and pet Mo, a large German Shepherd, through the open window. Mo and Alex were my first pet-person match, and I love seeing the giant dog riding shotgun in the mail truck every day, his pink tongue hanging out. "How you doing, good boy?"

Alex moves to the back of the truck. "More food for you, Ellie," he says. He pulls two large boxes from the trunk and walks them to the porch.

For the past few months, I've been getting monthly ship-ments of food from an anonymous donor. The first time the boxes came, I'd been elated. Not only because feeding animals is expensive and I'll take all the help I can get, but because I'd been sure the donation was from Mark. He found out about Ellie's Animals! He wanted to make amends!

That was the night I'd broken down and pulled up his Facebook page, sure I'd see something positive, maybe, possibly, a message to me. An overture. Something. But no. Instead, posted front and center on the page was the Taj Mahal picture. Further sleuthing led me to the name of the donor: S.A. Jami-son. I couldn't find out who S.A. Jamison was or where he (or she) was from, but one thing was clear, the donor was *not* Mark. Clearly. He was too busy whooping it up in front of the world's fanciest building.

"Thanks, Alex."

He returns to the mail truck, retrieves a stack of envelopes, and hands them to me. "Here you go, Ellie." He nods toward the stack. "Looks like a wedding invitation in there."

"Nah. I'm too old for weddings," I say, meaning it. "No one I know is getting married. I'm pretty sure." I wave to Alex. "See you. Thanks."

"Sure thing, Ellie." He gets back in the mail truck and drives off. I move to one of the rockers on the porch, sit down, and pull out the big envelope, the one Alex must have thought was a wedding invitation. I feel the envelope between my fingers, thick and expensive with my address spelled out in perfect calligraphy. It does look like a wedding invitation. With a start, I think maybe it's Mark. Maybe he's getting married.

I puff out a breath.

No. No way. That would be crazy. Even if Mark were getting married, why in the world would he invite me to the wedding? How would that even go? Hey new wife, this is Ellie, the woman I had an intense one-week relationship with. No. The wedding can't be Mark's. It must be someone else.

Curiosity piqued, I slide my finger under the envelope seal and pull out a breathtaking floral invitation. I scan down the names. Gavin Brady and Brandy Martinez. Getting married in Scranton. In six weeks.

Chapter 39

Mark

I sit at the edge of the bed in my hotel in Brussels, phone in hand. "Any good mail?" I ask Addison over FaceTime.

"Let me see." Her form bobs as she moves to the kitchen. She turns the phone to Sara and Sharon, both sitting at the table, craft supplies strewn in front of them. They wave in unison. "Still having fun in Belgium?" Sara asks.

"Wonderful," I say. "I'm bringing back tons of chocolate."

Sara cheers.

Though Lee was less than enthusiastic at the idea for my landmark course and it's likely I'll never teach it, I'm putting it together anyway. It's an excuse to travel, and something to do with free days that extend across my calendar ad infinitum. I've come to Europe a few times over the past several months and seen dozens of landmarks including the Taj Mahal, Big Ben, the Eiffel Tower, and the Colosseum. I'm here in Brussels to check out the Grand-Place, a large square surrounded by ornate and insanely old buildings, including a bell tower which spirals into the sky. I've loved it here and I know I'll include the Grand-Place in the course.

Addison orients the phone to a pile of mail and goes through it so I can see each piece. Bill. Bill. Advertisement. Bill. Advertisement. Then a large envelope, the writing on the front in fancy script. "What's that one?" I ask, intrigued.

"It's a wedding invitation," Sara yells from off screen. "We both got one too." She moves her finger between her and Addison.

A wedding invitation? I cull my memory for anyone I know who might be getting married just as Sara yells out. "It's for Gavin."

Gavin. Getting married. "Who to?"

Addison slides her finger through the invitation seal and pulls it out. "Brandy Martinez. The wedding's in Scranton."

I smile. I'm happy for Gavin and Brandy. They make a good couple. I think about them and a split second later, think of Ellie.

She'd be invited.

Right?

Maybe.

I haven't had any contact with her since she blocked my number all those months ago. I tried to respect that she didn't want me in her life. I wrote her a letter, a sad attempt to see if I could convince her to change her mind. I addressed it to Caleb's vet clinic in Rye, sealed it, stamped it, and then stuffed it in a drawer unsent. I started coming on these trips shortly after.

Travel has helped fill my days but hasn't helped me stop missing Ellie as much as I'd have thought. There are more reminders of her than I'd thought possible after just one week together. I thought of her and that ridiculous pink hand mold when I saw a wax museum in Amsterdam. At Big Ben, I was reminded of riding with her on the Orlando Eye. A dog in France looked exactly the way she'd described Peanut.

Drinking glühwein — hot wine — at the Christmas market in Switzerland and strolling by dozens of booths of handmade goods and delicious treats made me think of her because the whole thing was such an Ellie activity. In Brussels, I'd thought of her every time I ate chocolate. So, every day. In Paris, I broke down and bought her a pink floral scarf because I knew she would love it. It ended up sitting dormant on the table in my foyer for so long that Addison asked about it. I ended up giving it to her. It was too embarrassing to tell her the truth.

"You still there?" Addison prompts.

"Yeah." I jerk my attention to the present. "Just zoned out there for a moment. Great for Gavin. And I'll see you in a few days."

"See you then." There's a chorus of goodbyes. I hang up and try to push thoughts of the wedding and Ellie from my mind. It's months away. She might not be invited, and she might not come even if she is.

I stand and leave my hotel room. Fresh air and old buildings are a sure way to get my mind off the distant wedding and whatever guests (i.e. Ellie) may or may not be there.

I leave the hotel. It's my plan is to go to all the places I've seen so far and take pictures for the course. I walk over cobblestone streets lined with chocolate and souvenir shops, the smell of fresh waffles in the air. I reach the Grand-Place and take it in. I stare again at the belfry, a massive bell tower three-hundred feet high with a sculpture of St. Michael at the top. I angle my phone camera at the massive tower just as someone knocks into me. I turn around and see a woman with a phone outstretched in her hand in the opposite direction.

"Oh." She twists around and faces me. "So sorry."

"No problem." I hold up my phone. "We were both taking pictures, I think."

"A tourist hazard, I guess." The woman smiles.

She's pretty, I realize, and likely my age. She gestures around the plaza. "I just can't get enough of these old buildings. To think they are still standing and still so beautiful after so many years."

"I'm the same. I love baroque architecture."

"Me too." She pushes out a hand. "I'm Jeanette."

I shake her hand, small and slim. "Mark."

"I'm a sucker for old things." She gestures around. "It's why I love Europe so much. I used to be a history teacher."

I bug my eyes out. "I was a history teacher too."

"No way."

We gush over the coincidence, and I tell her about my idea for the landmark course.

"What a wonderful way to make history real." She pauses, then points to a Starbucks. "You wouldn't want to get a cup of coffee, would you?"

I digest the invitation. Since my return from the Ellie trip, I've gone out of my way to avoid any chance of a romance. A romance of any kind would feel like cheating, which I know is ludicrous since Ellie and I were never really a couple and certainly aren't one now. Still. It feels weird. I turned down an opportunity to be set up with a woman Sharon said would be perfect for me and have avoided somewhat botched attempts at flirting by Carolyn, a woman who sits near me in church.

Jeanette waves her hand. "Never mind. You're probably busy. Or need to get back to your wife or something." She adjusts the strap of her purse and gives an awkward wave. "It was nice meeting you."

"No wife," I say and take a quick glance at her ring finger. Bare. "I'm here on my own," I add. "I'd love to get some coffee."

We get coffee and biscotti at Starbucks and sit at an outside table that overlooks the Grand-Place. It's a stunning, sunny day and it's nice to be sitting with someone, rather than being alone.

Jeanette fills me in on the classes she taught; I do the same. She shares that she's from Connecticut and was widowed two years ago. Her two children, boys, don't live nearby and she's traveling to combat loneliness. I tell her about Scranton, my sister, and the girls.

The similarities between us and our situations are impossible to ignore. It's early, but Jeanette seems like someone I could travel with, someone I'd enjoy getting to know. It would be nice to have a meal companion, and it would make tours more enjoyable to share them with someone. Like I did with Ellie.

"I'm here in Brussels a few more days." She tips her head and picks up her coffee. "You?"

"Two more days," I say. "What else are you doing?"

"This morning, I'm planning to walk around Brussels. Later, I'm going on a tour of Bruges." She sets down her mug and angles her face toward the sun before shifting her gaze back to me. "There's probably room on the tour if you're free. It's a big tour company."

I hadn't been to Bruges yet, but I'd wanted to go. They have a belfry there almost as famous as the one in Brussels. "I'll look into it."

She texts me the name of the tour company.

A dog without a collar walks by our table, a small mangy thing. He sniffs Jeanette's sneaker, and she shoos him away. The dog scurries off, its tail between its legs. "Sorry," Jeanette says, looking in the direction of the dog. "I'm not a dog person."

"Oh." The statement surprises me. I don't know why. I barely know Jeanette.

"Too much fur and slobber." She sets her mug down with a bang. "Anyway. Would you like to walk around? See what we see?"

"Sure," I say, and stand, weirdly off-balance by Jeanette

234

shooing away the dog. I mean, I've spent time with plenty of people, and dated a few, who didn't own dogs, who may have not been "dog people," whatever that means. It's just a small thing; it shouldn't bother me. But I can't help but think that, had Ellie been here, she'd have scooped up that dog and demanded that I google nearby shelters. Or she would have walked along the square, unabashedly asking every person if they knew the owner. She'd probably have bought the dog a collar and gotten him a meal.

I smile at the thought.

"Just being here makes me smile too," Jeanette says.

"Right," I say awkwardly.

I follow her toward the entrance of what looks like a fancy mall. She steps inside and we amble down the covered corridor. Shops on both sides look expensive and upscale, the kind that would make Ellie squeal. In one shop window is an outfit like the one she'd chosen for me on our shopping excursion, and I'm immediately transported back to that day. "Well, aren't you just a tall glass of iced tea?" she'd said. I'd made a show of turning around like a model and she'd whistled. "Well, butter my butt and call me a biscuit, you clean up nice, Mr. Moore." A laugh escapes.

Jeanette turns in my direction "What?"

I shake my head. "Nothing. Sorry."

She waves her hand in the direction of the store. "No way on this one."

"There seem to be some nice things," I say, looking at a pretty blue dress in the window. One I know Ellie would pick if she were here.

"Too impractical."

She moves on and I notice, for the first time, she's wearing sneakers with thick soles. Practical shoes. Not Ellie ones.

I follow her into a chocolate store where we both buy gifts

for our children. We wander in and out of other stores, but all I can see are things Ellie would like. Bangle watches with flowers on their faces. A bright orange purse, big enough to fit all her stuff. Fuzzy pink slippers. An animal-themed cuckoo clock. Waffles and chocolate ice cream. Suncatchers. Bright red lipstick. High heels. I've thought of Ellie a lot since the Bahamas, but this, right now, is on a new scale. Maybe because I'm walking with Jeanette?

We turn a corner, and the same mangy dog from Starbucks is sitting with a man who appears to be homeless. There's a bowl in front of them with a sign for donations for the dog. Jeanette reaches into her purse and throws a big pile of Euros into the bowl. She looks the man in the eyes and smiles. "Have a good day, sir."

I look at her, and my surprise must be evident on my features.

"What?"

"Nothing," I shake my head. Nothing other than I'm an idiot. A pretty woman who shares my interests and lives on the same coast drops from the sky, and I was about to blow her off because she's wearing sneakers and isn't a dog person. Idiot. Idiot. Idiot.

She checks her watch. "I think I should get ready for the tour. Did you want to go?"

"Yes," I tell her. "I'd love to."

Chapter 40

Ellie

Both of us in outdoor boots and jeans, Maude and I pull hay over to our newest resident, Buttons. Buttons is a cow "donated" to Ellie's Animals after the owner of a nearby hobby farm decided to give up the venture and move to Bluffton, South Carolina. The same donor also donated two goats and four chickens. I'd almost said no to Buttons as a cow was not an animal I could easily match with an owner, but Maude talked me into keeping her. Something about her eyes. "They're soulful," she'd said, then added, "plus, how do we know she won't be sold to a factory farm?" Well, that did it. Sam converted the barn, and bam, we take farm animals now.

We finish feeding Buttons, then move on to the goats and chickens. Maude claps her hands together when we're done. "You'd better get packed if you're going to get to that wedding."

I put my hands on my hips. "Nice try."

We walk out of the barn toward the house. "Why not?"

"I told you why not." A few days after I'd received the invitation, I'd told Maude all about Mark over a bottle of wine. She's been bugging me to go to the wedding ever since.

"And I said, why not?" Maude says, stopping on the front porch. "Maybe Mark is free and just waiting for you to contact him. Or maybe he's not as great as you thought he was. Going to the wedding is a way to get him out of your system one way or another."

The mail truck pulls up and I wave to Alex and Mo, thinking on Maude's point. Mark might be waiting on me. Doubtful, but maybe. And he might not be as great as I'd thought — more likely, given my taste in men.

But neither of these issues is what I'm worried about.

I'm worried Mark will be as great as I remembered, and that he'll be there with someone else. The other two options, I can handle. It's door number three that's keeping me away.

Alex hops out of the truck. "Another food donation."

"Great."

He pulls out a giant box, another one from S.A. Jamison, and puts it on the front porch, then hands me a stack of mail. "Have a good one, Ellie."

"You too." The truck putters down the road and I turn back to Maude.

"So? Yes?"

I shake my head. "Even if I wanted to go, I RSVPed no."

"No, you didn't," Maude says quickly.

"Maude?" I squint my eyes in her direction.

"I changed it to yes." She waves her hands. "Sorry not sorry. I also got you a reservation at The Cedars. It's a luxury hotel outside of Scranton. My treat."

I put my hand over my heart. "Maude." I'm flattered that she cares this much about me.

"Whether you go to the wedding or not, go to the hotel. You deserve it. You work your tail off to keep this place going."

When I don't answer, she continues. "I booked you a facial and a massage for tomorrow morning."

"You work hard too," I say, and she does. Having Maude and Sam help with the rescue has been a godsend.

"You've let Sam and me stay here for free for the past six months. He's doing so much better. I couldn't be more grateful." She takes one of my hands in both of hers. "Please, let me do this for you."

Her face is etched with sincerity, and I can tell how much me taking her up on the treat means to her. "Okay," I say and put a hand on her shoulder. "You don't have to ask me to stay in a luxury hotel twice."

I pack, including a dress just in case, and drive to a town outside of Scranton where The Cedars is located. I pull up to the hotel, a stunning structure nestled in the Pocono Mountains with a chic, rustic vibe. I check in and get the keys to my room. I take the elevator to the second floor, slide the key into the lock, and step in. The room is gorgeous with wall-to-wall picture windows overlooking a lake surrounded by lush woods. The bed is enormous, dressed in fancy white linens and adorned with fluffy pillows. The furniture is a dark brown with the kind of sheen that makes it seem as if it had just, moments ago, been shined. The carpet, a dark gray, is deep and lush. I remove my socks and shoes, let my bare feet sink into the plush fibers, and inhale a deep breath. Maude was right. Just being here will be good for me. A touch of luxury goes a long way.

I step into the bathroom, shed my clothes, and run the water in the enormous marble shower. I stand under it, letting the liquid stream cascade over me. After, I towel off, put on the hotel robe, and dress for dinner. I choose the fancier restaurant because why not? A cheerful hostess seats me at a window table for two, a candle in its center. Couples surround me on every side, toasting and laughing. Six months ago, their presence would have bothered me. Six months ago, I'd have been mortified to sit alone. Not now. I've learned to enjoy my own company. And I need time to think about the wedding.

I'd love to celebrate with Gavin and Brandy, of course. But I don't know how I'll handle seeing Mark again. I'd fallen harder and faster for him than any man, and finding out he wasn't who he'd presented himself to be? It hurt. Deeply. I've rebuilt my life and my confidence over the past six months, and I don't want to slide back into that hurt space. It may be better to enjoy my time at this spa-like hotel and go home.

I order chicken marsala and wine. I eat every morsel of the meal — delicious — and finish the wine. After, I go back to my room, get ready for bed, and slip under the covers. It's a luxury to just fall into bed without feeding a menagerie of four-legged creatures. I love the rescue, but this is a break I needed. I make a mental note to book Maude a room here. She needs a break too.

In the morning, I eat a light breakfast, take a walk around the property, and go to the spa for the treatments Maude scheduled for me. The treatments are perfect, and by the time I'm back in my room, I'm so relaxed, I think I could see Mark with a harem of women and be unaffected. I decide, in my Zen-like, massage-induced coma, that I will in fact go to the wedding.

I pull out my pink dress, tea-length with a fitted bodice. I take my time getting ready because, if I'm going to do this, I'm at least going to look my best. Once I'm dressed and ready to go, I snap a picture and send it to Maude. Her response is immediate: *You go girl.* I smile. It's been years since I've had a girlfriend like Maude, and it feels good.

I drive to the location of the church and get lost along the way. When I finally arrive, I'm a little late and more than a little frazzled. The last thing I want is to make a scene of myself running in at the last moment. Maybe I should just leave. Maybe this is a sign. A big fact warning: Turn back now.

But I've come this far, and I look good if I do say so myself. Why not? If you can't take a chance in your seventies, when in the heck are you going to take one?

I get out of the car, hurry toward the church, and enter the vestibule. The wedding appears not to have started, Brandy and her bridal party nowhere to be seen. I forego being seated by an usher and slip into the back pew of the church instead. Now that I'm here, my desire to see Mark, to know if he's here, intensifies. I crane my neck and look for him, row by row, person by person. My eyes dart from the back of one head to the next. No. No. No. No. None of them look like Mark. Or at least not like the back of his head. Maybe he's not here? Maybe he's on a Taj Mahal-like trip?

I sit back against the pew and puff out a breath. That's it. He's not here. I'd been worried for nothing.

Then a man in one of the front pews stands and switches places with the woman next to him, her now on the aisle.

It's Mark.

And a woman.

I watch them, moving my head right and left to see between the masses of people in between us. Mark and the woman lean their heads toward each other; I assume they're talking. She rubs his back with an open palm. My heart stills.

He's here with a date.

He's moved on.

I didn't mean anything to him.

I knew it.

I grab my purse, ready to slip back out and return to the hotel. I should do that. Save myself this heartbreak. I can live out the cliché and get a pint of ice cream on the way.

No.

The word jolts my consciousness. No. NO. The old Ellie, the one whose validation came only from the men in her life, would leave. But the Ellie I am now? She's going to see this through.

Chapter 41

Mark

I switch places with Jeanette so she can have the aisle seat. She and I never became romantically involved, but we've been friends since meeting each other in Brussels. She's collaborated with me on the landmark course, and we've floated the idea to a few colleges and universities. We'll see, I guess.

Anyway, Jeanette's son, in the middle of a tumultuous divorce, just moved home and emotions are spinning out of control in her household. She needed a break, and I had a plus one. So, I invited her. I assume Ellie won't be here, but on the outside chance she is, and the likely chance she has a plus one on her arm, Jeanette will be a friend for me to lean on. Win-win. Sara and Addison are here too. Gavin invited the whole family.

Gavin and his best man move to the front of the church. He looks handsome, and older, and I wonder what he and Brandy have been doing for the past six months. If they went back to the counterfeit business or stayed away. That experience, Ellie and me helping them make the exchange, feels so long ago and so surreal that if someone told me it never happened, I'd believe them. We never got caught. Brandy and Gavin never got caught. The whole exchange was a blip in time that changed the course of my life. Without the exchange, Ellie and I wouldn't have stayed together in the Bahamas, and without that trip I wouldn't have fallen in love with her. I'd have remembered her fondly, but that deep love? That came from the time we spent together on the trip.

Canon in D by Johann Pachelbel sounds from the organ and I, along with the rest of the guests, twist around to look at the back of the church. Brandy's bridesmaids are ushered down the aisle by groomsmen, each in different but coordinating green gowns. Brandy stands behind them, a man I assume to be her father by her side. She looks radiant and I shift my gaze to Gavin. His eyes are on Brandy, totally transfixed. I love this for them. There was a time when I would have gotten married had the right woman been in my life. Turns out I met the right woman decades too late.

Brandy starts down the aisle and everyone stands. She passes the back pew, and my breath catches. But not for Brandy, though she does look gorgeous. My breath catches for Ellie. In the back row, looking every bit as stunning as she did when I first met her. I shift around, my heart in my throat. Ellie is here. My heart beats harder. Though I knew there was a chance, I hadn't expected her to be here. I don't know why. But it was her. Wasn't it? I try to reconstruct the woman I just saw in my mind. It might not have been her. It might have been a woman who just looked like her. This wouldn't be the first time I've thought I've seen Ellie, only to have it turn out to be someone else.

Brandy and Gavin stand in front of the minister and the wedding ceremony begins. I don't pay attention. I'm too busy thinking about whether the woman in the back is Ellie or not. I force myself not to turn around and check. That would be ridiculous. And what would I do if it was her? Wave? Smile? Mouth "I'm sorry"?

The ceremony continues, each part seeming incredibly long. There are two readings and two songs, both of which go on forever, and the minister's sermon feels endless. When they finally get to the exchange of vows and the minister says, "You may kiss the bride," I stand, thinking the ceremony is over. Jeanette tugs my arm, and I plant myself back down, realizing the error. "Someone's in a hurry for the reception," she whispers.

Or not, I think, because I have no idea what I'm going to say to Ellie if that is her.

When the minister says, "ladies and gentleman, may I present to you Mr. and Mrs. Gavin Brady," everyone claps and stands. I jolt from my seat and look for the place where Ellie or the Ellie imposter was sitting. She's not there. The pew is empty, not a soul standing in front of it, end to end. I look around the general area for the pretty woman in the pink dress. I don't see her. I must be a pathetic man, if not a crazy one. I'm still so in love with Ellie that I fictionalized her out of thin air.

Jeanette and I move to the aisle and wait for the receiving line, Addison and Sara ahead of us.

"Beautiful ceremony," Jeanette says.

"It was," I say, though I'd been so impatient for it to be over, I don't know if it had been beautiful or not.

When we reach Gavin and Brandy in the receiving line, I introduce Jeanette and give each of them a big hug. "Ellie's here somewhere," Brandy says with a casual wave. "My sheep."

"Great," I force out. Relief and worry compete for space in the vacillating emotions that have no business in a seventy-something-year-old psyche. Relieved that I'm not crazy enough to have imagined Ellie; worried about what I'll say when I see her.

At the door, two flower girls give us bags of rice tied with green ribbons.

Jeanette leans into me. "Strange tradition, right? Throwing rice?" She holds up her bag.

I don't, can't, answer because I'm too busy acting like a high schooler.

"Mark?"

"Throwing rice is meant to signal prosperity for the couple," I say before being pulled away by a former student of mine, then a second.

When I return to Jeanette, she's talking to Ellie.

Chapter 42

Ellie

The woman, Jeanette, met Mark in Brussels. She's a former history teacher like him and loves landmarks and old things the way he does. A perfect match. She probably even reads about plagues.

"Mark," she says, waving him over.

He smiles and my heart feels like it might break because the smile is for her, his perfect match, and not for me, the fling. Like Harrison's Lilith, I'd have felt better if she was a floozy or young, but the woman before me is clearly cultured and smart.

"Ellie," he says, reaching us. "How have you been?"

"Sweet as a peach." I force cheer into my voice. "How about you?"

"I'm good," he says, then repeats the word. "Good."

Brandy and Gavin appear at the church door at that moment, and we all line up to throw the obligatory rice. I refuse and grip the unopened rice bag in my hand. The last thing any bride needs is rice in her hair and down her dress and inside her whatevers. What a stupid tradition. Honestly.

Jeanette holds her still-tied bag and whispers, "I hate this custom too."

"Definitely dreamt up by a man," I say with an eyeroll. Jeanette laughs, and all I can think is damn, she's nice too.

In a flash, Gavin and Brandy run through the airborne rice to a waiting limo. The crowd disperses immediately after, and Mark touches my elbow. "See you at the reception?" He asks the question tenderly and my heart squeezes.

"Yes." I spit out the word without thinking, and driving there, every fiber of my being wants to back out. But Maude was right. I need to go to the reception. I need to solidify that Mark has moved on. I need to let this chapter go once and for all.

The reception is inside a stunning renovated farmhouse, modern-looking despite its rustic exterior. Wildflowers in vases sit on tables with light green linens. White party lights are strewn across thick wooden beams in the ceiling, giving the space a festive, fairy-like glow. A five-piece band plays music in front of a small dance floor.

Name cards sit on a table near the door, and I scan unfamiliar names for my own. I see my name and pluck it from the table. And then I see it. A name card with S.A. Jamison in fancy calligraphy. My heart speeds up. S.A. Jamison. The mysterious donor who has been sending packages of food to Ellie's Animals for months. A coincidence. Maybe. But S.A. Jamison is not the most common of names. Not like Jane Doe or Jim Smith or even Mark Moore. I scan the table for Mark's name, the somewhat reaching and hopeful thought that he's the donor still in my mind. But there it is. Mark Moore.

I stake myself next to the table as people walk into the reception. Whoever S.A. Jamison is, I'm not going to miss him. Or her. One card gets picked up and then another and another and another. I start greeting people with a "howdy" and a "have fun, y'all" because it feels better than standing there dumbly, waiting for the person who may or may not be Ellie's Animals mysterious benefactor to pick up the card. Mark and Jeanette show up and I point to their place cards. "Have a ball, y'all," I say.

Mark looks at me a long moment, then smiles and says in the same tender tone he'd used before: "Only you, Ellie."

I would dwell on his tone and the smile and likely read into both, but I can't because right then a man strolls up and picks up a bunch of cards all at once, including S.A. Jamison. I leave my post and follow him. He passes out the cards to a group of people, but I don't know which person has what name.

Guests are asked by a band member to take our seats, and I wind my way around the space to table six. As luck would have it (kidding) Mark and Jeanette are seated there too. I force a smile and sit. Right after, a woman pushes a second woman in a wheelchair up to the table. She haphazardly drops two name cards in front of their seats, one of them S.A. Jamison.

Mark cranes his neck across the table. "These are Sara and Addison," he says. "My nieces."

Sara waves in his direction with the kind of pshaw gesture I'm famous for. "Daughters."

I'm momentarily speechless and forget all about S.A. Jamison. These beautiful women are the children Mark raised. The ones I'd convinced myself were fictional.

Mark continues the introduction. "Girls, this is Ellie."

Sara's eyes go wide. She seems as stumped by my presence as I am by hers. "You're Ellie? The one from the cruise?"

"Guilty as a raccoon at night."

Both girls laugh.

The same band member who'd asked us to take our seats clinks a glass, and after, he introduces the wedding party, but

I'm not paying attention. Mark's nieces are here. He was telling the truth. At least about that.

Over salad and the subsequent dinner, I learn from the girls that Mark did raise them. That he did, in fact, make towel animals in the hospital. And not just easy ones. Fancy ones like monkeys. He participated in tea parties and did crafts with the girls at an old kitchen table. He'd rigged his bike to be able to pull Sara on the back. And he always juggled his work with her medical appointments, never making her feel that she, or her diagnosis, was a burden. His go-to phrase, said with humor: "What the heck else am I going to do?"

With each story, my heart dips further down in my body until I'm fairly certain it's lying on the ground. This is the Mark I thought I'd met on the cruise. A good man. Quiet and kind. One with depth. And I pushed him away. First in the Caribbean, and then when he'd called. I hadn't given him a chance to explain. Maybe if I had, it would be me sitting by his side instead of Jeanette.

I excuse myself to the "little girls' room" because one more heartwarming story from Sara and Addison might just kill me. I never get it right. I thought Harrison would love me forever and that Sebastian would fly to the US and sweep me off my feet. No and no. And Mark? He's the one I'd thought was a fraud. He's perfect instead.

I plunk down in the seating area of the spacious bathroom. My triumphant I-don't-need-a-man return just shattered to pieces. Not because I need Mark—I don't, I've proven that—but I do want his company. I want to be a part of his life.

Too late.

I wallow in the bathroom long enough that a search party may come looking for me. Finally, I push myself off the cushiony seat and put my proverbial big girl pants on. When I walk out of the bathroom, Sara is by the door.

She holds up a manicured hand. "Hey."

"Hey," I say, then remember the whole S.A. Jamison saga.

"Weird question," I say, because why not, I need to know. "Do you go by S.A. Jamison?"

"Jamison is my mother's last name. And mine." Her mouth splits into a broad smile. "Are you getting the care packages?"

"Yes, thank you, but—" I tip my head, a dozen questions on the tip of my tongue, all some variation of why.

"Let's move to the back patio," she suggests. "I'd rather speak there than right outside of the bathroom." She rolls her eyes.

"I knew I liked you," I say and start toward the door.

We move to the covered stone patio in the back of the space. It features a bar, a fireplace, a flat screen television, and a few different seating areas. A few people crowd around a baseball game; Sara and I move to the seating area on the other side.

"I found a letter," she starts. "From my dad. He'd mentioned you when he'd been on the cruise and Addison—my sister—and I had been so excited because we thought he'd found someone. And he deserves it, you know." She picks up a drink from the cup holder on her wheelchair and takes a sip. "Anyway, the envelope was sealed but it was stuffed in a drawer and the longer it stayed there unsent, the more I wanted to know what it said. So, I steamed it open." She holds up a hand. "I know. Invasion of privacy."

"Are you kidding? I jest. "I'd have ripped that thing open the second I saw it."

She laughs. "Good to know."

I wait, but she doesn't say anything further. The silence stretches on. "You're killing me here."

"Ellie," she whispers finally, "it was the most beautiful love letter I've ever read. Oh my gosh. I've lived with my dad most of my life and I can tell you, he's not someone who lays his emotions out there like that. He's usually more ordered with things, even his feelings."

I smile. Ordered is the perfect way to describe Mark.

"I don't know how he came to feel that way about you so quickly," Ellie continues, "but it was clear he loved you."

My heart drops. Loved. Past tense. A window had been there; I'd shut it.

"Anyway, after the letter, I looked up your social media and found Ellie's Animals. I sent the first package as a thank you for making my dad feel love, but then you posted about how grateful you were for it, and I fell in love with the mission. A pet for every person. I love that."

I put a hand over hers. "Thank you for those kind words. And those packages have been a godsend."

"I'm so glad."

"And your dad," I start, because I need to know, because even if I'm not the one, I want Mark to be happy, "Things are good with him and Jeanette?"

Sara scrunches up her face. "If by good you mean geeking out about history and old things, then yes." She pauses. "But they're just friends. You know that right?"

Friends. The word repeats itself in my mind, my heart lifting each time it does. Friends. Friends. Friends. Mark and Jeanette are just friends. "They're not dating?" I confirm.

"Nope." Sara shakes her head. "My dad is a totally free man."

Chapter 43

Mark

An old friend of Jeanette's is coincidentally at the wedding and the two of them move to the bar to get drinks. "Want anything Mark?" she asks. "Another scotch?"

"No. Thank you." I shake my head and glance around the venue, hoping to see Ellie. I'd like a chance to catch up, but she's been gone for a while now. Would she leave without saying goodbye? I don't think so, but I don't really know. She may have intended that her presence at the wedding be a quick in and out. Enough to congratulate the couple and that's it. She may not want to catch up with me. I wouldn't blame her.

The music turns slow, and Addison touches my shoulder. "Do you want to dance?"

"Absolutely. Best offer I've had all night."

I stand and we take our place on the dance floor. "How are you?" she asks.

"I'm good," I say, and I am for the most part. The bouts of loneliness are less now. I slowly developed a new routine to replace the old one. I eat with Sharon and the girls Sunday and Wednesday when I'm not travelling. I'm a volunteer at Rock-Steady-Boxing, a gym which assists the Parkinson's population, and some of the guys there have become friends. I joined the neighborhood poker group, finally. I started a vegetable garden. Plus, I have Darnell. Two walks a day like clockwork.

"And how is it seeing Ellie again?"

"Hard," I blurt out.

Addison's eyes flash surprise. I'd always said my time with Ellie had been casual.

"My feelings for Ellie ran deeper than I said," I tell her. I may as well. It's not as if they're going away.

"I knew it," she whispers, and then asks, "does she know?"

"At one point, yes. But I'm sure she'd be surprised to know I still feel that way."

Addison pulls back and looks me in the eyes. "You need to tell her." She moves her head around the space, like she's looking for Ellie.

"Don't. I messed things up. She doesn't want to be with me."

"Are you sure?" Addison steps back and Ellie steps around from behind me.

"Now what's this foolishness about me not wanting to be with you?"

"I" I start.

"Come on, Dad. Dance with the woman." Addison nudges me forward.

I take Ellie in my arms. "What is happening right now?"

"I think we're dancing, Mr. Moore."

"That we are." I put my hand in the air and Ellie does a spin, the skirt of her dress flaring out as she moves. I pull her close and even as I can feel Ellie in my arms, I can't believe this moment is really happening.

Gavin and Brandy sashay by us. "Go Sheep!" Brandy calls, and we laugh.

"I've missed you, Ellie," I say in her ear.

"I've missed you too."

We dance another song, get drinks, and move on to the patio. Jeanette waves from the bar, still talking to her girlfriend, and Ellie and I take seats by the fireplace. It's dusk. A red sun dips behind puffy clouds, its rays jetting lines of pink, yellow, and orange through the darkening sky.

"I got it all wrong," Ellie says and takes a sip of her drink. "You are exactly the man I fell in love with."

"You didn't get it wrong. I should have told you. Knowing everything you'd been through, I should have known that truth was a priority. I should have respected that."

"And I should have given you a chance to explain."

Neither of us speaks for a long moment. Ellie breaks the silence. "Well, aren't we just dumber than a sack of hammers? All this time we've lost."

"No more," I say. "Catch me up."

Ellie tells me about the settlement money and how she started Ellie's Animals. Sara had told me about the rescue, but I didn't realize how extensive it had become. Or what a good job she'd done matching pets and owners. "I can totally see you doing that," I say when she's done.

"I might be a tad pushy," she admits, "but when someone needs a pet, they need a pet. No one's brought one back yet." She taps my hand. "How about you?"

"I adopted Darnell," I say.

"Darnell!" She smiles broadly. "What a lucky dog."

I tell her about the landmark course and my travels. She insists on seeing pictures and we sit, our heads together, as I scroll through my phone. She seems interested and asks so many questions that I keep scrolling. All the way back to the picture of the letter I'd written her. Strange that I took a photograph, but I'd planned to send it. I'd poured my heart out into that letter, and I'd wanted my own copy. Proof of my feelings, or something like that.

I snap off the phone as soon as the letter picture comes up and look at Ellie.

She raises an eyebrow. "Letter from a lost love?"

"Sort of," I say and smile. "It was a letter for you. I chickened out sending it."

Ellie doesn't say anything, but the request is clear in the silence. She wants to see the letter. I turn on my phone and pull it up. I may as well lay it all on the line right now. It may be the last chance I get. "I want you to read it," I say and forward the letter to her via text.

"Wait," she says, "and this is a long time coming." She presses a few buttons on her phone, to unblock me, I assume. "Send it again, please."

I send the letter again, the telltale swish whooshing through the air and my heart along with it. I watch Ellie a moment, then step away. "I don't think I can watch while you read it."

I move around to the side of the farmhouse and lean back. I pull up the letter and re-read the words I'd written all those months ago.

Dear Ellie,

You are extraordinary. In just one week, you went from a woman I was hiding from (aka the woman with the purple suitcases) to one I cherish, adore, and love. How? Maybe it's your beautiful eyes, your kind soul, or your wicked sense of humor. All good candidates, but I don't think any of those are it. It's your essence. Vibrant, electrifying, sparkling. You light up rooms and people with your energy and love. And if all I get with you was one, glorious, incredible week, it was still worth it, and I'll never forget you. But I hope you'll give me more time.

. . .

I am sorry for not sharing all of me with you from the start. I was enjoying our time together so much, and I didn't want anything to mar it. Selfish, I know. You didn't deserve to be blindsided the way you were. I understand if you don't want to give me another chance, and if you don't, I won't reach out to you again. I respect and love you too much for that. But if you do grant me more time, I promise I'll be a man worthy of you, your love, and your trust.

Yours forever, Mark

I read the words again. I feel like I ripped open my heart and spilled it on the page. Part of me is embarrassed that Ellie is reading these words *right now* but most of me wants her to know. Even if she doesn't feel the same way, she deserves to know how special she is and what she means to me. Telling her is long overdue.

I click off my phone, tuck it in my pocket, and move back to the area where I'd left Ellie. She must be done reading by now. She's still on the couch, her image illuminated by bright moonlight.

"Hey," I say softly.

She looks up, her face tear-stained. She wipes it with the back of her hand. "I'm mad at you, Mark Moore," she says. "This," she holds up the phone, "is the nicest thing anyone has ever said about me."

"It's all true." I slide next to her on the couch. She takes my hand.

"Why didn't you send it?" she whispers.

"I didn't think you felt the same way."

She squeezes my hand. "Of course, I felt the same way. I

feel the same way. And I'm sorry. I should have let you explain. I just — " She looks away.

"It's okay," I say. "I understand. Is there anything you want to know or need to know about me to be sure?"

She pulls my head to hers and kisses me. "The only thing I need to know, Mark Moore, is that you're in my life for good."

I pull her to me and whisper, "I am, Ellie. Always."

Epilogue

One year later
Ellie

Mark enters the sunny kitchen of his Scranton home in khakis and a light blue shirt. He holds out his arms. "So how do I look?"

"You look like an esteemed professor."

He tips his head. "Yeah?"

I put my coffee mug on the table, stand, and move toward him. "Absolutely," I say and kiss his cheek. "They're going to love you."

"Thanks."

We move to the foyer. He grabs his keys from the bowl on the table and puts his hand on the doorknob.

"Professor Moore?"

He turns around.

"You're going to need this." I hold up the folder, his lecture tucked inside.

He slaps his head. "Thanks." He kisses my cheek. "I'll see you this weekend," he says. "Can't wait."

"Me either."

Last year, The University of Scranton hired Mark to teach his History and Landmarks course. Today is his first class. The seats had filled up in no time, and then the waitlist filled up too. He's been incredibly excited. And incredibly nervous. He gave me his trial lecture on the Taj Mahal at least six times. It's good. Or at least it was the first time.

Darnell rubs up against my leg and I pet him. Mark will bring him along when he comes to Rye this weekend. I'm hosting a gala, a fundraiser for Ellie's Animals not unlike the ones I used to sneak into when I was a worker at Zoo Atlanta. Maude and Sam live in the house and I do too, when I'm not here in Scranton. Mark comes to Rye, or I come here. Neither of us could leave our hometowns. Me because of the rescue, and Mark because of his daughters, and now, teaching. But it's all good. Old Ellie wouldn't have been secure enough to live apart from Mark, but new Ellie's just fine with it. I love Mark, but I have a life outside of him. He does too.

I set my mug in the sink and move upstairs to pack. I'm having breakfast with Sharon and the girls this morning before leaving for Rye. I've become close with all of them, joining them for spa days, girly movies, and mall trips, sometimes dragging Mark along, sometimes not. And once he got over his distrust of Mark, Caleb became good friends with him. They're both avid Steelers fans and passionate barbecue chefs. When Mark is in Rye, they often grill together and always watch the Steelers, first minute to last, never missing a second of the game.

In the bedroom, I pull out my suitcase, grab my clothes, and start to pack. I still overpack and each time I come, I leave more and more things here at Mark's. The reverse is not true. Mark always packs exactly what he needs — no more, no less.

I zip the suitcase shut and my eye catches a framed photograph of Mark and me in the Caribbean last January. We called it a honeymoon, not because we're married, not yet, but because we're committed. Mark is my person, and I am his.

I trust my gut on that one.

Because why not?

THE END

Acknowledgments

I had a ton of fun writing this book and want to thank all of those who made it possibly.

To Shelly Davis, thank you for your careful copyediting and for catching the things I never do. You've been such a help.

To Jena Collins—your cover design is once again perfection. I'm endlessly grateful for your talent.

To Wendy Rich Stetson - thank you for reading an advance copy of this book. Your insights are invaluable.

For the "Goldens." I have a guilty pleasure of watching shows in the Bachelor series with my daughters. The stories of the "Golden" men and women of the show (those over 60) touched me and served as an inspiration for *Why Not?* So thank you, Goldens, for sharing your stories and reminding all of us that love is worth pursuing at any age.

To my friends and extended family, thank you for cheering me on at every stage of this journey. Your encouragement, listening ears, and gentle nudges to keep going gave me strength when I needed it most.

To my children, Ryn and Kevin, thank you for your insights and encouragement as I shaped this story. And to Cassidy— your humor inspires my writing. If a scene will make you laugh, it stays in the book.

Most of all, to my husband, Jake—you are my constant support and my biggest believer. Thank you for standing by me as I chased this dream. I love you.

And finally, to my readers—thank you for picking up this book, for inviting these characters into your lives, and for sharing this journey with me. You are the reason I get to do what I love.

About the Author

Leanne Treese is an award-winning and bestselling author of women's fiction and romance. Her books have each independently been described as having "all the feels." When she's not writing, Leanne loves running, forcing her family to play board games (Settlers of Catan anyone?), and spoiling her beloved dogs. Leanne's favorite locations include her backyard, the Jersey shore, and anywhere that sells books or coffee, preferably both. A lifelong learner, Leanne's dream life would include going back to college and majoring in everything. More about Leanne and her books can be found on her website: www.leannetreese.com.